THE SECRETARY

A totally addictive psychological thriller with
a shocking twist

SADIE RYAN

Choc Lit
A JOFFE BOOKS COMPANY

Revised edition 2024
Choc Lit
A Joffe Books company
www.choc-lit.com

First published in Great Britain in 2019
as *Behind Closed Doors*

This paperback edition was first published
in Great Britain in 2024

Cover art by Nick Castle

ISBN: 978-1781896792

To my wonderful children, Harry and Charlotte,
I'm so proud of you both.

To Stephen, my second set of eyes, my sounding board.
You have never stopped believing I could do this. You never
let me give up. You pushed me when I didn't want to be pushed.
Thank you for pushing me over the line.

CHAPTER ONE

From: Alexander Bamfield
To: Tina Valentine
Subject: Need to speak with you.
Dear Tina
　I had a visitor today, here at my office in Braitling, who has informed me of some rather startling information which needs to be addressed with the utmost urgency. I would appreciate it if you would phone me to discuss this matter.
　Alexander

I instantly forget how to breathe. My past rearing its ugly head like this is not something I had accounted for. I delete it, go to the trash and further delete. With any luck Alexander will think the email address is no longer in use and stop writing to me. I know once I acknowledge that email something bad will happen. Wanting somebody dead is not a crime, certainly not the last time I checked. But wanting somebody dead and them dying is different. Especially if you have probable cause. The trouble is, I did. It was an accident. Clean and simple.

When Glyn walks into the bedroom from the en suite with his towel wrapped round his waist, I get a warm tingly feeling all over, there are other things on my mind besides Alexander Bamfield and I shove him away back to the corner of my mind where I've kept him until this morning. All mornings should start with the man you love striding into your bedroom fresh from his shower. I smile serenely as he runs his fingers through his wet hair. His strong confident manner is what first attracted me to him.

I flick a finger down his straight nose; his cheeks have a rosy hue to them from the heat of the shower. I find it endearing and kiss each one. Glyn flashes me a seductive smile and kisses me back, his warm breath against my lips gently caressing. He strokes my face, sending sweet sensations down my neck that make me shiver. I tilt my head back losing myself in his touch as his lips trail a hot, lingering sizzle down my neck until he gets to my breast. I flop backwards onto the bed giving myself up to the gentle touch of his lips against my skin. His tawny close-cropped hair turning silver at the temples drips droplets of water on my skin and I can almost hear them hiss.

'Hey, my gorgeous girl, are you feeling frisky this morning?' He bites my earlobe in jest. I feel shy that he can read my mind so obviously. The corners of his mouth twitch upwards. I can't help the rush of heat coursing through my body and all I want to do is lose myself in his arms. 'You look so beautiful fresh from your sleep.' He kisses me and I feel guilty for being so happy and in love with this man. 'You're so perfect,' he says, stroking my thigh. I try to protest but he shuts me up with a kiss. 'To me you are perfect. I love you and always will.'

I study his face and wonder how true his words would be if he knew my secret. Would he really stand by me if I told him? Would his love really be strong enough? But that's an irrational thought. Glyn will never know. Because I will never tell him. My eyes are fixed on his and I know he wants me to believe what he says. Like all good lawyers, I'm able to lie convincingly and my face does not betray my inner thoughts. I lace my fingers through his and kiss him back.

Glyn knows very little about my past. He would never understand if I told him and I couldn't stand what he might think of me. We all have secrets, don't we?

* * *

I walk into the noisy kitchen some twenty minutes later, wearing my emerald green trouser suit, my auburn hair twisted in a chignon and grab a coffee. I open the bi-folding doors letting out the stifling air. I can feel the gentle breeze of the early morning, but still I wipe the back of my neck with some kitchen roll.

I slide a slice of bread in the toaster and pull out the orange juice from the fridge, fill the kids' glasses and pour out their cereal while racing round the kitchen checking school bags and swimming bags.

Buttering my toast, I eat it on the go. Our six-year-old Matt is a straggler. He is not a morning person. He drags his feet over to the breakfast table to join Laura, his sister, who's reciting her times table.

'Come on, sweetheart, hurry up and eat your breakfast. Ali will be here soon to take you to school.' I kiss the tip of his nose and breathe in his scent, brushing his long auburn hair to one side. It's such a beautiful colour far nicer than mine. A tear leaks down his cheek. I know he's going to struggle today, I've been home for a week with a bad cold and he's got used to me being around. I wipe the tear away with the sleeve of my shirt, marvelling at his long eyelashes. I take his scent deep into my lungs and my heart tears as it does every morning when I have to leave them. He gives me a wet kiss on my cheek. The wrench gets harder every time.

Glyn sits at the table next to Laura pouring himself some Crunchy Nut cornflakes. I watch my children, they sense me looking at them and both look over at me.

'You sure you're well enough to go back today, darling? By the way did you do the online food shop?'

'Do you love me as much as Matt, Daddy?' Laura interrupts while reciting her times table.

3

'Yes.' Glyn reaches over enveloping her in a huge bear hug. 'I will always love you to the stars and back and Matt as well. You are my princess.' Laura drapes her arms around his neck and kisses him on the lips.

'I *am* your princess, Daddy, so can I have some sparkly shoes like a genuine princess?' I can't help but smile. Laura and Glyn are so alike. So much so that she already at her young age knows how to twist him round her finger. Glyn can never resist her.

Glyn laughs. 'You choose a colour and at the weekend we'll go and find them.' He pulls her chestnut brown ponytail in a playful tug. Taking one last mouthful of his cereal, he sweeps Matt up in his arms and rushes upstairs for teeth brushing and hair combing. 'Come on, Laura, teeth time. Tina, I'm going in my car today, I've got to go see a client first thing.'

I throw the dishes into the dishwasher and grab my jacket just as Ali knocks on the front door. I open it. 'Hi, won't be a moment.' She's a godsend, I've known her most of my life. I wouldn't trust my children with anyone else. She allows us to do our jobs without worrying about pickups and after school activities. I couldn't do my job without her. I wouldn't. By the door I spot Glyn's paperwork for today's meeting. There are two brown manila wallets, one with a piece of paper clipped to the outside. It's a CV for a secretary at the firm. Ordinarily, they inform me of staff departures.

CHAPTER TWO

The journey into Manchester typically takes me anything between forty minutes and an hour depending if there have been any incidents on the motorway. Not going on the motorway from where we live isn't an option. My phone Bluetooths to the car; I select a music track and hit shuffle.

I can see the numbers climbing on my car temperature gauge and it's only 8:00 a.m. My shirt sticks to my back and my eyes sting from my eyeliner sliding into them. My make-up feels as if it's melting from the heat inside the car; I turn up the air conditioning. I join the motorway from the slip road and cruise along, changing lanes until I'm in the outside lane.

The traffic flows. I sing along to the song, images of driving down the Californian coast road from San Francisco to Los Angeles in a convertible with Glyn flood my mind. It's on our bucket list, together with a million other things we want to do.

My mother always wanted to visit California but never made it. I go and sit in the park every year on her birthday. I had a bench put there in her memory. I'm glad she never knew how I paid for her time in the care home. In the end she didn't know me. After my father abandoned us, she was never the same.

I reach for my sunglasses from the glove compartment while mumbling through the words of the song. When I look back at the road, I hit the brakes, savagely. For a moment I think it's all over for me. Red tail lights from the car in front speed towards me with alacrity. I stop just in time. My car snaking to a standstill, propelling me forward then flinging me back into the seat as my seat belt tightens across my chest, crushing me. 'Shit.' I glance in the rear-view mirror and brace myself for the impact as the car behind hurtles towards me. I can't take my eyes off it. It takes the same evasive action. At the last second, I shut them tight and wait for the inevitable sound of metal smashing into metal. When it doesn't come, I open them and look. He too managed to stop in time. Thank God.

I arrive at my office underground parking still a little shaken and park my Mercedes in my allotted space. I take deep breaths to slow my heart rate down before going upstairs.

I walk through the tinted glass front doors of HVP & Associates, the law firm Glyn and I both work for. He's one of the partners.

'Hi, Cheryl, how are you today?' I say to the receptionist. She's nineteen and very friendly, always willing to help. She's on an apprenticeship. Howard, our senior partner, likes this, he feels he's doing his bit to help the youth of today. 'Do you think you could get me a coffee from Starbucks across the road when you get a moment? I had a bit of a nightmare on the motorway this morning.'

'Morning, Tina. Yes, of course, you look terribly pale. Do you want a croissant or something sweet to go with that?' she asks, tucking her slate-black bobbed hair behind her ear as she scrutinises me in case, I imagine, I keel over.

'Just the coffee, please.'

Mindful of somebody readjusting their position on the sofa to the right of me, I incline my head in their direction.

Cheryl whispers, 'She's here for a second interview with Howard for the secretarial position; he's in with John Priest.' That's the other partner. A taciturn man, tall and gangly with flaxen, floppy hair that I constantly want to cut. He wears thin steel rimmed glasses that match his voice.

I remember the CV and without showing my annoyance for not being included in this recruitment, I bend forwards and say, 'I wasn't aware any of the secretaries were leaving.' I put my briefcase down on the floor and pick up my post from the pile on reception, flicking through, waiting for an answer.

Cheryl doesn't pass comment, simply nods and calls through to Glyn's secretary, Rachel. I frown and wonder why she isn't calling Cathy, Howard's secretary.

I look up at the clock on the wall; I have one hour before my first meeting of the day. They are recruiting for a secretary and I'm out of the loop. Why? Hiring staff is my remit. My day is getting better by the second.

'If you could pop out for that coffee as soon as, I'd be very grateful. Make sure to direct the phones through to the secretaries and warn them first.' I pick up my briefcase, tuck the mail under my arm and see the interviewee watching me. She gives me a penetrating look, sharp and obvious. I smile a fake smile and stride past her, confused at the hostility I feel coming off her.

'There you are, Tina,' Howard says striding into reception just as I'm exiting. His booming voice carries through the room like a lion stating its claim; every word uttered charged with authority. He pats me on the shoulder like we're old buddies. Howard does this as an apology. He never apologises. 'We only found out we needed a secretary last week, and Rachel was lucky enough to know of a candidate.' He nods his head towards the blonde sitting on the sofa. 'You were off sick, time was of the essence, you know how it is. You understand, don't you, Tina?' I can feel her eyes burning a hole in my back. I turn and she smiles. Puzzled, I turn back to Howard.

'I hear you're interviewing her for the position?' I say in a flat, steady voice, but tight as a plucked wire. He notices my pale complexion.

'Tina, are you OK?' He looks at Cheryl.

7

'She said she had an incident on the motorway; I'm going across the road for a coffee for her.'

'What sort of incident? Where you involved in an accident?' He examines me up and down as if he might discover bits of me missing. 'Come and sit down, my dear. Did you bang your head? Are you sure you're all right?'

'Yes, thanks, I'm OK.' He manoeuvres me to the sofa but I stand firm to stop him pulling me along. It doesn't take a genius to know why he is interviewing her. I swallow to stop the rising annoyance from spilling over. Of course I'm not all right about this interview situation. But without sounding petty, what can I say? He is the senior partner after all.

'Well, what are you still doing here, Cheryl? Go on and bring her a few pastries too. The girl looks as if she's close to falling down.'

Hardly. 'Howard, I'm OK, or I will be once the coffee gets here. I need to get on. I have a meeting in an hour.' I glance at the blonde — Barbie or femme fatale? Either way Howard won't mind. Since his divorce he's been acting like a dick.

Howard pats my shoulder, which irritates me. He hands me a glass of water. I have no choice but to drink. I gulp down a little and ignore his caring attitude.

'We'll talk about the interview later, shall we?' I say.

'Right, we will, Tina,' he says. 'I'll see to Miss Pearson, shall I?' His eyes gleam.

It's a rhetorical question.

Ten minutes before my meeting Glyn turns up in my office. I tilt my head from the mountain of paper and smile. 'Hi, meeting go OK?' I know he will have been told about what happened but I don't want any fuss.

He nods. 'Tina, are you sure you're OK?'

'Yes, thanks,' I say, breezily, my incident now forgotten.

'Darling, I've just been told about your accident.'

'God, it's like Chinese whispers. It wasn't an accident, Glyn, it was an incident and yes, I'm OK.' He looks at me, closely, a bit like Howard did. 'Stop looking at me, I'm fine.'

'What happened?'

I don't want any fuss, and I don't want him worrying over me. The lines on his forehead deepen as he looks at me. He will worry, I know he will. He's got enough on his plate with his annoying client who does nothing but lie to him then expects Glyn to get him out of the mire. 'You know, sudden braking and as usual I was off with the fairies listening to music.' I wave it all away with a flap of my hand.

He tuts and shakes his head, sitting down in one of the two seats in front of my desk. 'How many times have I told you to concentrate when you're driving, Tina.'

'I was . . .' I shuffle some papers round on my desk. 'But I got distracted looking for my sunglasses and that's when it happened. I know, I know. Sorry, darling, stupid of me. I realise that now.'

We exchange a smile while I pull apart my croissant and sip my now cold coffee. 'I'm fine though, really I am. It was just one of those things,' I say in an upbeat voice, then push a piece of croissant into my mouth and follow with, 'My meeting starts in a few minutes; can we talk later?' I offer him the rest of the pastry. 'By the way,' I say, 'why didn't you tell me we were interviewing for a secretary?'

'Rachel informed me a few days ago she was leaving and dropped the CV on my desk recommending Megan Pearson. She thought that with the short notice and finding somebody to fill her place, I wouldn't be too upset.'

'Are you? Upset I mean, and why is Rachel leaving?'

'Yeah, she's been with me a long time. Between you and me, and she doesn't want the office to know, her husband has been diagnosed with prostate cancer. Rachel wants to leave by the end of the month. How can I say no?'

Something shifts inside me and I feel gutted. It makes my issue ridiculously petty.

'Why didn't you mention it?' I ask feeling hurt that he kept something like this from me.

'Because we had so much on here and you were feeling so poorly with that virus, I thought why bother you, we needed to find someone quick. What could you have done from your sick bed? It's not a big issue, darling.'

'Hmm, OK.' He had a point, I had felt lousy last week. 'Well, Howard is interviewing her at the moment. She's here for a second interview. Were you aware of that? He seemed keen. Let me know the outcome, but I think we should call an agency and see what else is out there. She might not be the right fit. I know why Howard likes her, I take it you've met her?'

'I'll go speak to Howard and suggest it. Yes, I met her when Megan came for her first interview. She came to the office the other evening to meet with us. She had to travel up; I think she's relocated from down south. We briefly met her and, as you saw for yourself, Howard is extremely taken. You know what a dog he is since his divorce.'

'Blatantly so.'

'The other evening he couldn't help checking her out. The woman is good looking, no getting away from that and the tight-fitting clothes she wears are the sort Howard likes.'

I know that most men like that sort of thing. It was obvious how much Howard liked the look of this woman. I feel a stab of jealousy at the way Glyn describes her. It isn't the clothes that bother me, more the way she wears them. I remember the way Howard's hand had fallen on the small of her back as he showed her into his office. I don't like her. Something is off with her, I can't put my finger on it. But something is off with that woman.

The phone rings.

'Sorry, my client's here. You better keep an eye on Howard, if he's not careful I can see litigation looming on the horizon with his behaviour. We're not in the seventies any more. He needs to remember that.'

'It's not that miserable woman that always ends up screaming at you, is it?'

I nod.

If I knew what was to come I would have begged to stay in this moment forever. In the safety of my loving family and growing career. Disjointed flashbacks hurtle towards me, faces and horrific scenes slam one after the other so power-fully that when Glyn has left my office I collapse back into my chair. My lungs gasping for air.

* * *

When my meeting wraps up, I walk to the secretaries' office to find Megan Pearson standing opposite Rachel at the next desk. The other secretaries are busy on calls or wearing head-phones listening to dictation. It's an open-plan office divided by low screens to give a level of privacy to each secretary, there's eight of them in total. Megan looks over and smiles. Something flashes underneath her expression but it shifts before I can decipher it, like the glimpse of a face in a dream just out of reach.

'Hi, Tina, feeling better?' she asks me. At 5'9", her tight-fitting charcoal dress accentuates her figure. With impeccable hair and make-up Megan knows most men think she is sexy. Her confidence tells you that. I run a hand over my suit self-consciously.

'Yes.' I can't remember what I came in for, it is clear Megan has been taken on without my consultation. Who made that decision? Did Glyn know about this? I'm surprised neither of them have consulted me. I thought today, at least, I would have had an input. To say my nose has been put out of joint is an understatement. Of course, I won't let that show as that would undermine me in the eyes of the staff. Instead, I grin and bear it.

'I believe you're leaving us, Rachel. Have we appointed Megan?' I can't help thinking about why she's leaving us. How would I cope if it were Glyn? They had so many plans for their retirement and now this. It seemed to happen to so many people. That's one of the reasons I want us to do our bucket list while we can. I can see she's putting on a brave face. I look away not wanting to make her feel uncom-fortable. After all, she doesn't know I know her reasons for leaving.

Rachel looks past me. 'Yes, we have. I'm taking early retirement.' Her eyes glaze over at the mention of retirement. 'Howard and Glyn decided to give Megan a trial period. They're working on the Farrington account today and didn't need the hassle of other interviews. They didn't want to bother you; I hope that's OK. Megan has loads of experience and I can give her a character reference.'

My voice carries a brittle edge. I can't help it. 'Hmm, and you've known her how long?' I hate how my voice sounds.

'Oh, about twenty years.'

I'm shocked. I was expecting her to say something like five years.

Megan's gaze is unwavering and blatant, her dark brown eyes follow my every move. I feel a chill and shiver as I pour myself a cup of water from the water cooler in the corner of the office. With my back to them, I ask, 'So, have you always lived around here, Megan? Rachel never mentioned you.'

'No, I lived in Kent.' I hesitate just as I'm about to drink. 'I moved up here six months ago. Are you familiar with the county? It's beautiful, truly the garden of England.'

Somehow and without wanting to my mind reels back in time and I'm flooded with the same disjointed images as before. I know I've done something that I would never have imagined myself doing. Something so bad my mind has blocked it out. And to make matters worse I feel a sense of justification surrounding it.

'That's where I come from, originally,' says Rachel.

'No, I've never been to Kent,' I reply as my hand shakes a little. I turn round. 'Rachel, I thought you hailed from these parts.' She never told me she came from the south.

'We moved up here when we married. My husband is from this area. It's no secret.' I wasn't accusing her of anything. I think again of her reason for leaving the firm, and it saddens me. I really don't know what I would do if something happened to Glyn. Maybe I'll ask Glyn if we can keep her on the payroll for another year, I know she will struggle financially, she's not due to retire for a few years.

'I suppose we all have secrets, don't we?' Megan says, interrupting my thoughts. My brows crease and I can feel my face tense at her words.

Megan moves round the table and comes to the water cooler where she helps herself to a drink. She stands close to me, so close I can see where she hasn't blended her foundation on her jawline particularly well. 'Well, I imagine some secrets are harder to live with than others,' she says in a hushed tone as if she doesn't want anyone else to hear her. 'Like Rachel, she doesn't want anyone to know why she's leaving. So sad, isn't it?'

I look at her over my shoulder and she smiles, warmly. 'Yes, very.' Her words unsettle me.

Rachel continues talking in the background, but I'm hardly listening. I'm too aware of Megan's presence next to me and what she might say next. 'I've known Megan a long time, her mother and I were friends. She decided to move up here after her father died.'

'Yes, Rachel has been like an auntie to me. I missed her when she came up here. So, when Dad died, I thought I'd make a fresh start.'

I watch Megan's face, but it doesn't change. I can't read anything in it. 'Well then, how fortuitous for you, Rachel, now you are retiring,' I say, wanting to get out of there.

I move over to Sally, my secretary, she's been with me from the beginning, loyal and trustworthy. Always unadorned by jewellery but smart in good quality suits, black or navy teamed with a white shirt. I don't believe I've ever seen Sally wear any other colour. She hammers away on her keyboard with her headphones on, her mousy hair flecked with grey pulled tight into a bun at the back of her head. I take a bunch of files off her desk; I don't know what they are, but I want it to appear as if I came in for something other than Megan's interrogation. I walk quickly down the hallway towards Glyn's office and catch up with him at the door.

'Hey.'

'Hey, I see you've taken Megan on? I thought I oversaw recruitment? After our chat this morning I thought I might have been kept in the loop?'

'You do. But Howard made the call. I've only met her briefly myself, he did the interview and told me he'd appointed her. She's on a three-month trial.'

I snort, understanding all too well why Howard made the call.

'You feeling better? You don't look great, still a bit pale. Maybe you should go home, darling.'

Megan strolls along the corridor towards us, I freeze in the doorway. She makes me feel so uncomfortable being around her. I squash the files I'm holding to my chest and press up against the wall as she walks past into Glyn's office. Her strong perfume lingering long after she has entered the room.

A compulsion, perhaps the same one that makes me pull the skin around my nails, makes me try to remember something that happened to me in my past. That email has jogged something loose, something I don't think I want to remember. But my mind is closed, it won't let me recall. That perfume is so powerful I fall back against the wall.

'Are you OK, Tina? Can I bring you anything? You don't look well.'

'Tina, are you OK?' Megan is by Glyn's side. 'Shall I get her a chair. She should sit down. She might fall and bang her head again.'

'No, thanks.' The perfume lingers around me like a spider's web. I don't want to sit down. I want to get back to my office.

Glyn looks at my pale face and grabs my arm to stop me falling to the side. I take a deep breath and regain my composure. 'I'm OK.'

I love this man with all my heart. He's a brilliant husband, father and lawyer. He trusts me. He believes I could never do anything wrong. He would lay his life down on that belief.

But I have done something wrong. I think.

CHAPTER THREE

I spend the evening preparing tea for the kids and a meal for Glyn and I, but I'm distracted all the time, unable to concentrate. This situation with Howard and Megan has unsettled me. It's unprofessional and his reasons for employing her could lead to a whole heap of problems. I'm certain if HR were aware they wouldn't be too thrilled. I think about the work waiting for me in my study but can't find any enthusiasm to do it.

I feed and then bath the kids, putting Matt to bed with a story.

Downstairs, Laura sits on the couch reading her book. When Glyn arrives half an hour later, he's greeted with shrieks of excitement from Laura who jumps up and clings to him, wrapping her arms round his neck. Every evening it is the same ritual, a bit like Groundhog Day. Except today, Glyn brings her the sparkly shoes she wanted. She flings off her slippers and puts them on and does a few little dance steps. Glyn makes monster noises and chases her upstairs where he tucks her up and they read together.

I've changed into loose joggers and T-shirt and sit at the table pressing a glass of cool wine against my neck to cool down as I wait for Glyn to eat our evening meal. I play with the stem of my wine glass.

'You OK, darling?' Glyn asks as he pours himself a glass and tucks into his food. 'You seem preoccupied. You're not still harping on about Megan, are you?' His voice is mellow and I can feel myself calming a little. His eyes show concern but I can see he's thinking there's more to it than merely the employment of Megan.

Pushing most of my untouched meal to the side of my plate, I pour us both another glass.

Glyn likes to think of himself as a wine connoisseur, he has a broad selection of wine on racks in the basement. He always selects the wine for the meal. I'm forbidden to touch these bottles as they're his pride and joy. I rely on inexpensive plonk from Tesco when he's not home.

'No, it's not that so much, it's just that she's a little weird.'

'She seems pleasant enough and I haven't detected any-thing odd about her behaviour. Maybe it's the incident you had today. It's likely made you feel a little vulnerable.' He reaches out and places his hand on mine. 'Because it could have been worse.'

I nod. But that's not what's worrying me. It's that bloody email and now Megan going on about secrets. I caught her watching me today on the few occasions our paths crossed. Creepy. I can't help thinking that email and Megan are con-nected and, if they are, how? 'You're right. I know it sounds foolish, but I feel scared. There's a deep gnawing in my belly, and I feel extra protective about the kids.' I need to stop talking like this. It's not real. I wouldn't be feeling like this simply from that accident.

Glyn squeezes my hand. 'Listen, darling, I'm not under-mining what happened, but you can't let this get to you. We're OK, our family is safe and we have a healthy part-nership in the law firm, but Howard will be watching. If you want to make partner in a couple of months be careful on that score. He likes Megan. Therefore, I suggest you be gracious and just get on. If he likes her, the last thing you want to do is rub her up the wrong way. He's pretty fickle.'

'What do you mean?'

'Professionally, he won't want to take on some flaky woman that's got it in for his girlfriend. He doesn't possess much patience, as you know, and it's close to decision-making time.'

'God, you sound negative about the whole thing, one incident and you think he's going to relegate me to the sidelines because of it? Is he going out with her then? But she only started today. Surely not.' I make a disagreeable sound.

'He isn't. No. Not yet. But it won't be long before Howard makes a move. He's a free agent and rich. He's playing all his cards. I've seen him in action, and am not being negative, just honest.'

He wants to say more, but I get up from the table and clear away our dishes, stacking them in the dishwasher. Glyn helps, putting away the condiments in the cupboard and re-corks the bottle of wine.

'That's disgusting. Has the man got no scruples?' I press the buttons on the dishwasher and slam the door.

'At this time in his life, he has the morals of an alley cat.' Glyn shrugs and puts away the table mats in the drawer next to me. 'Look, I know his agenda. I know how he considers prospective partners. Christ, he talks to me. Despite what you think, Howard has a rod of steel running through him. It won't require a great deal for him to question your strength as a partner.'

'But I bring in considerable revenue, second to litigation. Surely that suggests something?' I fling the dishcloth I'm holding into the sink.

He lets out a sigh. 'Look, Tina, just keep it together when you go in tomorrow.'

'Has something been said? Did he mention something to you today? I don't understand where this is all coming from.'

He grabs the bottle off the table to take it back down to the basement. 'Rachel mentioned your hostility towards Megan, that's all.'

His words sting. 'Hostility?' Thinking back, I was perhaps clipped and unfriendly. I defend my position. 'Well, nobody consulted me and they kept me out of the loop, how do you expect me to feel? Apparently, you and Howard decided to take her on. Without references, just because Rachel recommended her! So, yeah, I was frosty,' I snap.

'She has references, Tina, just not on her. Someone will ring her past employers tomorrow. We thought we wouldn't bother you about it today.'

My face burns with annoyance that he doesn't see how belittled this makes me feel. And now Rachel has irritated me by going behind my back to Howard.

'Why did Rachel even bother mentioning that to Howard? It seems trivial and unnecessary.' I hesitate for a moment. 'Almost as if she wants to sabotage me. Is she annoyed with me? Have I done something to cause her some distress, Glyn, because I'm unaware of anything?' My anxiety sits below the surface. I have always had an excellent relationship with the staff, especially Rachel.

'She hasn't mentioned anything to me. Look, stop fretting, you haven't done anything wrong. I want you to succeed as partner as much as you do. I'm only giving you the heads-up. Take it easy, don't annoy anyone at the firm, keep your head down and it should all go smoothly.'

'But if I've done something or said something to her, I need to apologise.'

'It's her situation at home that's probably causing her to be distant and maybe a bit short with you. I wouldn't worry. Will you please stop pacing!' Glyn blows me a kiss and walks off down to the basement, having to duck to miss whacking his head on the door frame.

I feel as if my life is starting to unravel. First with that email and now with Megan's arrival. These two coincidences haven't *just* happened. I feel sure they've been orchestrated.

CHAPTER FOUR

I have a terrible night's sleep. I wake up at 4.00 a.m. soaked in sweat. My dreams full of chaotic images mixed with enclosed rooms that I was trapped in. When I escaped one I found myself in another and another, never able to get away.

The temperature hardly drops at night. All the windows are open in the hope that a cool breeze will be forthcoming. I grab my glass of water off the nightstand and press it to my face. I'm not sure I can stand much more of this sweltering weather.

Glyn briefly wakes up and mumbles something to me. I keep silent, not wanting to wake him. I don't want him to know how I'm feeling as it will only lead to questions. Questions for which I don't have the answers.

Extracting myself from Glyn's arms wrapped round me, I climb out of bed, shower and dress quickly. I want to get to the office early and use the time before anybody arrives to do some research.

Glyn discovers me in the kitchen twenty minutes later finishing my breakfast.

'You're up early?'

'Yeah, I hope I didn't wake you. I want to get in early.'

'No, it was the empty bed that woke me. It's pretty early, though.'

'I know, sorry but I can't sleep. Sorry, I'm behind with a case. I had to postpone a meeting with a client yesterday and it's rescheduled for today. I can get a lot more done before the phones start ringing.' I hate lying to him. I feel he can see right through me so I drop my gaze.

'You OK? You seem a little on edge.'

I shake my head. 'No, I'm fine. Listen, I have to go, don't get the kids up earlier than their routine, will you? Ali will be round usual time to collect them.' I grab my stuff conscious I'm avoiding looking at him.

Glyn salutes me in a mocking fashion. 'No, Captain, I will do as I am told. Drive safely and text me when you get to the office, please. I think I'll indulge and watch the news, make a pleasant change, won't it?'

I walk over to him and wrap my arms around his neck. 'Love you, darling. I promise to be nice all-day long.' I can't bear the thought of Glyn ever finding out. I know it will break us. The thought of us not being close. Laughing together. Making love. Trusting each other.

* * *

When I arrive at the office, not long after 6.00 a.m. Howard's car is already in the car park. Upstairs, walking along the corridor, I notice his door is ajar.

'Good morning, Tina. How are you? Glad to see you putting in the hours.'

That irritates me. I say nothing, except, 'Morning, Howard, I'm feeling better thanks, thought I'd catch up on the Miller file as she's coming in today.' I soften it with, 'Would you like a coffee? I'm making myself one.'

'Excellent, thanks, bring yours in at the same time and we'll have a little chat.'

I dump my stuff on my desk, text Glyn that I've arrived and check my appearance in the mirror hung behind the door. My hair hangs loose today, I hope it represents a competent lawyer in Howard's eyes.

I place Howard's coffee on his desk and take a seat opposite.

'Tina, now this is a little awkward. I'm putting your behaviour down to the fact that you were involved in a minor incident yesterday and were not in the best frame of mind. However, this is a professional law firm, and we treat our staff with politeness and understanding.'

The colour rises in my face. I want to say that Megan's hiring just because Rachel recommended her was out of order. I realise I have taken a dislike to Rachel since she went behind my back.

Howard continues, 'When you're in the office you need to be professional all the time and that includes with the staff.' I want to say my bit. In lieu, I keep my mouth closed, annoyance bubbling inside me. I feel like a schoolgirl being told off by the headmaster. I'm an associate partner, and he should not be speaking to me in this way. Only because I want to make a full partner do I keep shtum. 'Rachel was upset yesterday with your cold shoulder approach towards her and Megan.' I want to roll my eyes, and it takes a lot of concentration not to. 'I'm aware that it was your best intentions to want to screen Megan. We have a lot of confidential work with our celebrity clients. I recognise that. But it's not only that, Rachel told me that you intentionally cold-shouldered Megan yesterday when she walked into Glyn's office.' This time my mouth drops open. He carries on talking, suggesting whether I would make a suitable partner after all.

I come away licking my wounds. Never in all the time I have been here has Howard used that tone with me.

I hurry down to my office and slam the door behind me. Sitting at my desk, I grab the file and flick it open. I am not in the mood for Mrs bloody Miller and her greedy sticky fingers. I take a few deep breaths to calm myself. I can't afford to have any more blots against me. My fingers curl tightly round the pencil on my desk, I can see myself snapping and losing it with Howard if this carries on.

Focusing my thoughts on my work, I push through the paperwork; Mrs Miller is tough, there is no reasoning with her.

I don't think she will settle; it looks like we'll be going to court after all. I have a couple of barristers that I will recommend to her. But no doubt she already has her own lined up. Her husband owns a large well-known logistics company; they've just won the Coca-Cola contract. This is big bucks for us if we win. I mean when we win. I want to bask in the glory that I haven't fucked up in Howard's eyes. I know the enormity of winning this case will leave me without any blemishes on my character.

'This is huge, Tina, our fees on this will do you the world of good as a partner,' Howard said to me when I discussed the case with him. 'Don't settle if you think we can get more, but if you go to court, it has to be a win-win for our client.

'You're the best for Mrs Miller, you were recommended by Mrs Swift and Mrs Miller is in a different league. Plus, this will deliver you straight into the heart of this wealthy circle of ladies. You know what women are like. If they do well out of a divorce, your number will be the first they dial.'

'No pressure, then?' I had joshed.

Howard hadn't missed a beat. 'There's always pressure, Tina, the bigger the case the more pressure there is and if your reputation precedes you, it will be exhausting.' As I left his office he said, 'Of course if you don't want to handle the big clients I can always give them to Lucy.' Lucy! My God, Lucy Rowley was a good divorce solicitor but not for clients like this. She didn't have the killer instinct that is needed fighting for this lot. I knew he was playing with me, but it still hurt.

I looked him dead in the eye without interrupting. Every word stung, fuelling the anger inside me. When he finished, I said, my voice almost a whisper, 'I have no problem handling the wealthy clients, Howard.' I could read between the lines; I knew that if I wasn't up for the big clients then by default I wasn't up for partner.

Later that morning, after working steadily on the case, I set my pen on my desk and decide I need a break and go to see Glyn. I locate him in his office sat at his desk with Megan standing by his side. 'Hi, darling, won't be moment,' he says.

I politely acknowledge Megan and sit down in front of him. Glyn is running through instructions with her. Is it just me? Or is she standing a little too close to him? Her tiny black skirt barely covering her knickers. I raise an eyebrow as she edges closer still until his arm is brushing against her. Glyn is unaware of any of this. I look up at her, and she gives me a smile, it's a pleasant smile, so why do I feel as if it's predatory?

'OK, Megan, I think we're done. Rachel can assist you with this if you forget any part of it. I know there's a lot to take in.'

Taking the files off his desk, she says, 'Thanks, Glyn, Rachel is extremely helpful.' At the door, she turns back and says, 'Excuse me, Glyn.' He's talking to me and stops.

'Has anyone told Tina that I'll be helping her today?'

Startled, I look from Megan to Glyn for an explanation. I can feel a hot flush on my cheeks.

'Sorry, yes, thanks, Megan. Tina, Sally called in sick this morning, something she ate. I recall you've got Mrs Miller in today and Megan kindly offered to cover for her.'

No way! I don't know what to say. Well I do. But I keep that to myself. I didn't know Sally was off, not having ventured from my office since I arrived.

'I'm sure it can all wait until Sally is back.'

'I don't mind, really I don't, Tina. The more I get involved the quicker I'll pick it all up.'

'Thanks, but I'll wait for Sally. You have enough to do with Glyn's work.'

I turn back and give him a questioning look.

Glyn says, 'We don't know if Sally will be back tomorrow and then she'll be playing catch up. Megan can take the load.'

I don't want Megan to take the load. I don't want that woman near me. Trapped, I agree, but decide not to action it.

When Megan leaves closing the door behind her, I say, 'I was going to ask Sally to carry out the checks on Megan today. I guess it will have to wait.'

'You could ask Rachel.'

'I could, but maybe she is too close to Megan. I'll ask Sally to obtain the references, if you don't mind.'

'What the hell does that mean, Tina? She's friends with the woman; it isn't a crime you know. What is she going to do? Lie? Fabricate references? That wouldn't do Rachel any good if she was found out, would it?'

I shrug my shoulders; I'm not sure why he is so defensive suddenly. I hadn't even considered those scenarios. I simply thought she wouldn't bother. In the hopes that by the time we received them everybody would adore Megan so much they wouldn't matter. Of course, that's only if she's lying, which I strongly suspect she is.

'No . . .'

'No, you're right. I don't know what's got into you; you seem to have it in for the poor girl. Just let Rachel sort it. Remember Howard is appraising you. If you're not careful, you're going to blow this. Don't be an idiot.'

'I'll do my best, but I will ask Sally when she returns. Remember I oversee recruitment and I will do it my way.'

Glyn doesn't miss the tone. 'Don't mess this up, Tina, I mean it. We're counting on this promotion. You're the one that wants the bigger house and garden. It's expensive round here, but we won't be capable of securing the necessary mortgage without your promotion. We're in a great position right now, the money you inherited has supplied us with a mortgage free home for a long time.'

I avoid eye contact; something has shifted between us. I'm uncomfortable with the way he looks at me. Maybe I'm being paranoid.

'Of course, I won't blow it. I had a chat with Howard this morning. He demanded I kept office politics out of it and win the damned Miller case or else it's cheerio partnership.'

'Right, good, I know you're under pressure from Mrs Miller and Howard to win this. You need to focus on the goal here.'

'God, I'm not under pressure. OK, focus I will. Sally can sort out the references when she gets back.' I raise my eyebrow in challenge. 'But I don't want Megan in my office and I don't require her help, is that clear enough?' I stand up keen to leave, sick of everyone hindering me.

'Chrissakes, Tina, do whatever you want.'

'Yes, I will, and that's my final word. Tell her what you like, I don't care. Oh, and for the record, please don't be so abrupt with me, Glyn, I'm not an office junior. I'm ambitious and covet this partnership. I will keep everyone sweet and walk on water if that's what's needed.'

It irks me we are having a tiff over Megan.

Glyn holds up his hands. 'Sorry, darling, I didn't mean to be bullish. I'm just anxious for you. In the last twenty-four hours you seem to have lost your focus.'

I sigh. 'God, this is absurd, we don't argue and look at us having words over something so trivial.' I lean over the desk to give him a kiss as a peace offering.

CHAPTER FIVE

That evening after I've completed the homework, made tea and read stories, I pour myself a glass of wine from the fridge, basking in the coolness of its interior for a few moments. Glyn will be home a little later tonight. He's meeting Howard after work for a drink. It's something they do once a week, *a boys' catch up* Howard calls it, whatever that means. I imagine the talk tonight will be about me. I know Glyn will stand up for me; he invariably does, but Howard has a roaming eye at this moment in time and it seems to have settled firmly on Megan causing him not to think clearly.

I leave Laura watching TV in the kitchen, telling her she can wait another half hour for Glyn then she must go up, it's a school night. I go into the study with my briefcase, pulling out the Miller file and opening my laptop. I look for the paperwork from today's meeting in the paper file. It isn't there. I start from the beginning and turn over each piece of paper one after the other until I reach the end. Still nothing. My heart leaps in my chest. I play back the sequence of events in my head. I wrote down what we decided to do and how. Mrs Miller gave me paperwork relating to bank statements both personal and business. She also provided me with a copy of the Coca-Cola contract. Shit, where the hell was it all?

I placed everything inside the file and put the file into my briefcase. I check my briefcase in case it has fallen out, but there's nothing.

A surge of panic floods me. I remember attaching the paperwork with a paperclip. I don't lose files. I'm meticulous. I also scanned it into the appropriate folders on the computer myself because Sally was off today. I would not lose original paperwork. I don't lose original paperwork. We're going to court in a weeks' time and need the originals. This is bad. I grab my briefcase and empty it. Shaking it upside down to double check, knowing it's a waste of time. I rummage in the pockets and check my desk in case I brought it in here and forgot. I grab my car keys, tell Laura I'm looking for something in my car and hurry outside. It's still daylight. Opening the boot, I look inside pushing supermarket bags out of the way. I search the front seat and the rear. Nothing. A cat screams and makes me jump and turn round. My eyes catch a glimpse of movement in the upstairs window of the empty house opposite. It's up for sale. I see a woman looking at our house. But she disappears when the low sun breaks through the light cloud, blinding me.

Back in my study, I log on to my laptop and sign in. The files can be accessed remotely, so if the paperwork is there then at least we have a copy. God knows what I'm going to say to Mrs Miller. Can she even get copies of the bank statements again? The little wheel spins slowly; our broadband connection isn't great here . . . eventually, I'm in. Looking across all the little yellow file icons on my screen, I click on Millers. It opens, but I don't see the statements. I refer to my paper file. The paperwork is the same as the digital copy. Identical. But no statements. I flick through in case I've misplaced them when I scanned them in. I know this couldn't happen; they would be at the front of the file. A sinking feeling drags from my chest to my feet.

I access the backup files, these are automatically backed up several times a day. I retrieve the file and click to open. Exactly the same. I lean back in my chair and think. I know

I scanned them in. I even looked at the damned file before leaving to collect the kids. I know they were in there. That means that between 2.30 p.m. and 5.30 p.m. something happened to erase the paperwork. I wonder if any other files have been affected? I also wonder if I left my folders open at work and this is what caused the files to vanish, like a cyber-swipe or something. I'm not techy, it is the best rationale I can come up with.

I hope Sally is in tomorrow. She'll be able to find them; she's techy. I really don't want to have to ask Rachel, she will go and tell Howard what's happened and that is the last thing I need. No, I need to keep this under wraps until I can find them.

The front door opens and Laura shouts, 'Mum, Dad's home, Dad's home.' Laura leaps into his arms and he smothers her with kisses. I love watching them together, the way she clings to him like a life raft, our beautiful gangly daughter is such a Daddy's girl. They have a special bond; they always have had, the day she was born he took her straight from the nurse's hands and held her close. Laura peed on him and Glyn thought that was the most amazing thing to have ever happened to him. He cried and kissed her and spoke so quietly in her ear the whole room went quiet. He won't tell me what he said to her. He said it was such a tremendous surge of love that he felt he had to tell her about it. They've been inseparable ever since.

I walk out of the study, apprehensively. 'You're back earlier than I thought.' My brain is going over the events of this afternoon on a loop. I did scan them, and I did put the papers in my briefcase.

'Yeah, well, Howard had a date.'

'Not with—'

'Yes, exactly. I told him he was moving too fast, and it wasn't really acceptable behaviour for a senior partner.'

'You did? And what did he say?'

'He told me to mind my own business. He's really taken with her. So just be careful what you say to her.'

'He's back in time, Mum,' Laura butts in. Glyn lowers her to the floor and she grabs his hand. 'Come on, Dad, I want to read a story with you and I need to get my beauty sleep, I have school tomorrow.'

Glyn laughs and looks over at me. I explain that this is a new phase that began yesterday. 'Apparently her friend, Penny, who according to Laura is beautiful, goes to bed early to get her beauty sleep and that is why she is beautiful.'

'Oh, I see,' says Glyn. 'Well then, we'd better get to it, hadn't we? I don't want to be the one who stops you getting your beauty sleep.'

Her face takes on an anxious look. 'Dad, this is important stuff.'

He begins with the monster sounds and runs towards her. 'Let's go then beauty queen.' They run upstairs and I hear Laura jump on her bed and then the door closing. Matt won't wake up. He could sleep through a bomb.

I walk into the kitchen and look at the oversized retro clock on the wall, Glyn should be down in ten minutes, so I reheat our meal that I prepared earlier. God, the bloody Miller case. I've lost my appetite. Standing at the sink I see a light go on upstairs in the house opposite. I can see somebody moving past the window and stop. They turn and look at our house. Then move away. It gives me the creeps.

I'm sitting at the kitchen table sipping my cheap wine after loading up the washing machine when Glyn walks in. He's had a few drinks this evening; I scowl at him for driving. I don't need to mention it, he can read my face.

'Penny for them, darling? And I'm not over the limit — nowhere near, we had two pints, that's all.'

I give him a sympathetic smile because I know he is genuine and I am being mean to even think of accusing him of drink driving. It's not something he would ever do, but the tension I know is written on my face. I walk over to him suddenly needing his arms round me and the reassurance that he loves me.

'I wasn't thinking of much, to be honest. Mostly about Laura and how quickly she's growing up. She'll want make-up next and nail polish,' I say avoiding my real problem.

Glyn hugs me tight, he's changed out of his suit into jeans and a blue T-shirt and spritzed some cologne. I inhale the scent deep into my lungs. It's my favourite, he's worn it for years.

'Well, nail polish is OK, isn't it?' He tilts my head up and kisses me, long and deep. 'I love you, Tina.'

'I love you too, babe. Yes, nail polish is fine. It will be lovely painting her nails for the first time. Secretly, I can't wait. I'm looking forward to doing little girlie things with her.'

'There's no rush, though. Let her ask you instead of suggesting it, if you don't mind. I don't relish the thought of our little girl growing up.' He hooks a strand of hair behind my ear. 'Why are you in your pyjamas already?'

'I had a bath, I felt tensed up when I got in this afternoon.' I laugh, thinking that was nothing to how I feel right now. I hug him tight unable to think of the right words to say. All that occupies my mind is where those damned papers are. I desperately want to tell Glyn, but I'm nervous this will compound all that's gone on at the office today.

He let's go of me, kisses the top of my head and heads towards the basement. 'I'll go and fetch us some wine. Shall we finish what was left yesterday? Food smells great, what we having?'

I stand by the hob twisting my wedding ring. 'Err.' I look over at the pan, my mind blank. 'A very quick coq au vin.'

'Mmm. You mean you used that cheap plonk of yours to get rid of it?'

I nod and take a sniff of the meal. 'It wasn't pleasant and my cheap wine had been hanging around for a while. Nothing like your reds. You've spoilt me with your wine. Hurry up, I'm going to dish up now.'

Sitting together he pours out the rest of the wine from last night, and I wonder how I'm going to get through this meal without blurting out what's happened.

'This is delicious, I think this is my favourite now.' I look at the label. 'Gosh, it's Rioja, it tastes like that Chianti we had the other day.' I exhale deeply, pleased my voice doesn't carry a tremor. I avoid Glyn's eyes. He knows me so well, I can't risk him suspecting I'm hiding something.

'No, it doesn't, Tina, it's significantly different.' He shakes his head in mock despair.

I shrug. 'Well, it does to me.'

'How did you get on today with Mrs Miller?' he asks, digging into his food.

I'm engrossed in my thoughts, again, going over what happened to that paperwork.

'Tina?'

'Yes, sorry, babe, I was miles away. What did you say?'

'I asked how Mrs Miller was today?'

'Oh, yeah, it wasn't as bad as normal because she brought in some paperwork she'd managed to find in her husband's office. So she was delighted. He doesn't know she's taken it.'

Glyn nods and takes a mouthful of chicken. Swallowing he says, 'Good stuff? Stuff that will support you in court?'

My hand shakes holding my glass. I try not to adopt the defensive mode that is normal when I'm in a corner: wary and belligerent. 'Yes, why do you say it like that?'

'Like what?' He laughs taken aback by my sharpness. 'I'm only asking. There's no hidden agenda, Tina.'

'She brought in contracts, especially the big one with Coca-Cola and company bank statements that sort of thing.' I nearly miss my mouth my hand shakes so much. I glance at Glyn in case he's seen but he's busy eating and clearly struggling with my outburst.

I force a smile, embarrassed.

The extended kitchen is full of that warm light you get in the late evening in June when the sun is going down. The bi-folding doors are open and it brings the garden into the house.

'Howard will be pleased.'

'Talking of which, I think he's an idiot and embarrassing.'

'I take it you're referring to his infatuation with Megan.'

'Of course I am. The man's having a midlife crisis. What's he going to do next? Buy a motorbike? Get a tattoo?' I eat my

31

food, even though my stomach is in knots, because if I don't he'll know something is wrong. 'I hope Sally's back tomorrow.'

'Yes, she's missed. Megan seems to know her way round our computer system, though,' he says, matter-of-factly. 'Picked it up very quickly, mind you, I think Rachel is a gifted teacher. She was looking for you today. I think you were in the loo before going to pick the kids up.'

'Who?'

'Megan.'

'Oh? Why?'

'She didn't say a great deal. She had some information for you, Mrs Miller had couriered over some paperwork. I told her to leave it on your desk. Apparently, you'd asked her to do something for you? Anyway, when she couldn't find you, she left everything in your office before going out on an errand for Howard.'

'Right. I don't remember requesting her to do anything.' I know I didn't.

He finishes his meal and sits back in the dining chair, his wine glass under his nose as he sniffs the delicate scents of the wine, until the tumble dryer bleeps and he gets up to sort the laundry.

'I forgot to mention I had an email today from Mum and Dad. They're coming over from Australia. They want to see the kids and do a bit of touring round the country,' Glyn calls out from the utility room.

I close the dishwasher door and switch it on, then sit down on the grey squishy sofa facing the utility. Christ, that's all I need. I should help him with the laundry, but he gets cross if I do. Tells me I fold everything wrong. So I let him have his way. The last of the sun has turned the yellow of the kitchen walls almost into an orange hue, making the room cosy. The weather channel says this heatwave is continuing into the weekend. I try relaxing by slowing my breathing, but it's no use. I need to go to bed to disconnect. My thoughts and emotions are all a jumble and I'm struggling to have a coherent thought. I want so desperately to tell, Glyn.

'When are they thinking of coming over?' I ask. Glyn's parents had emigrated to Australia ten years ago.

'Well, Mum has gone in for a routine operation, an abscess or something. So they were thinking soon?'

'What does soon mean?'

'They want to come in two weeks.'

Two weeks. Great. I lift my hair off my neck and twist my head to catch the breeze from the fan.

'The kids will be happy to see them. It's been ages and though they Skype, it's not the same.' I hate Skype. I hate that you can't cut the conversation short because they can see what you are doing. The doorbell can't magically ring. Or the phone. Neither can a mini emergency suddenly happen. Because they are there. Watching.

Glyn comes over to the sofa carrying the laundry basket full of folded dry clothes.

'Come on, let's get an early night, you've had a difficult few days. You need to re-energise. The Miller case is taking it out of you.'

I follow him out of the kitchen and upstairs. 'Do you know if the house opposite has sold?'

'No. Why? Do you know someone who's interested in it?' He distributes the laundry; I follow him, helping.

'No, but I'm sure I saw someone in there a couple of times tonight. At the window. It looked like they were watching our house.'

'Well, that's weird. I haven't seen any cars there. Maybe it was a trick of the light.'

'Maybe.'

Before I can go to sleep I have another look across the road from our bedroom window. The figure is standing in the same window, facing our house. My phone vibrates in my pocket. When I take a look it's a missed call from an unknown number. I look back at the house and see the person watching is on the phone.

CHAPTER SIX

My head is banging, and the kids are up before the alarm. Laura is shouting and screaming and I can hear Matt calling for me.

I wake up with a start, covered in sweat and in a panic. The full impact of those lost papers hits me. I haul myself out of bed as though I weigh twenty stone. I nudge Glyn and rouse him with a kiss. 'Darling, the kids are up and fighting and I've got a banging headache.'

Glyn gradually opens his eyes and mutters, 'Do you want me to go?'

'No, it's OK, I need some paracetamol. I'll grab a couple on the way.' I pull on my thin nightdress, which I discarded earlier, and leave the bedroom, quietly. They've woken up two hours before their normal time.

'Right what's going on?' I ask standing in Laura's room. 'Have you any idea what time it is? It's still sleep time.' I grab Matt off the floor, kiss his wet cheeks and smooth his head. 'Laura what is all this about?'

Matt sobs and snuggles into my chest. I stroke his head to soothe him and the all too familiar lump in my throat catches me out. I can't bear to see my children suffering. Matt looks so much like me with his auburn hair and fair skin. He's a gentle,

34

trusting little boy who I want to protect forever even when he's grown up. Laura too, of course, but she's tough and mentally stronger than Matt. I worry for my children. I worry every day. Losing my mother so early on is a pain I don't want them to ever experience. When my mother died a long painful death, I was consumed with grief. Long before she died, I began my grieving. What she went through after my father left us devastated her in a way no child should ever bear witness to. The unravelling of a once beautiful person is fearsome. The speed with which mental illness can strike is never obvious. This worries me. It always has.

'It's not me!' Laura says indignantly, sitting up in bed. 'He came in and started touching all my stuff and woke me up. Look what he's done with my hair ribbons? They're ruined, he's chewed them.'

I look down to where she is pointing. Two very wet and scrunched up pink ribbons lie on the floor. 'OK, I see, but it's not worth all this shouting. I'll go and wash and dry them. All is not lost, Laura. He's only little, try not to be so harsh with him.'

'Yes, it is. My beauty sleep is ruined. I'll be ugly when I go to school.'

I sigh, my head throbs and I'm losing patience. Sometimes she can be so stubborn. I hold back and when I know my voice is calm, I reply, 'If you go back to sleep for two hours, you can catch up and it won't make a difference. You'll still be beautiful when you wake up.' I put Matt on the floor, tuck Laura back in bed, kiss her forehead and turn off the light. I carry Matt to our room. Before though, I look out of his window and see a figure loitering by our front gate. I step back behind the curtain. The pounding in my head intensifies. I pop him in bed next to Glyn.

'Mummy, someone was in my room.'

'What? Matt you must have been dreaming. There's only Mummy and Daddy and Laura in the house. Snuggle up to Daddy, you'll feel safe here.' My stomach churns and clenches. A lot of the windows are open because of this heat.

35

Surely, nobody climbed in? As soon as I think it, I dismiss it. Impossible. Matt clearly dreamed it.

'All sorted?' Glyn says, still half asleep.

'All sorted, I'm getting up now, I can't get back to sleep. Matt is here next to you.' I don't know why I don't mention what I saw. The pressure of keeping these secrets is affecting me more than I thought. I'm behaving illogically. I know I should tell Glyn.

'Have you taken anything for your headache?'

'No, I'll grab something now.' He takes hold of my arm as I'm about to move away from the bed and gives me a gentle kiss and purrs, 'Love you, babe. You OK?'

'Yes, I'm fine. Love you, too.'

After checking the front garden and finding nobody there, the realisation hits me how stupid I've behaved. It could have been a madman in the garden. What was I thinking coming out here on my own?

Irritably, I wash Laura's ribbons and sling them in the dryer with some other stuff I pull out of the washing machine before taking a couple of paracetamol and falling asleep in front of the TV. I don't want to go back to bed; I know I'll be thrashing about and Glyn will ask questions. It needs sorting without him knowing anything about it. I berate myself for being so careless with those papers. I'm mortified how I am letting myself down.

Breakfast two hours later is a grumpy affair. Laura speaks to no one. Matt rubs his eyes and cries at everything Glyn and I do for him. I feel crap too. My neck kills and my eyes feel gritty. There's nothing more painful than doing all you can for your children and them not appreciating it. Mercifully, we are used to the mood changes and take it in our stride.

I finish my coffee and run upstairs to shower and dress quickly while Glyn finishes the breakfasts. As I'm coming out of our bedroom Glyn appears with Matt. Laura is getting dressed and Matt cries for me. He's so tired he's beyond grumpy. I dress him while I watch the clock. I'm going to be late. Matt is on go slow. The doorbell rings. The three of us finally rush downstairs ready for the day. Gratefully, I hand them over to Ali.

'Bye, guys, love you, have a great day at school.' I kiss them both on the top of the head and whisper to Laura, 'You look fabulous, so beautiful.' She grunts and Matt starts to cry again. My chest tightens. I wave happily at him so he can't see my own sadness as Ali walks them down and out of our drive.

Glyn comes towards me. 'Tina, you know you forgot to lock the French windows last night.'

'I did. I locked them when we went to bed.'

He shakes his head. 'You must have thought you did, but they were open this morning. Is it possible you opened them later, when you came down?'

'Glyn, I didn't.' To be honest I can't remember if I did or not.

We leave for work in two separate cars. Bad on the environment, but we often have to go to court or see clients and they can be anywhere from Manchester to Birmingham. Car sharing isn't an option for us.

I'm the first to arrive at the office. All the way over here I've been trying to think up a plausible explanation for the lost papers. I walk into my office and instantly detect that something is different. I scan the room and my desk. The photo frame of Glyn, the kids and me is missing. It is a 5 × 7-inch tall frame with four different photos of us all. It stands on my desk. Puzzled, I dump my briefcase and bag on the floor and sit down.

Nothing else is different. Wait, Laura made Glyn and I a Christmas bowl each. I keep mine on the little coffee table filled with potpourri and that is missing too. I wonder if Glyn has taken them, perhaps to show to someone. But he has his own so why take mine? I go to his office to check and sure enough his photo frame is on his desk and the papier-mâché bowl is on his coffee table. We have the same one, only his bowl is full of mints.

Back at my desk I sit mystified, willing myself to remember if I moved them yesterday before leaving. I can't worry about that now, I need to locate those papers. In the staff kitchen I switch on the coffee machine and fill it with water. I need my coffee buzz. Glyn is a tea man; he never drinks coffee.

Back in my office, I sit down. I drop the file on my desk and search my drawers. I discover nothing. A sense of shame starts to build inside me. How can I explain what I've done with them? I stretch out my legs and my foot hits something solid.

It's my photo frame, smashed. I pluck it out, gingerly, trying not to drop glass on the carpet. I shake the shattered pieces into the bin, picking out jagged pieces of glass still stuck in the frame. The support is broken and the frame leans badly to one side. I pull out the photos and bin the frame. Maybe the cleaners knocked it off and forgot to come back and clean it up. I leave the photos on my desk. God, I thought the coffee would perk me up but I'm so tired. All I want to do is go back to bed and crawl under the covers and sleep.

Sometime later, I hear voices in the corridor. I glance at the clock on the wall and see it's just before 9.00 a.m. Sally normally gets in at this time. I buzz through but there is no reply. My heart sinks. I really, really do not want to ask Rachel for help locating these files.

Fifteen minutes later I buzz through again and Megan answers. I close my eyes and count to five. I've been trying to occupy my mind with other work, but the lost files just keep nagging at me over and over. My mind doesn't stray far from the argument I'm going to have with Howard the moment I tell him. Shit.

It still astonishes me that I am up for partner. More so that I managed to become a lawyer after everything that happened to me. After my mother died, I went back to finish my university course. I struggled getting through my training contract putting all the hours in that they wanted from me. It overwhelmed me. I came close to having a breakdown and ended up on diazepam and seeing a therapist. I was eager to prove to myself that I could achieve what I had set out to.

I wasn't about to let my anxiety control me like it had my mother.

When I came here for an interview, I smashed it. I was proud of who I'd become and knew that my mother would have been too. I came off the pills and started dating Glyn, who was already a partner here.

'Congratulations,' he told me after calling me in on a pretext of needing other information from me. 'You have the job.' His relaxing manner and suave smile lit me up from the inside and I was transfixed. I remember every detail of that moment. I think I fell in love with him right there and then. He's been the only man I've ever loved. I felt foolish and anxious in his presence until I got to know him. He's the kindest man I've ever known.

'Hi, Tina, it's Megan, how can I help?' Her voice is breezy, light and full of good cheer and I just want to slam the phone down. I can't help it she just gets under my skin.

'Is Sally there, please, Megan?' My voice is toneless.

'No, sorry, she's still suffering with tummy trouble. Can I do anything for you?'

'Err, no, not at the moment. Oh, has Glyn arrived, do you know?'

'Yes, I've just taken him a tea; he's got a meeting at half past.'

'OK, thanks.' I put the phone down and swear under my breath. Damn, I am going to have to ask Rachel. But first as much as I don't want to, I need to tell someone about the missing paperwork. I head to Glyn's office.

'Hi, you got a minute?'

Glyn is on the phone; he waves me in. I take a mint from Laura's papier-mâché bowl and sit down.

'Sorry, darling, Howard is stressed over this case.' He puts the phone down and flicks through a mountain of paper littering his desk. Glyn is the untidiest person I know with paperwork. To look at his desk, you would think he wouldn't be able to find anything. But you'd be wrong. He knows exactly where it all is. Makes me dizzy. If he had lost the files,

I could understand it. But me, meticulous, organised me? I cringe and break out into a sweat.

'God, that means he'll be raging. I best keep out of his way.'

'Christ, yeah, lock your door and for God's sake, don't give him any negatives regarding the Miller case.' He grunts without look up.

'That's the thing, you see.' I get up and pace the room wringing my hands like some character out of a Jane Austen novel. Glyn makes throaty sounds that tell me he's listening but continues to check his paperwork against the computer.

'What's the thing, Tina? Sorry, darling, I've lost you.'

'Shit. Glyn . . . I've somehow lost originals for the Miller case; bank statements and the Coca-Cola contract.' As soon as I let the words out, my heart slams into my chest and I feel light-headed.

Glyn stops what he's doing. This time he does look up. 'What?' He sounds incredulous. 'Tina, how have you done that? You of all people!'

I want to stop wringing my hands. 'I don't know. I really don't. I scanned them into the computer and backed them up and took the file home. At least, I thought I did. I remember placing it in my briefcase. But none of it is there.'

'What? Not on the computer? Or the backup?'

'No, I've checked. It's gone.' I don't tell him I've known this since last evening.

'Has anything else disappeared?' He moves the mouse across the desk, his index finger clicking and clicking.

I know he's checking to see if any of his files have disappeared. I'm desperate. If Howard finds out about this he'll go ballistic in his present mood. I keep quiet.

'Tina?' He looks over at me.

There's a knock on the door. Glyn looks at me. I shrug. 'Come in,' he calls out.

John walks in, apologising for disturbing us. 'Tina, hope you're feeling better today,' he says to me, then flicks his hair and walks towards Glyn. 'I managed to clarify these numbers last night. The discrepancies you found look authentic, you were right, I think they're making all this up.' John turns to me, pushing his glasses up his nose. 'Sorry, I'll leave you both. Sorry for interrupting, I had to show Glyn these first thing.' I nod my response. He leaves before I can respond.

'Nothing gets past, John. Damn, he's excellent with the minor details,' Glyn says, then looks at his computer screen. 'Tina?'

'What? What else has gone missing?' In an instant I'm relieved, because if other files have gone missing then it wasn't me but something to do with the system. A surge of power or something of that sort. I breathe out loudly.

'Nothing's gone missing. The Miller file is here,' Glyn says, looking at me curiously.

'I know, but the bank statements and Coca-Cola contract Mrs Miller brought in are not.'

'Yes, they are. They're here. I'm looking at them now.'

Flustered, I stand beside him and look at the screen. 'But . . . I can't tell you how many times I looked at that bloody file. They weren't there!'

'Well, they are now. It's all there. You've been acting weird since that incident on the motorway, are you sure you didn't hit your head harder than you think?'

I pull back from his side. 'I'm definitely sure. Those papers were not in there. Next you'll tell me the originals are in the file.'

'Well, I don't know what to say. Go look. Is it possible you missed them too?'

Hurt by his accusation, I say. 'You come with me and see for yourself. I can't explain how the digital ones are back in place, but the originals are gone. Come on, let's go.' I walk out of the office and see Megan turn the corner towards the secretarial department.

'Tina, if you need time off, please tell me. We can't afford to screw this up.'

I whirl round on him. 'Glyn, stop it. I'm OK.' I storm into my office, Glyn following close behind. 'Right, here is the file that I pulled out of my briefcase when I arrived this morning. Go on, knock yourself out.'

Glyn sits in my chair and flicks through the paperwork. I'm huffing and puffing, pacing the room full of indignation he thinks I have head trauma.

His voice is tender when he speaks. 'Tina . . .'

I turn and stride over. 'Well then. They're not there, are they? And I haven't lost them. So, where are they?'

'Tina, they're right here. Look.'

'What! No, they can't be! I checked so many times.' The look in his eyes devastates me. 'Don't, don't you dare say I have a problem. Those files were not there last night or this morning.'

'You knew about this last night?'

I want to kick myself in the head for letting that out. They weren't there. I know they weren't. 'I didn't want to bother you about it last night. I believed I'd find them when I got to the office. But this morning they weren't here. Glyn, you must believe me. I'm not lying.'

Glyn strokes his jaw. 'Tina, the files are all here. Megan, did you move some paperwork from the Miller file yesterday for any reason?'

I spin round. How much has she heard? I look at her sternly. Then I remember Glyn saying she had been looking for me yesterday.

'No. I didn't, Glyn; I had no reason to go into that file. Tina didn't require my help.'

I don't know why but that feels like a smack in the face. What's left of my strength seeps out of me like a punctured tyre.

'Tina, you rely so much on Sally, perhaps you should have let Megan help yesterday and this wouldn't have happened.'

'Has something happened? Have I done something wrong?' Megan says, sounding upset as though she might be in trouble. Her voice wobbles. I stare at her, it actually, wobbles! Unbelievable.

'No, nothing, Megan, we thought we'd overlooked something, but we've found it now,' Glyn replies.

'Why were you looking for me yesterday?' I ask. I don't need to see Glyn's face to know he is frowning at me for asking.

'Yesterday? I don't think I was.' She moves closer to us.

'Yes, Glyn mentioned you were looking for me before I left to pick the kids up. That you had some information I'd requested? What was it?'

'Oh, that. Yes, it was Sally; she phoned in to ask that you not call her. I couldn't find you to tell you, then I forgot, sorry.'

Megan smiles and looks to Glyn before she leaves. It irks me that she does that.

I can't believe Sally said that. 'Wait, but what information did I request from you?'

She smiles benignly. 'Tina, you asked me to find out the availability of the two barristers for Mrs Miller.'

I did not ask her that. I'm about to say this when Glyn cuts in.

'Right. OK that's all, Megan, thanks.'

When we are alone, he wraps his arms round me. 'Tina, if you want help with this case, will you ask? I know what you're like. Anyway, the thing troubling me is your memory, please go and see the doctor. Maybe you don't remember banging your head.'

'Don't remember *banging* my head! And I don't remember where I put those files and I suppose I don't remember having a picture frame on my desk like yours, either.' I turn away to hide my watery eyes.

We both look over at my desk in one swift motion. The frame is back in place and so are the photos.

I extract myself from his embrace and go towards the photo frame. 'This morning that was broken. I stood on it under my desk. I'll show you; the broken one is in the bin. Look . . . I don't understand. It was here this morning.' I can barely look at him. I look round my chair. Everything is tidy.

In a second, Glyn is standing by my side. He clasps my hands and strokes the knuckles with his thumb. I don't want sympathy. I want him to believe me.

'Don't you dare say it. I know what I saw. And I don't believe Sally asked me not to phone her. That's not like her.'

Glyn watches me closely. 'I want you to call the doctor right now. I'm staying here until you do. And maybe Sally just feels crap and doesn't want anybody calling. Have you thought of that?'

I scowl. 'No, I haven't. I still think that's odd, though.' I make the call in the excruciating silence of my office and then power walk out. Head down. I throw my handbag over my shoulder and barely notice my surroundings or Megan walking past. I manage a tight smile and exit into the lobby. I press the button for the elevator. Once inside I let the tears out and gasps of air escape in ragged tones. I'm a mess. A crazy mess.

CHAPTER SEVEN

I wince inwardly when I tell my doctor why I'm sitting in his office. Of course, I don't say I've been losing things or misplacing stuff. I keep it simple. 'I banged my head. A little. I think.'

'Have you experienced any blackouts? Loss of time? Memory loss? That sort of thing,' he asks.

I say no on all counts. He examines my eyes with a pen like torch. Then he checks my ears.

'Why are you checking my ears?'

'In case of brain bleed. It's just a precaution. Did you attend the hospital after the car accident?'

'It wasn't a car accident. I told you. It was severe braking at high speed. I was jolted viciously and slammed back into my seat by the seat belt.'

'Where did you strike your head?'

I touch the back of my head. 'I was slammed backwards. I didn't bang it as such.'

'But you've exhibited symptoms as though you have?'

'No.' I sigh heavily. 'My husband has asked for me to come and get checked out. He thinks I may have injured my head.'

'What would cause him to think that other than the obvious? Have you shown signs of possible loss of memory or head trauma?'

I'm grateful that Glyn isn't here with me. He would be making out that I was having a brain bleed for sure.

My doctor, a quietly spoken Asian man, looks at me as if I'm wasting his time and he could be doing something better, like going on holiday, instead of talking to a woman who hasn't banged her head but thinks she might have.

He asks me if I know what day it is and to repeat the months of the year backwards. Then he asks me to touch his finger with my finger, which he holds out in front of him and then to touch the tip of my nose very quickly.

I pass all the tests.

'I'm not concerned, Mrs Valentine, I'm not referring you for a CT scan. But if you do develop any signs of what we've discussed, please come back and see me.'

'Thank you, Doctor. I will.'

I am relieved it's over and I can honestly tell Glyn I have been checked out and there is nothing wrong with me. Maybe now he will believe I am not imagining things.

Leaving the surgery, I head to school. I find a parking spot close by. All my parking buzzers go off as I slip neatly between a Land Rover Discovery and a Fiat 500.

Ali walks past my car, headphones on, arms swinging at her sides. Never one to forgo an opportunity to exercise, she's dressed in trainers, leggings cut off below the knee and a tiny T-shirt. She doesn't notice me. I'm not surprised; it is a rare event to find me here at this time. I'm usually a last-minute arrival. I jump out trotting along in my heels to catch her up. 'Hey, stranger,' I say as I run up behind her, tapping her on the shoulder and trying not to show how out of breath I am.

She lets out a little squeal and jumps away from me. 'Tina! You startled me.' She pulls her headphones out and we hug for a few moments. 'What brings you to the school gates punishment? You look smart in your suit.' Ali is one of those women who looks great in anything. I envy her blonde shaggy Californian hairstyle. I know what I look like in leisure clothes and it's nothing like Ali.

I laugh. 'Thanks. I had to go to the quacks for a check-up. Glyn insisted.'

Ali goes serious for a moment. 'Is everything OK? Or shouldn't I ask?'

'Of course, you should ask. You're my best friend, aren't you? There was an incident on the motorway, that's all. You know when you're travelling along doing seventy miles an hour and then suddenly the traffic in front of you stops? Well, I hit the brakes, hard, and hit my head on the headrest. Glyn thinks I might have banged my head a little too hard.' I roll my eyes. 'So, to appease him, I've gone for a check-up and all is well.'

'Does your head hurt?' she says, looking at my head for signs of bumps, bruising or bleeding. Why does everyone do that? It's so annoying.

'No. I didn't black out or lose time, although listening to Glyn you'd think so.'

'So why did he send you to the docs?'

'Oh, it's a long story. But you're looking great, have you lost weight?'

Ali laughs. 'No, but I've joined the gym and have a personal trainer and I'm trying to walk everywhere now. I think I let myself go, the trigger was when I couldn't easily fasten my jeans.'

I look her up and down. I've only seen her in passing for the last two weeks and haven't really looked at her; I can't believe the change. 'Well, you always look great, but whatever he's doing, you look even better now. I could do with losing some weight.' I pull on my waistband — sometimes I have to unfasten the button to get some relief. 'I think all this wine drinking at home is piling on the pounds and I've got hooked on those new crisps you brought round a few weeks ago. I can't stop eating them. Maybe I need to go to the gym too.' I scrunch up my face. 'God, I can't face it, not really. By the time I've finished with the kids I'm whacked. Pretend you didn't hear that.' We both laugh conspiratorially.

'Let's have coffee instead or better still let's go to that lovely little bar that's opened in town, you know the one on the corner. James is going away next week. My mum could babysit. Think you could get out?'

'That sounds like a great idea, we haven't had a night out in ages. Talking of mothers, Glyn's parents are coming over.'

'From Australia?' I nod. 'Are they staying with you?' I nod again, Glyn's mother is not my greatest fan as she thinks I should be a stay-at-home mum. It's a topic she always brings up on Skype and I choose not to engage in. When we had Laura and I returned to work we had a huge tiff and didn't speak for two months. It took Glyn a long time to persuade us to talk again. He told her it was our choice and the subject was taboo. She doesn't stick to the rule, but I've learnt to avert the conversation when she starts.

'Yeah, for a bit. Then they're doing some touring of the country. We hope to take advantage and get some evenings out.'

'I'm looking forward to it already. Have you met your new neighbour yet?'

I tilt my head to the side; I wasn't aware any of the neighbours were leaving.

'No. Who's gone?'

Ali lives on the opposite end of our road where the houses are smaller three-bed Victorian terraces. On our side of the road; the houses are four to five bed semi-detached or detached — ours is detached, with a basement and decent garden that is long rather than wide.

'The house opposite you, silly, the one that's empty. I only knew about it because I saw the removal van there last Friday lunchtime bringing in the new people. It was a small van. So maybe a young couple or first-time buyers. They didn't have a lot of stuff. It's been on the market for a long time.'

'That makes sense. I thought I saw someone in there the other day. It gave me the creeps. It looked like a woman but I can't be sure. Both times she was looking across at our house.'

I shiver. 'The place is full of rot and damp. It lets the whole street down, and I hate looking at it each morning when I come out of my drive.'

'Hey, come on, we have about five minutes before our life is no longer our own. So, tell me what's been happening to you. I don't think we've chatted properly for weeks.'

I laugh and nod in agreement. 'True, we haven't.'

'So? Anything fab happening in the Valentine household? How's that handsome husband of yours? He still causes a stir round here when he does a pick up, you know. He's so tall I can always find him, usually with a gaggle of mums round him. I consistently receive envious looks fired at me when I say hi and he bends to kiss me on the cheek. I love it!' We both giggle like teenagers.

I get a buzz knowing he's mine and how much attention he attracts at the school gates.

Ali has remained my dearest friend since school. The only time Ali and I have not been together was when I went away for a while to look after my mum. She knows me better than anyone. Even Glyn.

The kids are suddenly free and everyone is looking for their children. Laura comes bounding towards me like a colt.

'Mum, Mum can I go for tea at Katie's, they're having pancakes.' She pulls at my sleeve. 'Pleeeease, Mum.'

I look at Ali, and shrug. 'Fait accompli, as the French say.'

Laura flings her bags at me then goes to chat to Katie who flings her own bags at Ali. Both girls waltz off down the street arm in arm, chatting like they haven't seen each other in years, when in fact they've spent the entire day together.

Ali seizes my hand and pulls me towards her. She whispers so the other mothers standing around can't hear, 'I have something to confess to you later.'

CHAPTER EIGHT

'I'm sure Glyn thinks I'm turning into a basket case.' We've fed the kids and deposited them in the back garden. I take off my jacket, finally, enjoying the through breeze from the open windows on my skin. I fill Ali in on the last two days and include everything I can remember. Except Megan. I can't quite bring myself to talk about her. What am I? Twelve? Moaning about some woman who's annoying me? I need to get a grip. So I tell her, she's my best friend, I need her frankness. Saying it out loud *does* make me sound a little loopy.

Ali lets out a deep sigh. 'Wow, I see what you mean.'

'Oh God, you think I'm crazy, too!'

'What? No. I haven't said that, have I?'

'Well you have, actually. In that sentence, "Wow, I see what you mean."'

'No, that's not what I think. Tina, you need to stop overanalysing everything. Just deal with each problem on its own, otherwise collectively you will drive yourself mad . . . sorry, terrible choice of words,' says Ali as she sits next to me. 'I could do with a glass of wine, what about you?'

'Me too, but it's a bit early, yet. Don't you think?'

Ali looks out of the window; I follow her gaze. They're all playing happily. Matt is digging in the flower bed and the girls are inside the pink Wendy house that dominates Ali's back garden.

'It's nearly five o'clock. I won't tell if you don't.' She brings over two glasses. 'They're only little ones and you've eaten all that batter which will soak it up.'

I take a deep drink and enjoy it slipping down my throat. 'Don't I know it. I've had to unfasten the button on my trousers.'

Ali raises an eyebrow and sighs. 'Nothing for it, Tina, you'll need to make time for the gym now.'

'Yeah, maybe. But seriously, Ali, tell me what you think is going on. Am I going crazy? I'm doubting myself and it terrifies me. I think I left the back door unlocked last night and don't remember. I'm sure I locked it.'

'Have you told me everything?' Ali asks.

I nod. 'Definitely everything.' I enjoy a welcome breeze caressing my neck. I take a sip of my wine and wonder if to tell everything to the woman who has been my confidante since I was a child.

'Tina, you're not losing your mind. Maybe you're pre-occupied by this case.'

'I'm not,' I add in my defence.

She furrows her brow; there's silence for a few moments before she says, 'OK, let's take this one step at a time. Have there been any meetings or any new people that might have messed with the system without you knowing?'

I laugh. 'Don't be silly, Ali, we don't let strangers on the system. Everybody that uses it are staff . . . and Megan, of course. She's new.'

'The same time you started losing things she started?'

My brain is either firing off many unhelpful thoughts or freezing on me right now. None of which are helping. Why did I not think of this? When I voice it aloud in my head it sounds ridiculously obvious.

'Yeah, but that's a coincidence, right? No way she can have moved that paperwork. Having said that, she seems to have blind-sided Glyn and Howard and the rest of the staff.

51

I know that sounds silly, but they all think Megan is lovely. Especially Howard, he fancies her and has invited her out.'

'No way! And you say she's just started there?'

'She's fuddled his brain for sure. The man's having a midlife crisis, that's what I told Glyn. But you should see her, Ali, I mean she's a tease. Not at all like any of the other secretaries. She's a long-time friend of Rachel's, well Rachel was a friend of Megan's mum and a sort of auntie to Megan and, of course, Rachel can do no wrong now.'

Ali nods and blinks rapidly then asks, confused, 'Why?'

'I forgot you didn't know. Her husband has been diagnosed with cancer, and she's taking early retirement to look after him.'

'Oh, that's tragic.'

'It is, and Glyn and Howard tiptoe round her. I can't believe the change in her. I think it's the worry. She looks grey and lost.'

We are both silent for a few minutes.

'What's this woman like, then? Megan.'

'A Marilyn Monroe lookalike, with swollen pouty lips. She wears tight clingy clothes that leave nothing to the imagination, no VPL, so nothing going on in that department. And every time she looks at me, she launches daggers.' I present her with a look of bemusement.

Her eyes are wide, staring at me as she listens. 'Has she hit on Glyn?'

I flinch remembering her standing next to him. 'Absolutely not, but she's provocative and I don't know why, but I get the feeling she's trying to provoke me. Why? What have I done? Crazy, isn't it? The woman is intimidating me in my own office.' I avoid looking at her. I can't risk Ali suspecting that I'm not telling her everything. She knows me too well.

Ali pats my hand. 'Do you know anything about her? Have you ever met her before? For all you know she might be someone Glyn knew in the past?'

I scrunch up my face. 'What! No! Christ, he'd remember her, believe me. She isn't someone you forget.' My face is full of disgust like I've just stood in dog poo. 'Besides it's Howard she's drawn to.'

'I know, but you said she was weird with you. What about someone in the background? Someone he met and dismissed. Maybe a friend of a friend? Or something like that. Could she be out for revenge against him for snubbing her?'

I think about this, but I can't see it myself. 'No, Ali, I see where you're going with this. But no. I think she's just a flirt who doesn't like me.'

'What if she's the wife of an ex-client or a wife of a client the firm went up against and sued?' Ali throws her hand up in dismay. 'Perhaps she's out to hurt the firm. Maybe she hates you all. Maybe . . . you are the first one on her list.' When she sees my confused face, Ali finishes with, 'Oh, I don't know, it's just the way my mind works. Maybe it's none of those things.' She starts to laugh. 'Maybe she's just a psycho . . . like Norman Bates. Maybe she's a psycho Barbie.'

I smile, but I feel a chill in my blood. 'Great, you really have sewn a seed. Thanks.'

Ali grabs a cushion holding it close to her chest. 'Look, don't take this the wrong way, Tina. But is it possible that you are overlooking things because of this incident? Wasn't it a close call? You once confessed to me that watching your mother die was a life changing moment and death terrifies you.'

I contemplate what she is saying and the tears trickle down my face before I can stop them. I'm thrown, I'm not actually sure who I'm crying for. My mother or what happened surrounding her death.

Ali throws the cushion to one side and hugs me. 'Tina, I'm sorry, I think because you might have died that day it has made you have a sort of mini breakdown. I know you're terrified of death and losing your family. Holding the fear inside is maybe messing with your brain a little, to protect you from going into a state of panic. That terror might be what is muddling you up now.'

Unable to find the words to articulate, I feel the old feelings inside begin to well up and I push them down.

Shove them deep. But I can already feel them bubbling, rising upwards threatening to come out. I close my eyes and concentrate; I need to try harder to put them away before they get a hold of me. I find sealing them away works well for me most of the time.

I wasn't always like this, only when my mum died, before then I was in touch with my feelings. Now I keep a close guard on them in case they try to take over as they are right now and cause me to lose sight of my goals. Maybe I have taken it all out of proportion. And yes, losing my family *is* my greatest fear. I miss my mum and I hate that every time I think of her, I see her dying. I battle to force myself to see her before the cancer. When we were happy. Not that there were many happy times. I remember bursts of happy moments when she was lucid, but her mental health cast dark shadows over our happiness. The fear of loss is always so close by, hovering, skulking in the gloomy corners. Crazy, I know, and maybe it's because of this fear I'm losing sight of what is real. I don't want to go there again. To that dark confused place.

Ali hugs me and keeps her eyes on mine to keep me focused. 'You're not going to die, Tina, you need to move on. Nobody can take your family from you, remember that. Nothing is going to happen. You're not going back there. You're well now. That was all in the past.'

I breathe deeply. She doesn't know that, not for sure, nobody can predict that. I'm glad she has my back, though. 'Glyn mustn't know about . . . you know.'

She squeezes my hand. 'I know and he won't. Nobody knows. Just you and me and that's the way it'll stay.'

'Thanks.'

'Tina, I'm here for you, you know that, don't you? You can talk to me and tell me anything. I'll stand by you, whatever. You do know that, don't you?' Ali lets go of me and tightens her grip on my hand. 'But after you went away, you were never the same when you came back. You've lived with her death for a long time and the guilt. It's been a massive weight you've carried, but you need to let it go. It wasn't your fault. You did what you could for her. She had cancer, she was always going to die.'

'You make it sound as though it's easy to forget.'

'Not forget but put to one side. Achieve closure. Maybe go and speak to someone like a therapist, it helped once before.'

I break eye contact, withdraw my hands and stand up. 'You're right. I'll do my best.' Never one to linger on a point, I move on. The last thing I need is to go back into therapy. What I've found after my experience is that once you're in the system it's difficult to get out. Labels, the medical profession love to put labels on everyone. Clinically depressed they called it. Ali is great, and I cherish her, but she likes prodding me a little too hard. I don't enjoy getting too close to my feelings; they get in the way of my linear thinking.

'You like to manage everything in your life. You were like that as a child; you always formed a plan that we had to follow and when it didn't turn out the way you wanted you got upset. But life has its own plan, sometimes very different to what you think. Look at me. Who would have thought I'd be divorced and a single mother at thirty-one? I definitely didn't believe I'd meet a remarkable man like James who would care for us as much as he does. My plan was to go it alone. Thank God it never worked out like that.' She laughs and stands up, gives me a kiss then walks to the back door. 'All three are in the tent. They've probably dressed Matt up in some sparkly dress. The poor lad, he's so sweet, they do take advantage.'

'Hey, in all this drama I forgot to ask what it was you had to tell me,' I say switching the topic from me, and grateful for the escape.

Ali smiles, sweetly. 'James has asked me to marry him.'

'Oh, my God, that's fab, Ali, I'm ecstatic for you. You don't look ecstatic. What's wrong?'

'It's only with my last marriage turning out so badly, I'm nervous.'

'James is nothing like that tit. He's a good man; he's proved that to you. You've just instructed me to let go of the past and here you stand hanging on! Let go, girl. I'm so excited. I can't wait to tell Glyn. Do you have a date?'

CHAPTER NINE

I welcome the weekend with open arms; a lie in and a cosy body spooned up against me. Glyn's hand is on my thigh and moving. It's still early, and Glyn's body is snuggled up to me and he appears to know we have time before the kids wake up. It constantly amazes me how he gauges the timing so perfectly.

He moves his hand to my waist and gathers me against him, kissing my shoulder and neck whilst his hand gently caresses my tummy. 'I hope you're feeling less anxious, babe. I think you really let go last night and relaxed.' He chuckles making me grin subconsciously. 'Allowing my hands and body to de-stress you is the best cure.' He nibbles the back of my neck. I shove my bottom backwards and he groans. I let him think that. Don't get me wrong, I love him touching me. Except sometimes it does nothing for me if I have things on my mind, and I do. I'm still not convinced I overlooked the files, either the electronic versions or the paper ones.

'You know you always do that to me. I let off a lot of steam with Ali, that helped, too. The pair of you are great at de-stressing me.' It would upset Glyn if he knew that right now, all I'm thinking of is how it all happened.

'I'm sure it did and the doctor giving you the all clear helped. But primarily it was my magic fingers that did the trick.' His hand wanders down my tummy and between my thighs.

'I don't want to talk about the doctor.' I turn round and kiss him. His stubble scratches my face. His untamed hair and sleepy face do turn me on; I love this man. But I'm distracted. Glyn looks sharp in his business suits, but I much prefer him like this, first thing in the morning, sleepy, warm and cuddly. I kiss his lips and suck the bottom one. He kisses me back, greedily. We manage to make love before the kids wake up. Matt bursts in the room with a toy truck and throws it on the bed narrowly missing Glyn.

Glyn lets out a pretend 'ouch' then grabs Matt and they begin to play wrestle on the bed. That's my cue to get up, jump in the shower and pull on my dressing gown. It's another lovely day out there. I consider what we can do today as a family. We've enjoyed four days without rain. I leave my hair down this morning, grab my straighteners and get rid of all the curls and waves.

Glyn is still rolling on the bed with Matt.

'Did you know someone had bought the house opposite?'

'No, have you met them?' He says tickling Matt on the belly who shrieks with delight.

'Ali said she'd seen a removal's van, she thinks it's a young couple.'

'That's odd, I haven't spotted any movement there?'

The toy truck falls off the bed. Matt rushes out of our room. A few moments later he comes back with arms full of trucks. 'Play, Daddy,' he says, sorting out two rows of trucks at the foot of our bed. Both Glyn and Matt start crashing trucks into one another. Matt squeals and laughs, shouting, 'Again, Daddy, again.'

'There was a woman in the window looking over at our house.'

'Really?'

'Yes, I caught a movement from the corner of my eye and when I looked, I saw her for a second then she'd gone. It might have been nothing, though, shadows or a trick of the light. I can't be certain.'

He doesn't respond with words just a grunt. He's involved with the car wreck going on.

'Well, I'm sure we'll meet her in good time,' I say. Something about that house bothers me.

'We will. Come on, basher, lets go get some breakfast,' Glyn says. He grabs Matt and hoists him up onto his feet. Matt pulls a face. Glyn comes across to me and gently loosens the belt of my dressing gown discreetly slipping his hand over my breasts, kissing me. He turns to Matt. 'Let's eat, then we can carry on afterwards.' Glyn pulls Matt towards the door. Looking at me over his shoulder, we both know he'll have forgotten all about their game once he's downstairs.

I finish my hair add some earrings then step backwards; I trip on the trucks, catching my thigh with the sharp edge of the digger, tearing my skin. Pressing the wound with a tissue, I rush to the en suite, swab it, put on a Band-Aid, then slip into a pair of jeans and T-shirt.

* * *

I decide that today is a good day for a barbecue. After breakfast, I inform the Valentine family we are having a barbecue and paddling pool party this afternoon. I make a mental list of what is needed from the supermarket and scribble it down.

'Wow, how to clear a kitchen in one fell swoop, babe,' says Glyn, finishing his tea and looking up at me in surprise. 'What's brought this on?'

'I thought it would be pleasant to have Ali and James over. James has just got back from his trip, plus we haven't seen them as a couple for ages and Katie loves playing with our two. And Ali revealed to me that James has proposed.'

'That's marvellous news. You'd better get moving and don't forget the champagne; the supermarkets are a madhouse on a hot weekend.'

'Rammed. Can I leave you to blow up the paddling pool?'

He pulls a mock-sad face. 'Really? Blow up the paddling pool all on my own? Are you sure you can delegate such a responsible job to me without your supervision?' He's mocking me. The last time I entrusted him with the barbecue he charcoaled everything. So now we prepare everything inside but still call it a barbecue.

I send a quick text to Ali before slipping my arms round his neck and kissing him gently on the lips. He tastes of tea and Marmite. 'No, darling, I'm asking James to support you, obviously. If you get through that, you can wipe down the table and chairs along with laying the table.'

Glyn grabs me when I pull away. 'Are you sure about me laying the table, you know how odd you are about that?'

I grimace but smile regardless. 'I'm sure you will do a brilliant job of it. Just make sure it's—'

'I know, I know, promise you won't have a hissy fit if it's not?'

'I won't, well, I'll try not to.'

'So, this paddling pool and all the blowing. Will you make it up to me later? I'll have sore lips from all that blowing.'

'Mmm, will you require me to kiss them better or will they be too sore for any kissing?'

'They will need kissing better,' he says and kisses me back.

His words make me think about that missing file. You see I know that file was not misplaced, because I am meticulous and organised. Granted, I do suffer from a little OCD, mostly at home. It manifests itself with odd little tendencies such as setting the table, everything must be balanced, all cutlery spaced out equally. Same with pillows on beds and cushions on sofas, similar distance apart. My handbag, too. Everything enjoys its own place. Purse at the bottom under my telescopic umbrella and make-up bag, just in case of pocket thieves. Like I said, not radical. It all started after Mum died. I manage my anxiety now. Initially, it freaked me out because this was how Mum started after Dad walked out. Except she couldn't control it in the end.

My phone pings with a text back from Ali saying they'll join us for the barbecue and she'll come to the supermarket with me. I text her back that I will pick her up in a few minutes while running upstairs for a jacket. Although it's a scorching day, it's always freezing in the supermarket and I hate that just as much as I hate supermarket shopping. When shopping by myself I tend to time how long it takes me to get round, each visit I try to beat the last. So, when they decide to move things and swop the aisles, I want to throw a mini fit. Jacket in hand I pick up my bag from the console table by the front door. The doorbell rings. It's Ali and James with Katie already in her bathing suit.

'She couldn't wait,' says Ali nodding at her and noting my look of surprise.

'Hi, Katie, Laura's in her bedroom, go up. Glyn's in the back garden, James. Congratulations, by the way,' I deliver a friendly punch to his shoulder.

'Thanks. This woman needs taking off the market; she's too precious.' James pecks me on the cheek and blows a kiss to Ali. 'Nice to see you, Tina, it's been a while.'

'Yes, too long. We'll do some serious catching up today, though.' I kiss him back as I leave.

Reversing out of our drive I see a woman in the house opposite sweeping the drive, wearing baggy T-shirt, shorts, trainers and baseball cap. The front of the cap is pulled down to hide her face and her hair is swept up underneath. 'Oh, there's the new owner,' I tell Ali. 'Shall we go over and introduce ourselves?'

Ali glances over her shoulder. 'Where?'

'Oh!' Dropping my sunglasses down the bridge of my nose I look behind me again. 'She must have gone back inside, she was sweeping the drive. Maybe we should invite them over when we return.'

'Good idea, I'll go over later when we get back while you unload the shopping.'

* * *

'I see you're getting on with the job, quickly,' I say, dropping the shopping bags in the kitchen. Both men hold a half blown up medium sized paddling pool with two empty bottles of lager by their feet. 'Do you think it'll be blown up by lunchtime?'

It irritates me they haven't finished. Take a deep breath, Tina. My therapist used to tell me breathing exercises bring stress levels back down. I would like to get some little pills from the doctor instead of relying on my breathing exercises right now. But I'm nervous of getting hooked like before. I have that kind of disposition, I think. If temptation was put in front of me right now, I might.

'I think so, darling, refreshments will help, of course,' Glyn says dangling the empty lager bottle.

Over my shoulder I say, 'I'm just saying, not wanting to rush you or anything, but you won't get fed if the pool isn't filled up. Oh, by the way, Ali has gone over to ask the new neighbours if they'd like to join us.'

'That sounds like a brilliant idea,' says Glyn.

'It'll be lovely to see that old wreck done up. It's such an eyesore,' says James.

I hand them both another bottle. 'Glyn, did you remove my debit card from my purse for any reason?'

'No, why would I do that?'

'Ali had to pay, I couldn't find it anywhere. Can you reimburse her, please? I must have left it at the office.' I don't remember doing that. Thank God Ali was with me today. 'I rang the bank and cancelled it just in case.'

By midday all the food is ready. I've arranged the table how I like it. Ali has returned informing us our neighbour is a single woman who will probably join us. Glyn brings out some of his special wine from the basement and Ali and I dry the kids off and settle them in their places. James transports the food from the kitchen for me and places it in the middle of the table. I pull up the umbrellas to shade us; the temperature is in the high twenties already.

We open a bottle of champagne and toast our good friends. 'To a fab life together, you both deserve it,' I say.

The four of us clink glasses. I'm so happy, I want to cry. I try not to notice that Laura has moved her place setting and it's now not quite opposite Glyn.

Ali jumps up and hugs me then Glyn. 'Guys, you are the best friends I've ever had.' She turns to me. 'Tina, you're like a sister to me, will you be my maid of honour?'

I screech with excitement. 'God, yes, so long as I don't have to wear a peach dress.' We hug, and Glyn and James perform manly things with handshakes and fist thumps.

'Once you've eaten you can get back in the water,' I tell the kids.

'So, what's the new neighbour like?' Glyn asks, biting into a corn on the cob.

'She seems charming. I think I caught her on the hop. I didn't think she was going to answer the door until she caught sight of me tapping on the window and realised I'd seen her. She's on her own though, no husband or partner. A bit glammy.'

'I wonder if she's getting contractors in for the work or doing it herself.'

'Oh, I think she'll get contractors. She doesn't strike me as the sort to get stuck in.'

'Really? What sort of glammy?'

'Well, to start with, her nails. Long with extensions in vivid red, matching her lipstick.' Ali sculpts with her hands the outline of a voluptuous figure.

We all say in unison, 'Oh.'

James laughs. 'Well, maybe we should invite her over for dinner if she's on her own. Don't you think, Ali? To be neighbourly? There's only so many ping ping meals a single person can live off.'

'Maybe,' Ali replies. 'Let's see how today goes. I get the feeling she might be a handful.'

'You said she was charming,' I say.

'She is, she was with me, but, well, I don't know how to say it if I'm honest. Anyway, she'll be here soon, you'll see for yourself what I mean. I think they call it high maintenance or something like that.'

Again, we say in unison as if we fully comprehend but not so sure we do, 'Oh.'

The doorbell rings just as Glyn is getting up to fetch more wine. 'I'll get it,' he says. I pour myself another glass of wine and pass the bottle across to Ali.

'Shall I bring up some more wine while you get the door, Glyn?' James offers as he empties the one he's holding.

Ali and I laugh. 'Not if you value your life,' Ali tells him, watching Glyn's face grimace.

'Thanks, I'll grab it on the way back,' Glyn replies.

'Can we get in the water now, Mum?' Laura asks. I look at their plates and give them the nod.

'Is he still precious over his wine? I thought that was only in the beginning,' James asks, helping himself to more couscous.

'Nope it's the same. I keep some cheap stuff in the fridge in case he's home late and I want a drink. I wouldn't dare touch his wine. Bit OCD about it.' I giggle. Who am I to mock OCD? I feel light-headed but serenely relaxed and very happy for my friends.

'Do you think that's our new neighbour at the door?' James asks.

'She said she'd come,' Ali replies. 'She was unloading packing boxes when I knocked. Strange though, she seemed to recognise who I was when she opened the door, then smothered it with a coughing fit. She offered me a drink and hurriedly put away some files inside one of the packing boxes.'

'Really? Maybe they were naughty photos or something. What do you mean she seemed to recognise you?' I remember the woman in the window looking at our house. 'Maybe she's seen you about, picking up the kids.'

'I don't know, but I'd swear she called me Ali, but most likely it was me imagining she said Ali. She probably said hi. She had the radio on loud it was difficult to hear.'

'So, you didn't have a chance to snoop?' I ask. 'That's not like the Ali I know who is fond of looking in people's medicine cabinets when she goes to dinner parties.'

Ali laughs. 'I'm not that awful!'

James and I both chip in, 'Yes you are.'

Not bothered, Ali continues with her story. 'She seemed embarrassed enough about hiding them. I moved over to the box when she fetched me a drink, *being the inquisitive person I am.*' She giggles and strokes the side of her nose with her finger. 'I was peering in to see if I could discover anything when she suddenly appeared next to me and closed the flaps on the box. Scared me half to death. I was mortified she caught me. So, she might not come over. She might think we are all a bunch of nosy parkers.'

James hugs her. 'Ali strikes again. I've told you before your snooping is going to get you in trouble. You know what happened to the curious cat?'

'Oh, shut up, James,' I laugh. Ali and I giggle from too much wine.

The three of us are chatting merrily when Glyn arrives back at the table with our new neighbour. 'Would you like a glass of wine, no need to worry about driving home today.' He pours her a glass from the open bottle on the table. 'Look who our new neighbour is!' he says congenially.

CHAPTER TEN

Ali jumps up and air kisses her. 'Great that you could make it, sit down.' She moves a napkin from the empty chair opposite. 'Wow, you clean up well, don't you?' She and Glyn run round like worker bees, clearing a space and finding clean crockery while I observe it all as if I've been punched in the gut. My fork is halfway to my mouth as I witness the scene. The bite-sized chicken on my fork suddenly doesn't appeal.

She sits down and smiles broadly at me. I look beyond her at Glyn who faffs like an old woman explaining the vintage she is about to drink. I manage a strained smile. Ali plates food for her like she's the bloody Queen.

Megan is wearing a corn-blue off the shoulder dress with her ample bosom pushing out of the top. The men try to avoid looking. But with her blonde hair, her predatory body language, she's sucking them in anyway. In an instant I feel frumpy in my shorts and T-shirt. Even Ali, who always looks great, resembles someone who has dragged her clothes from the nearest overflowing pile of ironing.

Glyn is oblivious to the storm cloud that has come over our pleasant afternoon. James is the only one as perplexed by their behaviour as I am. Sat to my right he whispers, 'Is she someone famous?'

'No,' I remark, unable to say more.

'She's a bit overdressed, wouldn't you say?'

My hazel eyes narrow, taking in her low-cut dress that untastefully exposes her boobs. When she leans forward to accept the glass from Glyn, I have a sudden urge to reach forward and catch them, like falling melons off a counter, they precariously balance in the ribbon of fabric round them.

'Just a bit,' I reply to James and set my fork down on my plate.

Her eyes watch and smile at me. I can feel my happy feelings floating away and dark clouds gathering. I take a deep breath and within a few moments, Glyn is talking and smiling at me as though I should be overjoyed by our new guest. Has he lost his mind? I know he needs to be a courteous neighbour, exhibiting the niceties good neighbours are supposed to exhibit, but he's also aware how I feel about her. The thing I find difficult to swallow is how confident she is amongst my family and friends.

'What a surprise this is, Tina? What a small world, don't you think?' He nods and I think he wants me to agree. Of which I don't. I can't. I'm too hard-pressed focusing on my breathing and wondering what alien parasite has invaded his brain to make him think like that.

I lean back in my chair ignoring Glyn and say in a tone anything but friendly, 'Megan, what are you doing here?' In fact, I am sure it sounds hostile.

She raises her well-defined eyebrow, the sort that arch in the middle offering a surprised look all the time. She has a tinkling laugh. It's irritating. Her voice is husky. I hadn't picked up on it before. It comes across as suggestive and vulnerable. She's about as vulnerable as a great white. I'm temporarily thrown back to the last couple of days and my anxieties at the office — off they go again. Pulse racing. Brain swirling in confusion how to handle this bloody vile woman in my house without coming out of it looking like the bad guy. The all-familiar flush begins creeping up my chest to my face.

'Tina,' she says excitedly like I'm a long-lost friend. 'Ali popped over the road and invited me over; I had no idea you and Glyn lived here. Imagine my surprise when Glyn opened the door. Beautiful house. So big. So spacious.'

I give her my best cheesy smile and I'm rewarded with a frosty look from Glyn. I don't care. Why is this woman in my bloody house? Sitting at my table, mingling with my friends and family?

Ali stops what she's doing and looks at me. Her eyes wide with astonishment. She sits down next to me and squeezes my leg under the table. She whispers, 'I can't believe it. Is this *the* Megan you were talking about?'

Megan's eyes are fixed on me making me uncomfortable.

'Yes. What the hell is she doing here?'

'Christ, she's the new neighbour, Tina.'

'I gathered that. How is she my neighbour? Isn't that a bit strange and coincidental?' The hairs on the back of my neck stand up. Something isn't right here. She's not who she says she is. She's lying, but I can't think why? For what purpose?

Ali drinks her wine and turns slightly towards me, I can see she's embarrassed about all the fuss she made over her. Glyn sits down next to her.

Megan waves her hands animatedly while she talks in that breathy voice. Christ, it's like a magnet drawing him in as though he were metal filings. Why had I not noticed that before? She flicks her blonde hair over her shoulder, *oh, please*, whilst chatting about wine to Glyn. He is thrilled there's someone at the table as enthusiastic as himself. It's all a show. I can see it in her face. Why can't anyone else? It's obvious. She's not even discreet about it. Who comes to a barbecue dressed like *that*, anyway?

Megan looks concerned suddenly, she places a hand over Glyn's on the table and her smile disappears. My eyes drop to their hands and I have a tremendous desire to drag my husband away. By his hair. What is wrong with him? James isn't smitten. Has she given him a pill of some sort while we weren't looking? She says, 'I'm so sorry, Glyn, I was going to bring a bottle of champagne with me but I clean forgot. I feel terrible intruding on you like this. Shall I go back for it?'

Yes, go back, you made up Barbie and stay in your own house.

He grins broadly and shrugs. 'Don't worry about it, we have plenty of wine.' He shifts his hand and I relax, a little. I'm still cross with him.

'Are you sure? I feel terrible, sitting here drinking your wine and eating all this lovely food that Tina's prepared.' She simpers and turns her gaze on me. 'Maybe I should go back for it.' She prepares to leave the table.

'It's OK, honestly, have us round another time to make up if that makes you feel better.'

It doesn't make *me* feel better.

'If you're certain.' She emphasises the *you're.* Then as an afterthought she looks my way. 'Tina, thanks for inviting me. You'll have to come over to mine next time, once I'm settled in.'

I grimace.

'We look forward to it, don't we, Tina,' Glyn says, waiting for my answer.

I try understanding the uncomfortable feeling worming its way inside me. This woman despises me and I have no idea why. I can feel it coming off her in waves.

It takes me a few moments to reply. 'Yeah, one day we'll do it.'

Megan dismisses my jibe and talks and talks, she jumps from politics to fashion to TV dramas. Her chatter is relentless, and reels in James talking about motorsport, which thrills him, this being his favourite topic. Christ, she sounds as if she's been up all night with Trivial Pursuits or profiling. I see Ali visibly bristle.

Talking with Ali and half listening to their conversation I glance over and she smiles but it doesn't reach her eyes. A warning? I desperately want another glass of wine but know it will take me beyond my comfort zone. Ali half turns and says quietly, 'Let's clear some of this away, I want to talk to you.'

'Can I help, Tina?' Megan asks as Ali and I begin to collect plates. 'Or would it be too crowded in the kitchen?' *Anywhere would be too crowded with you, weirdo.* I catch my thoughts before they gain momentum. I can't let them. I need to control them and focus on not getting stressed. Stress can trigger OCD tendencies to spiral out of control. Like my mother. With me it all began soon after the funeral, or at the funeral to be precise. The order of service had to be placed on the pews all facing the right way up. All in a line. When people began arriving and disturbed the layout, my breathing accelerated and I nearly passed out. That was the first time I knew something was changing inside me.

'No, it's fine, we can manage. I'm going to fetch the coffee. I take it you've had enough to eat,' I say and pull away the plate from in front of her, raising an eyebrow when Glyn's face questions my actions. *What? She shouldn't be here in the first place, eating my food.*

'That's a great idea, I've had far too much wine.' She looks cheekily at Glyn and giggles. 'You're very lucky, Tina, to have such a wonderful husband and family.'

I look at her and she looks back at Glyn who is holding court on the merits of European wine verses New World wine. Glyn has drunk too much, I can tell. To divert the conversation and move him away from Megan, I ask him to add some more water to the paddling pool.

Ali and I clear the table. When we're in the kitchen stacking the dishwasher, she looks over her shoulder, sure we can't be overheard and says, 'You didn't say she looked like that, Tina.'

I look round my kitchen; it's such a mess, how does it always end up like this? I need to clear it up. There's too much mess. Everywhere. The bin needs emptying. The recycling bin is overflowing. Bottles and glasses litter the work surface. Pans and dishes overflow the sink. I don't know how it's so bad when I loaded the dishwasher before we went out into the garden. I tell myself this is the mark of a busy family life. But suddenly it all looks chaotic.

'I did. That dress is so short, I bet it would fit Laura,' I say, pulling on my rubber gloves and diving into the sink to degrease the pans before re-loading the dishwasher.

Ali is immediately stern faced. 'I don't like her one bit. Who dresses like that to a barbecue, especially if you don't know the hosts? There's something off about her, I understand where you're coming from, now. Creepy. Thinking about it, she was really keen to hide those photos and paperwork from me at the house.'

'You see. I thought it was just me.' I rub my thigh where I cut myself with the toy truck.

'Absolutely not, no, definitely creepy. She won't be invited over to our house.' She shudders. 'She's like a cougar ready to devour our men.'

I let out a deep breath. 'Oh, Ali, thank God you see it. Thank God. You can see why Howard is gaga, can't you? Christ, the pheromones oozing from her!'

'Definitely, oozing, and oozing all over Glyn. She's trouble, Tina.'

'She reminds me of those Venus fly trap plants,' I say at the same time as my rubber glove snaps on. 'She's so rude. Who would come over like that after what's gone on at the office? It's not rocket science to see I don't like her. I can't stand the woman and want her out of the office and our lives.' I scoff. 'And why would she think we'd go over to hers? She's crazy. I don't trust her. I have a deep feeling . . .' I touch my stomach '. . . a bad, deep feeling.'

'Hi, Tina. I thought I'd come and see if there was anything I can do to help,' Megan says standing in the doorway, smiling, holding a glass of wine in one hand and a small silver picture frame she's picked up. 'Families are special, aren't they?'

I try to look welcoming. But I know I don't pull it off. How much *did* she hear? Did she hear that I hate her? Don't trust her? Oh, I don't care if she did or not. Why am I even worrying about it, for heaven's sake? I'm the associate partner in the firm; she's a bloody secretary. Yeah, but she's doing it with Howard and that gives her more power.

Ali continues loading the plates in the dishwasher and mumbling, 'Did she hear do you think, I don't think she heard. Pretend like we've said nothing bad about her.' I give her a tiny shove to shut up. She heard all right.

Megan, not missing the nudge goes straight to the tap and pours herself a glass of water, which I think is rude, but I don't say anything. Ali rolls her eyes and keeps quiet, continuing with the loading. 'You have such a great house; it's beautiful. I'd love having a house like this, mind if I look round? My family lost their house. Repossession, you know.'

'No, I didn't know. Not today, Megan, it's a mess, I haven't had time to tidy up.'

'Oh, Tina.' She slaps her hand against her chest. 'I don't mind that. You should see my place. In fact, you really must come over. Both of you. I'd love getting some ideas on interior design. This place is just gorgeous.'

'Another time, Megan, today it's impossible. Sorry.' What am I apologising for? I reprimand myself. I dislike and mistrust this woman and should not feel obliged to be nice to her. Ali has stacked the cutlery arbitrarily. I bend down and do it in an orderly fashion. Knives together, forks together, spoons and teaspoons together. There, better. My pulse slows.

Megan smirks at me when I straighten up and begins to wander round the kitchen opening cupboards and straightening the cushions on the sofa. They were straight before, now she has messed them up. I clench the urge to walk over and put them back. I raise my eyebrows at Ali; we have an unspoken message which we use when we're out together on a girlie night and get hit on: we've used it for years, and it comes in very handy, it says — *what the fuck is going on? Time for a quick exit*. Ali takes her cue; she looks round for a distraction and grabs the coffee cups I left out on the worktop and shoves them in Megan's hands.

'Here, you wanted to help, didn't you? Well, let's go, coffee is ready.' She virtually frogmarches Megan out of the kitchen.

Like a boomerang a moment later she walks back in as I'm walking out with the coffee. I stand blocking the door, wondering what she's up to now. 'It's so nice to be here with *your* family, Tina, thanks for inviting me.' I smother a laugh not knowing what to make from that sentence. Then she adds, 'Sorry, I need the loo, is it upstairs?'

'No. It's by the front door. You can't miss it. There's a wooden heart hanging on the door.' I have no choice but to go outside and leave her inside my house. Something doesn't feel right. Do I need to go keep an eye on her in case she moves anything?

I set out the coffee cups and Glyn goes back in the house.

'Where are you going?' I ask abruptly, suspicion ripe in my tone. I'm on edge and uncomfortable with her inside my house. What if she's looking at stuff and reporting back to Howard? Stop being crazy, Tina. What can she find? My *Psychologist* magazine for one. She might report to Howard I'm reading it. So? So, plenty.

'To the loo, why? Do you want to come with me?' He gives me a cheeky chortle, and I dismiss him with a wave of my hand, he's drunk. Not drunk, drunk, just tipsy. 'You need to chill, darling, you look all stressed, have more wine.' He points at the bottles on the table, then heads inside and all I can do is look at Ali in a panic. At that point I see her eyes move from my face to the side. I turn and see Megan leaning against the door frame watching me while she talks to Glyn. The sun had dipped behind a cloud when suddenly it emerges, blinding me. I shield my eyes with one hand, when I can see clearly again, both Megan and Glyn have disappeared.

CHAPTER ELEVEN

I tactfully offer an excuse about making more coffee and, leaving Ali and James at the table, go back inside. I feel strangely uncomfortable looking for Glyn and Megan and I don't know why I should, it is my house for heaven's sake.

I hear giggling coming from the basement; the door is ajar. I navigate my way down well-worn stone steps, quietly, fully aware of wanting to sneak up on them. Scowling, not happy the way my thoughts are going, I justify a bona fide reason to myself for sneaking downstairs — to see if I overhear anything, she might say about me, that's all. It's a substantial basement with wine racks at the far end. From their vantage point they will see me coming down the steps before I see them. Their voices are muffled; the only audible sound is Megan's laugh, which irritates me like a hair shirt.

Megan is facing me when I reach the last step, she looks straight at me with an amused look, one I wish she would remove.

'Tina,' she says, 'Glyn has enlightened me on his wine collection.'

Glyn jokes, 'Tina thinks I'm a little OCD about it.'

Oh, ha ha-ha, very funny Glyn. I don't think he realises what he's said. He's definitely had too much wine.

'I do not,' I say in my defence and come to stand next to him. 'We'd best get back to our guests, darling,' I emphasise the last word and link my arm through his.

'Tina loves the French Viognier, don't you, babe.' Glyn points to several bottles of the wine.

'Don't you get tempted to sneak down here and help yourself?' Megan asks, running a finger along the bottles.

'No. This is Glyn's domain; I never touch the wine in here.'

'Crikey, I hope it's insured. There are so many bottles, can you imagine if the kids came down here and knocked them all over.' She places the palm of her hand against her mouth in mock horror.

'That wouldn't happen. The kids are not allowed down here.'

Glyn squeezes my hand knowingly. 'You're right, come on, let's go back upstairs. I've enjoyed talking to you about my wine, Megan. We mustn't neglect our other guests, though.'

'The pleasure is all mine, Glyn.' She lunges forward and pecks him on the cheek. Next, she looks at me and says, 'It's so lovely we're neighbours.'

I don't make a comment. I can't. My lips have welded together. I need fresh air.

We leave in single file up the steps, Megan leads and I follow. I turn to glare over my shoulder at Glyn who offers me a *what's the problem* look. Why can't he see what she's doing? Is he really so dense?

Back upstairs, I brew more coffee and carry it outside to find they have relegated me to the head of the table. The kids have re-joined us and nibble on breadsticks plus small biscotti biscuits. Megan sits next to Glyn.

I'm fuming and astounded how easily this woman is working her way into my family. Her familiarity with my husband is winding me up.

'Did you work for a law firm before?' James is good at getting information from people. We always laugh at his approach and have suggested on numerous occasions he should bring a questionnaire with him.

'I have done, but I've worked in various businesses over the years.'

'What sort of companies have you worked for?'

'Oh, you know, all sorts. I worked for the NHS for a while. The last place I worked was at a law firm in Braitling.' My head snaps up. 'It was a modest office, you couldn't really label it a law firm, mostly a one-man band, you know the type. The old gentleman did mostly Wills and Trusts that sort of thing.' She looks directly at me. 'It proved to be incredibly enlightening. How long have you been married, Tina?'

'Err . . . about six years.' I sip my coffee, where is she going with this?

Megan pulls a face as if she's calculating some difficult mathematical sum in her head and then looks at Laura and Matt. 'And how old is Laura?'

'Laura is eight,' I snap, knowing full well where she's going. I don't justify myself but let her pursue her line of questioning. If she thinks she is going to humiliate me, she's mistaken.

She pulls the look that says, *ooh, I've just done an extremely difficult sum in my head. Want to know the answer?*

I'm not embarrassed, because I've never hidden the fact from anyone that Laura was born out of wedlock. I keep my eyes on her and defy her to carry on. Why would she think I'd be embarrassed? What century does she think we're living in?

But instead of coming on the attack towards me, she goes all-empathic with Glyn. It's never bothered him before, but right now I wonder if that was real or if he just went along with it. With all the wine swimming inside him and Megan's flirting, I worry he will declare something shocking. She places her hand on his arm. Leaning her head to the side like a dog, she asks him, 'Was it a shock when Tina announced she was pregnant? Or were you both planning it from the start? I imagine, it was love at first sight, was it?' She twirls a strand of hair and doesn't take her eyes off him. My heart leaps at his hesitation like a car when it stalls. I want to chuck my biscotti at her.

Finally, after a lengthy pause he says, 'I suppose it was a natural thing for us. Yes, it was love at first sight; I was thrilled. Tina and I are blissfully happy together, aren't we, darling.' Glyn blows me a kiss, removes his arm from under Megan's and reaches over for my hand where he drops a casual kiss on my knuckles. I want to cry at the loving gesture. But he did hesitate. Is that normal? Should he have or should he have come straight out and said, no it wasn't a shock. She's messing with my head. I can feel her inside. She's fricking crawling around in there, rummaging and looking for the right buttons to press.

'Mmm,' she says, 'Does Laura know you weren't married when she was born, but you were when Matt came along?'

I tear a chunk from my biscotti with my teeth. Luckily, Laura and Matt don't notice, they are far too busy squabbling over the last biscotti. 'As much as we *like* you, Megan, I don't see how any of this is your business,' I snap. 'Why don't you tell us where *your* family are? Are they all still in Braitling?' *There, let's find out about you, madam.* I place my coffee cup in front of me with the handle to the right and central on the table. I slip the teaspoon under the handle.

Megan shoots. 'I don't have any *family* left. They're *all dead.*'

'Oh, I'm sorry to hear that. It must be tough to be on your own,' interjects James. What the . . . has he missed her behaviour moments ago? Why the sympathy? I want to snort and say I don't believe her. She's making it up to grab sympathy from my friends. I play with the tiny teaspoon. James looks at me and swiftly moves on. 'Have you always enjoyed working as a legal secretary? Is that what brought you to Tina and Glyn's office.' I can see he is trying to lighten the mood. My mood.

Megan studies James. 'Funnily enough, no. I worked for an estate agency, but then heard about Rachel and what she was going through and thought I'd move up here to be near her and help. She didn't want a big fuss making. She was a good friend of my mother's. She was always around when I was growing up, she's part of the family. When she moved here we kept in touch. She knows all about my family and what happened to them. Braitling is a small village. Difficult to keep secrets in a small village.' She picks up the bottle of wine and tops all our glasses up, except mine. I survey her face while her eyes focus on me. I shift uncomfortably in my chair. 'You shouldn't drink whilst taking meds, Tina.'

I blink. 'What? What did you say?'

'You can provoke a bad reaction if you drink while taking medication, haven't you read the leaflet in the packet?'

Everyone looks at me. I look at her. 'What are you talking about, Megan? I'm not on medication.'

'Oh, sorry, they said at the office you suffered from OCD and required medication to keep it under control.'

'I do not suffer from OCD. Who told you I did?'

She fans her face as if dismissing the whole thing. 'Oh, I don't know, it might have been Sally. It most likely was Sally come to think of it.'

Sally does not know about my OCD. Nobody does. She's lying. She's found that out from somewhere and is now trying to pin it on Sally. But it won't work, so I laugh to take the sting out of the accusation and make her out as a gossip hound. 'Well, you shouldn't listen to gossip, Megan, it can get you into lots of trouble. I am not and do not suffer from OCD and I am not on any medication.'

'But your desk. It's so tidy. I thought—'

'You thought wrong, didn't you?'

'Oh, dear, silly me, here have more wine.' She fills my glass and places it in front of me, then taunts me to drink it. When I don't, she raises her glass. 'Let's make a toast, to Tina NOT having OCD.' There's a stunned silence and then everyone raises their glasses, including me. 'Go on, Tina, you have to catch up with the rest of us, drink up.' I accept another drink not taking my eyes off her. She gently pushes the base of my refilled glass towards me.

'Have any of you been to Braitling?' She directs the question mostly to me.

I stay silent.

'No, we haven't,' declares Glyn a little more subdued than before. Why is he avoiding looking at me? Am I in the wrong here? Does he genuinely believe what she said? 'But maybe we should do a long weekend, Tina. It will be good for us.' He looks over at me and scowls at my stony expression. Good for us? Is there anything wrong with us? I twitch my lips to smile. 'Rachel always says how lovely Kent is. We could leave the kids with James and Ali? What do you think, Tina? You two wouldn't mind, would you, Ali?'

James is still on his mission to find out more information from her. 'How long have your parents been dead, Megan?' James enquires.

'Or better still,' pipes in Ali getting animated, 'why not the four of us go. Tina tells me your parents are due over soon and my mother is too, so why don't the four of us go? It's been so long since we had a break together.'

We used to do lots of long weekends together. When did that stop and why? I can't remember. It just happened. Kids. Your life changes, we should be more proactive about these things, Ali is right.

'My mother died nine years ago not long after my father lost the house. The stress and stigma were too much for her,' Megan declares, wiping a pretend tear from the corner of her eye. *Oh, please.*

I listen to both conversations at once and then suddenly I can't stand the mess on the table. It's chaos.

Megan continues, 'I think you would love it, Tina. I think you would have an affinity with the place.'

I still don't say anything.

James asks, 'Was it recently your father passed away?'

'About two years ago. He never got over losing the house and mum dying. He sank into deep depression and couldn't hold a job after she died. Then my grandmother told him she'd taken him out of her Will. She was afraid he'd squander her money. She'd been propping him up financially for years. She was wealthy. She had a house worth over a million pounds in Braitling when she died. She cut him out of her life too, so we moved to Cheltenham where he started a small book restoring business, but it went bankrupt. He found it difficult to get back on his feet after losing that. We ended up living in a council house on a terrible estate.' Why is she looking at me when she says this? Megan studies my face. I study the table. My hands curl into balls to stop me from getting up and clearing it away. How is she doing this to me? It's as if she's talking directly to me and not the group.

James looks solemn when he speaks again. 'I imagine that was very difficult for him. Losing his wife then losing his mother. How awful to be cut out of your parents' Will.'

'It was. He never believed she'd do it. It broke him when she died and he found out for sure he wasn't in the Will. I started work straight after finishing school. We moved houses several times. Eventually I was his carer when he couldn't manage alone any longer.' Megan can't help herself, she notices my balled-up fists, smirks and says, 'Did you know Tina had an incident the other day on the motorway and bumped her head? And now she forgets things.' It comes out of the blue and nobody is more shocked by her statement than me.

'I do not!' I state with authority. 'And I didn't bump my head, not really, my head hit the headrest, that's all. I had to brake severely on the motorway. I was just shaken up that's all. The doctor's given me the all clear.' I stare at her, tightening my fists.

'Oh, sorry, it was just with you misplacing files at the office and then thinking that a picture frame had been broken when it hadn't.' She addresses the others. 'You know I've heard that this sort of bang to the head can lead to long-term memory loss.'

'How do you know about that?' I ask her, furious she's again trying to undermine me.

'About the long-term memory loss? I read it somewhere, I think.'

Then I remember the French windows being unlocked. 'No. About the other stuff.'

'Oh, that. The staff are talking about it. It's only what I've heard. Is it not true?' She rests her arm on Glyn's again. The woman is insufferable. 'Sorry, Glyn, if I've spoken out of turn. I thought with Ali and James being your best friends they would know. Oh, dear, have I put my foot in it?'

'Who told you they were our best friends?' I demand.

'You did, Tina, earlier. Remember? When I went back in the house looking for the loo. Don't you remember?'

CHAPTER TWELVE

Later that evening when everyone's gone home, we tidy up and put the kids to bed. We're not speaking. Glyn tells me I'm irrational over Megan and must cease my animosity towards her. That it's all in my imagination. She's perfectly agreeable and friendly and I'm over sensitive.

'What about the OCD jibe,' I say, 'that wasn't agreeable.'

'What about it?' he says. 'Maybe people think you have OCD because of the way you like everything a certain way. Not like me. Nobody could ever say I had OCD.'

No, you couldn't, but I'm sure there's some disorder to compartmentalise him. I hate that he sounds as though he's taking the moral high ground here.

'OK, maybe, but who would say I was on medication? And why did you look so horrified as if I was and hadn't told you?'

'I didn't look like that.'

'You did. I saw it in your eyes; it was as though you believed her. As if I wouldn't tell you if I had to take meds. Glyn, we don't have a relationship where we don't tell each other stuff.'

'OK, so perhaps it crossed my mind. You have to admit that it has flared up again recently.'

'No, it hasn't.' He gives me a quizzical look. 'No. It. Hasn't. I have, I'll admit, been a little precise with things, but it has not taken hold of me again. It hasn't!'

I flick on Sky and scroll through the movie channels until I find something that will allow me to drift off. Glyn's gone down to the basement. He doesn't want to discuss it further, he said.

A little later he joins me when I'm falling asleep on the sofa. The evening has cooled down for a change; I close the French windows and lock them.

'Hey, brought you a little cheese and biscuits and a cup of decaf coffee. I noticed you didn't eat much today.' His voice has a hint of concern about it. 'I don't want to fall out over this, Tina.' He lights a couple of scented candles. I watch him, wondering what is going through his mind. I am not as convinced about all this being a coincidence as he is.

He sits next to me with his own cup of tea. I drift in and out of drowsiness and can't quite grasp what he's saying, but the mention of Megan spikes my blood levels. Why are we still talking about her? Then I understand. 'Sorry? What are you talking about, Glyn?'

'You were unfriendly. She's our neighbour and we work with her. We should make a concerted effort to get along that's all I'm saying, plus she's lost all her family. She's just being friendly. Trying to fit in.'

Fit in? I don't want her to fit in with my family and friends. He lowers the volume on the TV and I pull away from him sensing I'm not going to like what he's about to say next.

'Glyn, the woman seems to have infiltrated our lives. Don't you think that is weird? But you're right, maybe I need to be more tolerant.' It grates on me to say this, but if I don't it will create a wedge between us and I won't allow her to achieve that. 'I still don't think it's a coincidence that she's bought the house opposite.'

'How would she know we lived here? Rachel only spoke to her the other day about the job. Now you're reaching. See how wrong you are? At any rate, she's renting it.'

'So why didn't she say that? Why make out she's bought the place, asking Ali and me for interior design ideas?' No, something isn't right. I take a bite of vintage Cheddar. 'Don't you think it was odd the way she asked when the kids were born?' That was weird. It freaked me out. Who goes round accusing people you've just met of having kids out of wedlock?

Glyn laughs. 'Perhaps she has strict moral values and doesn't believe in children outside of marriage.'

'So, she's judging us?' Judging? Who does she think she is? 'Moral values! How can she have moral values then come to a barbecue dressed like a siren and fawn all over you?'

'She wasn't dressed like a siren, you're exaggerating again, Tina.'

'Really? You think? So, why did she have to come out with that peculiar comment about me telling her that James and Ali were our best friends? When I didn't even mention it. Why would I say something so stupid? I'm not a child . . . *ooh, they're our best friends, you know.*'

'I don't know, Tina. Are you calling her a liar?'

'Are you calling me a liar?' I finish the cheese and biscuits and set the plate aside.

'Of course not,' says Glyn. 'I'm merely saying let's try and keep the peace when we go back to the office. She lives across the road. We don't want to fall out.'

'No, that wouldn't be neighbourly.'

'There's something else.' His words tinged with sadness forewarn me and immediately I know I'm not going to like what he's about to voice a second time.

'What?'

'Earlier you said you'd left your debit card at work?' I nod and wait expectantly. 'On their way out this evening, Megan knocked over the handbag you left on the console table by the front door. As usual it was unzipped and the contents dropped out. Including your debit car. Ali found it.'

'What? Ali did?'

'Yes, it surprised her because you tipped out the contents in the supermarket to look for it, didn't you?'

'I did. And it wasn't there! Glyn, I'm telling you it was not in my bag. I searched it, thoroughly.'

'Tina, for chrissakes. That's what you said about the file and the digital copy at the office. But when we looked, it was all there. Just like today. What's going on with you?'

'Nothing, why don't you believe me? I'm telling you it wasn't there.' I know it wasn't there. I looked in every inch of that bag.

* * *

We all sit in the open-plan kitchen having Sunday breakfast while the sunshine pours through the windows; it's another magnificent day. I open the by-folding doors to let the glorious morning in. Glyn and I flick through the Sunday papers, careful not to catch each other's eye. The kids have theirs watching TV; it's a Sunday treat. I prefer them to chill out at weekends, I like having them around. I'm always averse to them doing any away from home activities at the weekend if I can facilitate it. For me, the weekends represent precious time with my family. I slide between Matt and Laura and pull them close. My mother's mental health problems worry me. What if I inherit them? What if this forgetfulness is the beginning? She used to imagine strangers were out to get her. Is that what's happening to me? When I had my therapy, it helped separate my mother with mental health problems and my mother that I remember, loving and nurturing. The mother I lost to the madness that consumed her before the cancer claimed her life was not my real mother. I hear Mum laughing in our kitchen when we were all a family, singing as she showed me how to bake. My father laughing and sneaking up behind us to steal the cup cakes we pull out of the oven. Me running after him, pretending to be cross. Our house was full of laughter. The three of us against the world my dad used to say. Until he left us. My arm that Matt is leaning on has gone to sleep. I pull it out and wiggle my fingers that have gone to sleep while extracting myself from them. They don't notice they're too engrossed in SpongeBob.

Glyn and I have scarcely spoken this morning apart from the perfunctory 'Good morning.' I'm still cross about how he accused me of forgetting and misplacing items. I am a little scared, though. It kept me awake all night, tossing and turning. Of course, he was prepared to set it aside for the sake of sex. I couldn't. Not last night. He said he was cool about it and I think he was to a degree, but my excuse was feeble in his eyes. Why do men constantly think sex will make everything great again? When it won't. He hurt my feelings by accusing me of lying, of absentmindedness. The last thing I wanted was to be intimate.

Our sex life is great. I know from friends and magazines we're unusual, especially when you have kids and the dread of that perfectly timed nightly call, *Mummy!* For us sex perpetually represents the one place we both go to make up. It's where we come together when we've drifted away from each other. Last night, I felt alone and being near him was the last place I wanted to be. This morning, I sort of regret it because now there's tension in the air.

Something has changed. In me? In him? I feel on edge. I have that wobbly feeling in my legs you get when you're apprehensive.

I sit buttering a slice of toast and adding peanut butter while scanning an article in the paper on divorce. It's predominantly about rich businessmen hiding funds from their wives with a view to avoid paying out large settlements. With my court date looming, I'm aware I need to do some work in the study later this afternoon. So, to make up, I'm wondering what we can do this morning as a family. I make Glyn a cup of tea and put a fresh coffee capsule in my coffee machine. He's brooding. He won't admit it, but not having sex last night will make him brood. And brood. And brood.

Something needs to be done or else this will become a problem. The kid's TV is overly loud, I turn down the volume.

'Mum!' screeches Laura. 'I can't hear it now.'

'Yes, you can, it's too loud. Don't turn it up or I'll turn it off,' I say, putting the remote on the granite worktop, out of her reach.

A typical male, Glyn won't broach the subject. He won't want to hear there might be a problem. And there isn't unless this silence carries on. It's crazy. Sometimes, I think men are crazy, driven mad by their need for sex.

I look out of our kitchen window at Megan's house and wonder what she's up to. She's crawled under my skin like a parasite causing me to want to scratch the itch. What other treats has the woman in store for me? I'm intrigued to sneak a look at those pictures Ali said she was eager to hide. First, I need to get inside her house. Figuring out how to achieve that isn't going to be easy, I can hardly invite myself round and start poking and prying.

Suddenly, her washed-out, blue front door opens. As if she senses me watching, Megan steps out with a yard brush and begins to sweep the path, while looking up periodically at our house. There's nothing to sweep, no leaves, no litter. She should start on the overgrown garden and broken pots lined up beneath the front window. They've irritated me for months, they need lining up. I have a feeling Megan isn't interested in cleaning up her house or her garden. As I watch through slightly open venetian blinds, I'm sure in the knowledge that she can't see me. But then she stops and turns abruptly, almost as if knowing I'm watching. It creeps me out. I step back and at that point she waves. Christ! I step back, again, instinctively.

The coffee machine bleeps that it's ready, startling me. I make my drink, and the kitchen fills with an aroma of fresh coffee making my taste buds spring to life.

I slide next to Glyn on the sofa. 'Hi,' he says, without looking up. Is he punishing me with his indifference? Maybe she waved *assuming* I was watching, there's no way she could see me. Naturally, I didn't wave back. I fumbled with the cords and pulled the blinds closed, slowly.

Yesterday's events run through my mind for the hundredth time. My lost debit card. I have never lost my debit card in the entire time I've had a bank account. I was in and out of the office on Friday and didn't always take my bag. I remember seeing Megan walking back and forth from Glyn's office to the secretarial department. Could she have slipped in and taken it? No, that's too brazen. Too bold. What if I or anyone saw her? There would be no way out. And yet she must have, there's no other way it went missing and suddenly appeared back in there yesterday. That's too much of a coincidence. Tossed in my bag, Glyn had said. A positive confirmation to me that I had not left it like that. I don't throw my cards in my bag. They all have a compartment inside my purse. He should recall that.

I want to get out of the house. I need to get out of the house. 'Let's have a day out, shall we?' I suggest to Glyn, now perching on his lap and pulling the paper out of his hands. I'm not letting her get between us. I need to rebuild my bridges with him. There can be no weak link, he needs to believe in me and harbour no doubts. I fold the newspaper and place it neatly on the table. There's an atmosphere hanging heavy in the air and we need to blow it away, so I place my arm round him and nibble his ear. 'Don't stay cross with me about last night,' I whisper.

'I'm not,' he says, but he doesn't squeeze me or provide me with any tender affection. Clearly, he is.

'Yes, you are. Stop it, Glyn, let's get past this, can we? We don't fall out.'

'I haven't fallen out with you, just disappointed.'

'OK, I don't want to talk about this now.' I notice that the paper is folded slightly crooked, so I refold it making sure the edges all meet. 'But you need to know I couldn't do it, not after you said those things to me.' I place a finger to his lips to stop him saying any more. 'Let's have a nice family day today, please?'

'OK.' He exhales. 'Where do you have in mind?'

'I thought we could go to Marbury Country Park, take the bikes and a picnic and make the most of this excellent weather.' My voice is chirpy. Too chirpy. I turn to the kids who have walked into the kitchen. 'What do you say, kids?'

'I'll go and get changed. But, Mum, do I need to wear a helmet?' Laura asks excitedly.

'You know you do, Laura. No helmet, no bike.'

She pulls a face. 'I don't want to go then.' She crosses her arms in an act of defiance.

'What? Why?'

'Because it will spoil my hair! I'll look stupid when I take it off. It squashes my fringe.' She presses her fringe with her fingers to demonstrate how it will look. 'I'm not going.' She stamps her foot.

'I going, Mummy. I want to wear my helmut,' Matt says, rushing over to us and jumping up and down in excitement while dragging a black and white wooden toy dog on wheels by a rope lead. 'Dog coming too,' he pulls Dog up and cuddles it. This is the current phase for Matt. Don't ask me where this fixation has come from, because I have no idea. Matt has had Dog in his room since Christmas and never taken a shine to it. Then a few days ago it was attached to him like an extra appendage. 'Dog needs a helmut, too.'

'No, he can ride with the picnic stuff, Matt. He'll be safe there.' I can see his bottom lip begin to wobble as he weighs up the fact he'll be parted from Dog.

Laura rolls her eyes. 'Well, you haven't got nice hair, have you, so it doesn't matter.'

I start to laugh. 'Laura, Matt has lovely hair, don't be mean.'

'I'm not going if I have to wear a helmet.' She flops on the sofa in protest.

'Helmut, helmut, helmut,' Matt says, jumping up and down, his auburn hair flapping. He reaches out for my hand. 'Let's go find my helmut, Mummy. I goin' to tell Dog he must ride with the picnic 'cause there's no helmut for him.' He picks up Dog and whispers to him.

'It's hel*met*, Matt, not hel*mut*,' Laura corrects, sarcastically.

'OK, Laura that's enough. How about you wear your helmet and don't take it off.'

'What, never?'

I can feel Glyn sniggering behind me. It's a relief. 'Obviously, not never. But while we're out. You can keep it on while we eat our picnic and on the ride. Take it off when we get home.'

She huffs. 'Can I keep it on in the car on the way home, too?'

'If you want to, but nobody will see you in the car except us.'

'And Dog,' says Matt, pulling Dog up close to him. 'Dog will see her flat fringe.'

'Shut up! You don't know that,' Laura says.

'No, no I don't,' I state.

'Somebody important might recognise me. Somebody from school.'

'That's true. OK, keep it on until we get home. Is it a deal? We OK to go?'

She nods, runs over to us, giving me a hug and kiss. 'Love you, Mum.' I stroke her hair and embrace her to let her know I understand her quandary. Looking at my children my thoughts often run to the love I still have for my own mum. My loss is more than my heart can take sometimes, still after all this time I experience the harsh and brutal pain. Loss represents the other side of love we never relate to until it happens. Looking at Laura my heart constricts with the knowledge that one day she will be in my place. Thinking of me and how I handled situations. Insignificant objects triggering thoughts and reminders. Sounds and scents winding her mind back to another time and place where scenes play out, the colours not quite as sharp as you'd hope. The edges frayed with a hint of something else, just out of reach and vanishing like a dream in the morning.

She must see Glyn sniggering because she finishes with, 'Daddy! A girl must always be prepared in case she meets somebody important. Don't you know that?'

Glyn has his hands on my waist and gives me a little squeeze. I smile, relief flowing through me, we're OK. He's OK. 'Right, you're right, Laura, you go and get dressed, Mum and I will get the bikes.' I can feel him trying to contain his mirth.

When Laura leaves the room, Glyn swipes a slice of toast from my plate and we go to the garage with Matt riding on his shoulders and Dog dangling. We're good. I know the uncomfortable moment has passed.

I help Glyn with the bikes and then escape, leaving him to load them onto the back of his BMW Tourer parked in the drive.

When I return with the kids and the picnic basket, a little while later, I find Glyn at the front gate talking with Megan. He smiles at me pleasantly; there's a look on his face saying, *Don't start, Tina*. What is she doing here? She's like a bloody boomerang. Has she been waiting in her front garden for us to make an appearance? Or worse, covertly watching from behind a curtain?

Megan is wearing tight three-quarter length pink leggings and a crop top the colour of custard. I could choose a nicer description for her yellow top, but I don't want to. Custard suits my mood right now, especially as she's jogging on the spot. Glyn makes an obvious attempt to avert his eyes by making a fuss of the children. Could she dress more provocatively? Could she? I mean, COULD SHE!

'Hi, Tina, thanks for yesterday.' She gives me the once over. I know I don't look as colourful as her in my white shorts, espadrilles and flowery T-shirt, neither do I want to look like a dessert at a kid's birthday party. Her voice is measured and her words drawn out as in, Ti-na and yes-ter-day. 'I was just telling Glyn how much fun I had. But all that good food and drink, I need to work it off.' She sighs and runs a slow hand, seductively over her tummy and down her thighs, throwing Glyn a look to check he's watching. How could he not, she's virtually on top of him. 'Isn't it a glorious, morning? Did you sleep soundly, Tina? You look a bit tired, hope nothing kept you up last night.' She smiles at me, casually, but only one side of her mouth turns up. Everything about her this morning is slow. Casual. Laid-back, reminding me of a vinyl record on a turntable played at the wrong speed.

'Great, I slept great, thanks,' I say in my chirpy, chirpy morning voice I've been using today, squinting as the sun gets in my eyes. I touch the top of my head for my sunglasses but they're not there, they are poking out of my handbag on the passenger seat. 'What would keep me up?' I put Matt on his booster seat on the back seat and hand him Dog then close the door.

She laughs. 'Oh, nothing, I thought Glyn might have kept you up.' She leans into Glyn and whispers loud enough for me to hear, 'Or did you have too much wine last night?'

I fire Glyn a look. A look he understands only too well because he backs away from her immediately.

'What are you talking about?' Where does she get off talking about stuff like that to my husband?

'Come on, Tina, we were joking about it yesterday. The boys and I,' she says in that slow manner, 'you know how it affects a man's libido, whereas with a woman it's generally the opposite.' By boys I take it she means James and Glyn. Boys. Hardly. Next, she'll be calling him Muscles or Cowboy.

Megan continues to jog on the spot. Laura, who appears by my side carrying her helmet is fascinated. I turn her away and jostle her to the car.

'Hi, Laura, you look pretty today? Such a lovely figure.' Laura smiles at her and Megan winks conspiratorially. 'Oh, don't forget what we discussed. If you want to come over later to get your nails done, I'm free.'

Laura turns to reply, but I push her a bit too hard into the car. 'Ouch,' she says scowling at me. 'That hurt, Mum.'

'It didn't hurt. Fasten your seat belt and Matt's too,' I say in a cross voice and close the car door. Why does Megan annoy me so much? Why do I let her do this to me? It's the calculated, cruel, cheeriness in her tone that does it, as if she thinks I will flip, here, in front of everyone, so she can turn round and say, 'see, that bump on her head has affected her,' well, I'm not going to give her that satisfaction.

'Megan's going to paint my nails, Mum,' Laura says opening the car window. I try to stay calm. I'm doing Laura's nails. Not her. Matt has placed Dog between them and fastened the lap belt round him.

'When did you discuss nails with my daughter?' I ask Megan in a loud, clear voice, as if I'm talking to someone hard of hearing.

There's silence.

I can't show her she's getting to me. I must stay calm. I open the boot to grab a bottle of water for the journey and take a couple of seconds registering the contents. Oh my God, it's a shambles. I want to pull everything out and arrange it properly. Neatly. *I don't need to do this. I don't. I can leave it. Walk away, Tina. Close the boot and walk away.* I do, but it's like pulling away from a gigantic magnet. It's as if all the forces are machinating against me to snap.

Megan says sweetly, with faux innocence. 'Oh, yesterday, she was admiring my nails and I said I would do hers if she wanted. I hope you're not cross; I didn't mean anything by it. I don't want to step on your toes.'

I look back at the car and see Laura peering at us through the back window. Do not engage. Do not get drawn into this minefield.

'That's right, Tina, I heard her, it was just before I showed Megan the wine cellar. You mentioned Laura would want them doing soon, didn't you?' Glyn butts in. He's at it again. Getting in the middle of it all. I think the bridge we built is about to collapse. What I said was between us, not the whole neighbourhood. Instantly, I'm in a difficult position. I want to do Laura's nails.

'Thanks, Megan, but I'll do Laura's nails. I've already bought some pastel colours for her. In fact, we're painting them later when we get back. You don't need to worry about it,' I say rapidly, without providing her with an opportunity to challenge me.

There's a beat.

'How wonderful. She'll be thrilled. She told me you didn't approve. Of course, I told her you wouldn't be so harsh and perhaps she had misunderstood.' Megan tilts her head to one side waiting for me to respond.

I don't. Instead, I breathe in like I'm sucking on a desperately longed for cigarette, and when I'm sure I can reply without gritting my teeth I say, 'Bye, we have to go now.' I snatch the keys from Glyn's hand and jump into the driver's seat, expressing my irritation by slamming the car door.

I pull out of our drive. Megan is conveniently blocking the exit. I edge the car closer and closer to her until the bumper is a fraction from her body. Why won't she move? If I take my foot off the brake, I could crush her. All the beepers are going off in the car. I could say my foot slipped. But knowing my luck, I wouldn't get away with it. Glyn slams his hand on the bonnet making me jump. 'Tina, stop.'

I press down firmly on the brake and roll down my window. 'Come on, Glyn, we have to go.'

'See you later, have a fun day.' Megan glances at Glyn and waves at the kids in the back even though she can't see them through the blacked-out windows.

CHAPTER THIRTEEN

By the time we get home later that afternoon, the children are tired and cranky. I haven't forgotten I said I would paint Laura's nails. However, I'm also acutely aware she has school tomorrow and they won't allow her to go in with nail polish. In the mood she's in, no matter how I present it, I will be the monster mother.

We put them both in the snug and turn on the TV.

The picnic proved a success. We even had ice cream, which Matt managed to spill down his shirt, as usual. I'm drained. I don't know where Glyn has ended up, the last I saw of him he was unloading the car in the garage.

The study is stuffy, so I open the windows to let out the stale air. It's south facing and catches the sun most of the day. The floral smells of the garden hang in the air. I catch a scent of rosemary from the line of bushes running along the path that divides the lawn. The begonias in the terracotta pots beneath the window are blooming beautifully.

While my laptop fires up, I pull out the files and flick through them, half expecting something to be missing. I suddenly think of Sally and have a need to speak to her.

'Sally, hi, it's Tina. How are you?'

She hesitates before she speaks. 'Hi, thanks for calling, Tina. I haven't felt this ill in ages. Sorry I haven't been in, I know we have a lot on with the Miller case, but I honestly don't know what I've caught,' she says cautiously. I tap my pencil against the edge of my desk. Something is up with Sally.

'God, I'm not calling because of work, I'm concerned how you are. It's so unlike you to be off ill. You must have caught a nasty bug.' In the five years Sally has worked for me she hasn't had a day off sick. She's a stickler for turning up for work, no matter what. I don't want her to pick up how desperate I am for her to come back in. She's a little apprehensive talking to me, selecting her words carefully.

'Most likely. It just happened so quickly, though. That afternoon after I drank my coffee, suddenly I felt terrible. I couldn't hold anything down. I hope I haven't given it to anyone. I'll catch up tomorrow, I promise.'

I try putting her at ease. 'Don't worry about it. Come back when you're better. It happens to us all. How are you feeling now? Are you getting over it?'

'Yes, I should be back in tomorrow. I can't wait. I've been going out of my mind with boredom. There's only so much daytime telly you can watch.'

Something is definitely off with Sally. I try lightening the mood. 'It's nice for a day, but after that . . . I know what you mean.' She sounds tired and worried. 'Well, I'm glad you're feeling much better and I'm looking forward to having you back in the office.'

'Thanks, Tina, I'll catch up on everything. Oh, I hope you didn't mind that I didn't call you.' Yes, I did find that odd. 'Tina, are you annoyed with me?'

'What! Sally, why would I be annoyed? Are you sure you're OK, you do sound a bit strange. Not yourself. You asked me not to call you, remember?'

'I didn't, Tina. Somebody from the office called me to say you were cross I was off sick. I couldn't help it. Really, I couldn't. I would have come in if I could. I don't take time off sick very often.'

'What! Who called you?'

'She didn't say. I didn't recognise her voice. But she told me not to call you.'

I envisage Megan making that phone call. The mother in me wants to soothe, Sally. God, she must have been worried sick on top of feeling crap.

A sudden surge of anger wants me to race over to Megan's house and have it out with her. I stab my pencil into the desk instead.

I should tell Glyn about this conversation. Tell him that somebody from the office called Sally, making out I was cross with her and the only person in the firm who would do that would be Megan. I should do that. But I know I won't. He won't believe me. Why would she do it? There is no reason for her to make that call, that's what he will say. His lawyer head will tell him, without proof it's heresy and I don't like her; therefore, I'm blaming her. Sally can't categorically say who made that call.

She's from Braitling in Kent. What she said about her grandmother and the house was pointed at me, I know it was. Why? My father lived in Braitling that's the only connection I have with the place. I went there a couple of times to visit him.

I leave the study and make my way to the kitchen. I've taken to watching her house as much as she watches mine. I have the feeling she knows I watch. I don't see much. She rarely comes out or to the window, except when I'm outside, which makes me think she's spying on my moves. I really need to get her references checked out and do some digging myself. Maybe she's psychotic. Christ. I get how I sound to Glyn but I can't get away from the fact that I have a gut feeling. A woman's intuition about her. I know I sound crazy. Almost as batty as my mother at her worst paranoid times. When she looks at me, when I catch her watching me out of the corner of my eye, I can't help the feeling she's plotting something against me. Like a revenge attack. I think about what Ali said about her. Could she be a disgruntled client? Sounds more plausible than a psychotic on the loose. Now I'm rambling.

I see myself rush over to her house. Bang on the door and insist she tells me just what the hell is going on with her? But I won't. She'll probably record it and use it against me to make out I'm the psychotic one. I imagine her reaction to my turning up on her doorstep. 'But, Tina, I don't know what you're talking about. I only want to be friends. I'm so grateful to Glyn for giving me the job.' I snort. Then I'll want to flatten her. Again, not a good move.

The way she was touchy with Glyn, I am surprised I didn't punch her.

My mobile rings, I see it's Ali. 'Hi, you OK?'

'I'm fine, thanks, how you bearing up?'

I smile, I'm not surprised Ali's called me. 'I'm glad you called. I feel I'm going out of my mind and that scares me.' I close the blinds in the kitchen leaving only enough of an opening to watch her house. 'She was here this morning. At the gate as we were leaving for our day out. Dressed in the most provocative jogging outfit you've ever seen, flirting with Glyn — again.'

'How was Glyn with her?'

'Oh, he was Glyn, you know? Pleasant and polite but he was uncomfortable as any man would be with a woman like that doing heavy flirting.'

'Can I say something, Tina? Without you hating me because I say it?'

'Of course, oh, Ali, I'd never hate you. Say it, please. I feel so bloody unbalanced at the moment. I'm beginning to believe that bump on the head is sending me mad. I know I say different, but this is real life not a damned movie. Glyn is trying to be supportive, but he can't understand why I'm so hostile towards her. All he sees is this kind, helpless woman who wants all of us to get on. I know what it looks like to the outside world. My world is turning upside down and I don't know what to do.'

'What I saw was Megan flirting with Glyn to wind you up. Make you jealous. She's certainly up to something. Look, after you left this morning, I went out for a walk with Katie to the park. She was at your house.'

'At my house? What do you mean?'

'She didn't see me. I sent Katie back home on the pretence to fetch something and I stayed to watch. At first, I thought it was you.' I'm confused. We don't look anything alike how could Ali think it was me? 'She had your sun hat and big Chloe sunglasses on and dressed in very similar clothes to you. She was reading a magazine, lying on your sun lounger with a drink.' I turn back to the window and glare at Megan's house. 'I knew you'd gone out. Glyn called James to tell us this morning. That's what struck me as odd that you'd stayed behind. I walked in and was about to say something when she took of her hat revealing her blonde hair. She had her back to me and didn't hear me.'

'I told Glyn we needed to put that fence back up, it leaves us so exposed. Although, it was a good job it was down otherwise you wouldn't have seen her.' I walk to the French windows and check the key is still in the lock. Then I check the spare in the drawer. Still there. 'My kitchen French windows were open the other day. Glyn thought I'd left them unlocked. Remember I told you? Do you think she's got a key? Oh my God. I'm not going mad. She is up to something.'

'I wasn't going to say anything, what with you having so much going on at the office. I didn't want to scare you. I've been going over it in my head and finally I thought I'd better tell you. Just in case.'

'In case what?'

'I don't know. Just in case that's all.'

I'm momentarily distracted when her front door opens and she walks out to her car. I open the blind a little more. 'Do you think she's dangerous?'

'I think you already know the answer otherwise you wouldn't ask me.'

CHAPTER FOURTEEN

Monday morning is always a drag; I have a scheduled pow-wow with Howard and this can take anything from half an hour to two hours, depending on his disposition. This morning, I'm certain he is not in the best of moods. But it's not always easy to tell. I have misread him before.

'Where are we up to with the Millers, Tina?' he asks me as I walk into his office.

I start to speak and settle myself in the leather chair opposite his desk. Howard's office is always dark. It's depressing. I don't know how the lack of daylight doesn't affect him; the blinds are closed only letting in enough light so you can discern it is daytime. He prefers electric light. Sometimes, I think he might be a vampire; I mean who doesn't like sunlight? It's so rare we get glorious days like these, why wouldn't you feast on them? It's early and already the room is roasting. Did I mention he likes the windows closed, too?

'I've received a court date through for the end of the month,' I say adjusting my bare legs from sticking to the leather armchair. 'We're trying to settle out of court, but Mr Miller is not cooperating.' I open the file on my lap. 'We've lodged an application for a financial order. He's with-holding financial information and we're waiting to receive his

Form E1. I have discussed with his solicitor that we are in possession of certain paperwork regarding Mr Miller's financial position.' I look up from my file to see if he is aware of what went on with this paperwork.

'Remind me again whom he's using?'

'George, McAllister & Owen. June Finnigan is handling the case.'

'God, she's the most unpleasant woman I've ever met. I've never seen her smile.'

'Or lose a case,' I add. A trickle of sweat runs down my cleavage. I wish he'd put his air conditioning on. The man is peculiar to say the least.

'No, you've got your work cut out with this one. We need everything, Tina. She is meticulous and the slightest cock up and she will slaughter you. Do you think we can settle out of court?'

'I'm not sure. I've engaged Tom Whitwham as Mrs Miller's barrister.'

'Good, good. Excellent choice. Do we know who they have?' He mops his brow with his handkerchief.

I shake my head; wouldn't it be easier and more pleasant for him if he switched on the air conditioning?

'Mrs Miller is worried her husband is going to hide many of his financial papers. She's informed me it won't be the first time he's done this sort of thing, he did it with HMRC. I have set her mind to rest and informed her if he is found to have deliberately misrepresented the truth, criminal proceedings can be brought against him for fraud.'

'Yes, yes, but we don't want to go down that route. What's your next move?' He perches on the end of his desk, facing me. His trousers ride up exposing spotted socks. That's not Howard at all. He's extremely conservative.

'I'm waiting to see his E1,' I tell him taking my gaze away from the socks. 'At that point I can reveal my hand if I discover any discrepancies.'

'As soon as that comes in, it needs showing to the forensic accountants.'

'I have a feeling they're going to hang on to this until the last possible moment.'

'Quite possibly. Therefore, put the pressure on and turn the screw if you find that's what they're up to.' He slaps his palms on his desk and levers himself up. Howard's signal that the meeting is over. I see all his recent dining out is piling the pounds on his waistline. I wonder if he's seen Megan over the weekend. Did she buy him those socks? 'OK, then. Anything you need to run by me, let me know.' He looks at his watch. 'I have a meeting in ten minutes and Glyn is joining me for that.'

I leave and walk to the secretaries' office.

'Good to see you, Sally.' I look over at Megan and Rachel who ignore me and appear in deep concentration with headphones on and typing. 'Can you come to my office when you get a moment and I'll run through a few things with you,' I ask Sally, secretly thrilled she is back at work.

'Five minutes. Let me close this file and I'll be with you.'

Later, as I come out of my office with an armful of files, Howard's door opens. I pass by without looking over. Glyn and Howard walk out with their client, followed by Megan. I make a point to keep looking straight ahead, I don't want to make any eye contact with her especially as Howard is there.

The four of them step into the corridor, it reminds me of *Boston Legal*, the American TV Legal drama. They are all in the loop. A party of four and I am uninvited. I can't help but wonder why I have been pushed out. Have I though? Or am I over thinking it all? It could be, of course, the sudden insecurity that I'm feeling since she arrived. It's ridiculous, I am a lawyer and she is a secretary, how can she push me out?

I recognise the client, Mr Kite, he's suing his employer for unfair dismissal citing ageism as the cause. He will be OK with Glyn, it is one of his pet hates.

Megan conveys something to Howard who immediately scowls and looks in my direction. Walking along the corridor she loses her balance and reaches out, Glyn turns quickly at her gasp catching her before she falls flat on her face. She shouldn't wear such ridiculous shoes to the office.

Moments later while I'm standing at Sally's desk, Megan walks in holding onto Glyn's arm and limping. She tells him she's twisted her ankle and asks him to look at it. Which he does. She glances over at me while he holds her ankle in his hands, I can't hear what he says to her but they both laugh.

I turn back to Sally who looks over at them, her blue-grey eyes kind and full of concern. I hand her the files and explain I want her to check out Megan's references. 'This is strictly confidential, between you and me. Nobody else in the office is to know,' I tell her in a low voice.

Sally nods and makes no comment. She won't say anything.

I walk out and ask Glyn to join me in my office.

* * *

In my office I collect my handbag and double check I have everything I need. 'Do you fancy grabbing some lunch?' I take off the small silk red and gold scarf tied at my neck and drop it on the chair. I'm far too warm. 'I want to pop into the department store across the road and grab some nail polish for Laura.' I wonder if I should take off my suit jacket before going outside. The temperature in the office is cool with the air conditioning on, and so hot outside, but then I will feel underdressed if I do.

He looks at his watch. 'It's not even twelve, Tina. I thought you told Megan you'd bought some nail stuff?'

Trust him to remember that. 'Yes, but when I looked last night, I didn't like them. Let's go to Kendals first, then lunch. I'm starving, I could eat a horse.' I can't believe he remembers that conversation. Glyn has an excellent memory for what's important, I've never known him to remember trivial pieces of information like nail polish before.

'All right, but I can't be out for long.'

We walk out together past the secretaries' office. Through my peripheral vision I catch Megan glowering at me. I link

102

Glyn's arm suddenly feeling light-headed with a desperate need to get away from her and this building. Don't panic, I tell myself. I need to suppress the panic. I remember the therapist mentioning to me that past trauma would trigger a flight-or-fight response. But I'm not remembering past trauma, am I? I close my eyes for a few seconds and push away the thoughts that right now are so desperately trying to awaken inside me and cause my anxiety to flare up. I breathe, deeply. I tell myself I am in control. That she can only harm me if I allow her. It makes no difference; my body is acting on its own. My mind must take control. Images of my mother flash before me. In the hospital. Then the funeral. I see the chapel before the cremation. I see the urn with the ashes and then I see me. Sat alone. Despondent. I block. I block. I block. NO! I won't think of it. I won't. I breathe. Breathe. Breathe. God, there's no room in my head to think of anything else. It's stuffed with images I don't want to see, shadows and faint pictures I know I don't want to remember. I focus on the office floor counting my footsteps to distract me and allow Glyn to steer me away. Then we're outside where a gust of warm air hits me like a wall as we exit the air-conditioned office block. The traffic noise fills my ears and people all round me dart past. The images have gone. I breathe deeply, relief coursing through me that the horror of those thoughts are now locked away again.

'You OK, Tina? You're hurting my arm.'

'Sorry . . .' I lift my head and enjoy the sun on my face. 'I was . . . I don't know . . . I wasn't aware I was, sorry.'

Walking along Deansgate clutching on to Glyn, I decide that I am going to follow through with my original plan to flush Megan out. To find out exactly who she is and by doing so I am going to ring the private investigator I found on the internet. You see it in the movies all the time, people ringing up private dicks. That's what they call them in the movies. I can't call mine a private dick. It sounds inappropriate. Like a metaphor for penis. So wrong on so many levels.

The shopping done, we grab some sushi from YO! Sushi, but I'm not very hungry after all. My small bag full of assorted pastel nail polishes for Laura swings from my hand. I unbutton my jacket and pull my shirt away from my skin, it's sticky. Back at the office, we step into the elevator to take us upstairs. The heavy steel doors close and suddenly as they are about to meet, a hand shoots between them and they spring open.

CHAPTER FIFTEEN

I gasp when the doors open and Megan stands on the other side. 'Hi, God, I thought I would miss it, you don't mind if I share, do you?' She directs her question to me. 'Tina?' Her voice fills the elevator. I run a finger along my top lip. Is that sweat?

I don't answer. I see her limp has vanished though.

Instead, Glyn replies, 'Don't be silly, of course, we don't.' He steps aside from me for Megan to stand there. Why would he do that? 'Looks as if your foot is better.'

'Oh, yes. Must be your magic fingers that did the trick.'

I withhold the urge to kick her.

Glyn nods and we ride up in silence. When the elevator pings on our floor, Megan turns to me. 'Did you paint Laura's nails last night? I bet she was over the moon.'

My hand tightens round the bag and a flutter starts just behind my ribs. Oh God, I can feel the terror rising again. What the hell is she going to say now? 'No, it was late when we got back and she was tired.' The doors open. I push past her to get out.

She makes a sad face. 'What a shame, well maybe at the weekend you can find time to do it for her.'

The flutter turns into a frenzied pounding.

Her words grate on me like nails down a chalkboard. I look at Glyn as I walk out and whilst he offers nothing in response, he scowls at her words.

'I will always find time for my children, Megan.' There's a shrill annoyance to my voice.

'Mmm, yes. I guess it's difficult though when you work full time. They say that children of working parents often feel neglected.'

A wave of irritation sweeps over me nearly knocking me off my feet and I hang on to the heavy glass internal doors for a little longer than necessary.

My frustration with this woman sits in my mouth like a stuffed rag. There isn't a mother alive that would not want to flatten her right now.

'That depends on the parents. Glyn and I do not neglect our children,' I fire back unable to help myself by taking the higher ground.

Megan is on my heels. I walk through the door pushing it closed behind me, dramatically. Unfortunately, it's designed to stop this type of behaviour and closes with the speed of thick molasses.

'I've read that small things like painting nails and dressing up, whilst the parents don't put much seriousness to them, they are actually damaging to children if ignored.'

I keep walking with my hand clenched round the bag so tightly my nails dig into my palm. My stride is strong and long. Surely this woman knows when to stop badgering? Doesn't she? Or is she pushing my buttons for a reaction? Does Megan know I was in therapy? Is that why she is pushing me?

When we arrive at the secretarial office, I say over my shoulder, 'Unless you've had children you will never appreciate how they work. Don't believe everything you read, Megan.'

Back at my desk, I slump in the chair and my eyes flood with tears. Christ. What is going on with this woman? Wiping my eyes with a tissue, I take out a piece of A4 notepaper from my handbag with the private investigator's details and lock it in the top drawer of my desk. I spent some time last night researching investigators while Glyn read the bedtime stories. The key to the drawer I put under the telephone on my desk.

There's a knock at my door.

'Come in.'

Sally walks in holding a notepad and her head bowed. From her gentle voice, I can hardly make out what she is saying until she gets closer. 'I have that information you requested,' she says without lifting her head.

'Great, let's have it then, don't worry, Sally, I'm sure it's not that bad.' I try being generous, hoping it's bad enough for me to do something about her. 'Did you make the call in my office?' Less chance of anyone eavesdropping. She nods. I extend my hand to take the paper from her. 'What have they said?' I ask too impatient to read the answer for myself and so sure her references won't be legitimate.

'They all provided glowing reports, Tina.' She looks at me from lowered eyes. 'All three of them couldn't say a bad word about her. In fact, one of them remarked they would take her back if she returned to Braitling.' Sally looks concerned that she's given me erroneous information. She fiddles with a button on her shirt waiting for me to speak. Hesitates, goes to say something else, but recognises the look on my face and thinks better of it.

My enthusiasm drops, annihilated by all hopes of discharging Megan while Sally's words travel through me like a bullet. A flush of pink highlights my cheeks. Well then, I'll have to contemplate another way to discredit her. I shift uncomfortably in my seat and cast an uneasy glance at her.

'Are you sure? Sorry, Sally, I know you're telling me the truth. It's just that I was so sure they wouldn't pan out.' I pick up my pencil and tap it against the desk while I think. I don't want to drag Sally into this. Not really. But the urge is too powerful for me not to ask something else. 'Tell me, have you noticed anything odd about her?'

Sally looks questioningly at me.

'What I mean is, she seems too nice. Too obliging. It's not normal behaviour, is it? When you come to a new job, you're usually a little shy, hesitant of talking to your boss in case you say the wrong thing. You observe and weigh people up until you understand the politics of the place. But she's done none of that. She's dived straight in and weirdly everyone likes her.' *Apart from me.*

Sally chews her lip.

'What is it Sally? You can speak your mind. I won't have a problem with it.' Secretly I'm banking on her providing me with some ammunition. Some gossip she's overheard that I can use as leverage against her with Howard and Glyn.

'They don't speak to me much. Rachel is distant with me. We used to get on, but I feel now like I'm encroaching on their friendship. I've heard them talking about you.'

'Really? Go on, what have you heard?'

She looks at the floor. 'They said that you forget things and lose paperwork. That perhaps this Miller case is stressing you out. Megan said she had an aunt who started like that and developed a mental health problem.'

My mouth drops open in disbelief.

'What?'

'Sorry, Tina, maybe I shouldn't have said anything. They didn't know I could hear; it was by the photocopier. I was coming out of the stationery cupboard and stopped to listen when I heard your name mentioned.'

I sigh heavily. 'No, it's not your fault, Sally. Thanks for telling me. Look, I don't want you to feel as if you've become my spy, but just let me know if anything else is said. You'd best finish those letters I've dictated, I'd like them in the post tonight.'

It's unfair for me to use, Sally. I wouldn't want them to start making her life difficult.

Before leaving the office for the afternoon, I drop in on Sally to reassure her that I'm OK with our earlier conversation. Rachel and Megan are at their desks and not wearing their headsets. I place my handbag on the floor by Sally's desk and ask Sally to join me in the compact kitchen where I reassure her all is well between us.

* * *

'I'll do your nails after tea and homework,' I tell a smiling Laura, who grabs the bag and sets the colours out on the kitchen table in a row. Delighted, she sits at the table ooh-ing and ahh-ing over which is her favourite colour. Matt is under the table building something with his Lego with Dog by his side.

'Can I have a different colour on each nail, please?'

'Sure, why not. But the deal is that at bath time we must take it off. You know you can't go to school with nail polish.'

'I can only wear it tonight?' She pulls out her bottom lip. This is Laura in a sulky mode.

'Just tonight, but if you're good about it, on Friday after school we can paint them again and you can wear them all weekend. Deal?'

Laura thinks for a second then nods her head. 'Will Daddy be home in time for me to show him?'

'Yeah, he'll be back in a few minutes. I need to nip out to pick up some milk when he arrives, I forgot to call and ask him to get some. As soon as I get back, we'll start. OK?'

'OK.'

I go over and check the fridge in case there's anything else I need to pick up. While I'm at it, I bin a few out of date yoghurts, and a pack of sliced chicken that smells a bit weird. I glance across the road and see Megan on the phone pacing to and fro in the lounge. I close my blinds a little. She's gesturing wildly with her free hand as though furious. Then she turns and looks directly at me. Instinctively I duck down. Shit. How does she know every time I'm looking?

'Why are you on the floor, Mum?' Laura asks standing on the other side of the open fridge door, peering at me.

'I'm not. I dropped something.'

'What? There's nothing there.' She bends to look.

109

'Oh, it, er, rolled under the fridge. I'll get it later. That's your dad arriving. Don't forget to finish your homework.'

When Glyn walks in, I shoot out with the briefest of salutations, to the small late shop we have a mile from the house. I pull out of the drive, glance at Megan's house and swear I see her dart behind the curtain.

I've noticed that Glyn is a little detached from me — we're back on talking terms again, but that still doesn't mean we are back to our good place. Our safe place. We don't seem to be able to discuss this issue going on at work. To say I'm annoyed he didn't take Megan to task today over how she spoke to me is understating things. For some reason I don't want to bring it up again in case he thinks I'm obsessing. Which I'm not. Nevertheless, I'm annoyed with him. For whatever reason, and I don't have the answer, talking about Megan causes us problems. Do I want to? No. Should I? Probably. I must face the facts that everyone appears to think I have some sort of problem. Except I don't. I'm not mental. I'm not delusional. Was I affected by the bump on the head, which wasn't a bump at all, which just evolved into an imaginary one by all the do-gooders round me? Obviously not. There was no bump.

When I finish at the late shop, I text Glyn to say I'm popping over to Ali's for a few minutes, and that I won't be long as I've promised to paint Laura's nails. I change the two kisses at the end of the text to one kiss. Then back to two. Then back again, because two means too much and right now I'm not in a two-kiss sort of place.

Ali is sorting laundry when I knock on the door. Katie lets me in then rushes back to the lounge and the TV.

The smell of damp clothes invades the kitchen. 'Gosh, do you want to do some of my laundry while you're at it? I forgot to put mine on when I got home this afternoon. I hope Glyn sees it and puts it on for me.' I lean over a pile of damp clothes just out of the washing machine. I give her a massive hug. 'How are you? Missing James already?'

'Yeah, I'm missing James, lots. What are you doing here? Not that you're not welcome, of course. I just wasn't expecting you. The house seems so empty without him and especially my bed.' She giggles, putting her mobile phone in the drawer in front of her. 'It's only for a few days, though, I'll cope.' Ali starts folding clothes, assigning them to piles on the kitchen table as she goes.

I'm happy for Ali, she's had it tough the last few years as a single mum after experiencing a traumatic divorce. She and James are so well suited. He's a university professor. Moved here from the Midlands and met Ali in the library of all places. She was searching for books with Katie, and he was there because . . . well he loves libraries. I thought that was a bit odd. I told her, too. I said, 'Don't you think it's a bit odd that a grown man *likes* libraries? Not books. But *libraries* themselves. I mean, if he said he enjoyed motor sport or golf or even train spotting — maybe not train spotting that's equally as weird. But libraries?' Anyway, she must have seen past the *love* of libraries because she hooked up with him. It's cute in a way. They are a fabulously cute couple.

'How has it been at the office with madam, there?' She bobs her head towards Megan's house.

I perch on the bar stool next to her and begin rolling socks. 'Nightmare. Sally tells me she and Rachel have been bitching about me. Saying that I'm forgetting stuff and losing paperwork. Making out this Miller case is stressing me out. She even told Rachel I had some mental health issues, that her aunt started like this and . . . well, you can imagine the rest.'

Ali stops folding clothes. 'You're kidding, right?'

'No, she told me. They've also alienated her. Rachel rarely speaks to Sally.'

'Weren't they close once upon a time?'

'Yes, very. Since Megan's arrival she won't go beyond the pleasantries with her. I don't want to say a great deal to Sally. The last thing I want Sally to feel is uncomfortable if they know she is blabbing to me. She needs this job and I'd hate to lose her.'

'Yes, but you would never sack her, would you?'

'Of course not, but they can make her life difficult and then she would leave.'

Ali nods, knowingly. She folds a bed sheet, places it on the clothes pile and picks up a pillowslip. She looks extremely young with her hair pulled into a ponytail. She appears to be getting younger rather than older. It's the James effect.

An image comes to me of my face reflected in the mirror; I'm looking older since all this began. The tension in my face actually hurts some days. Really, it does.

'If you want a drink, there's an open bottle in the fridge.'

'No thanks, I only popped in to confess something.'

Ali stops folding the pillowslip. 'What? Have you found out something?'

'I've hired a private investigator to check her out.' I bite my lip. 'Sally checked up on her references, I was certain that they'd be false. Instead, they came back glowing. Can you believe it? I was certain they would bomb.'

'Wow. I thought they'd be false too. I mean, she doesn't look like your typical law secretary. More like a pole dancer.'

I laugh, Ali laughs too, but mine sounds hectic and high pitched — a little peculiar. I'm not sure why it sounds like that. I look at my hands and they're not trembling. I don't feel anxious just a little on edge.

'At work her dress is conventional, clingy in all the convenient places, but conventional,' I say. 'I keep reminding myself she has lost both parents and that losing her father has affected her a lot.'

'What has that got to do with how she is with you?'

'I don't know. I keep trying to give her the benefit of the doubt, as they say. But she's just plain nasty. Like today, she had a go at me and Glyn, but especially me about my parenting skills!'

Ali gasps, her eyes widen and she freezes while folding Katie's pyjamas. 'No!'

'Yes, as low as that.'

'But why have you any sympathy for her? You are crazy, sorry, no pun intended.'

'I just don't get it, Ali, why me? And the astonishing thing is, somehow she's managed to make me come across as nasty.' I scoff. 'Howard won't hear a bad word against her and Glyn . . . well, I've no idea what's got into him.' I lean my head back. Dammit. I remember Laura's nails. 'I really must get back, sorry to dash.' I tuck the stool back under the counter.

Ali scowls. 'I didn't want to tell you. But when we left the other night, James told me she kept interrogating him about you. James thought she was inquisitive because you are her boss, and she looks up to you.'

'What! Are all men idiotic?' I laugh incongruously.

'I know, I said as much.'

'Nosey more like. Does she not think you'll mention this to me?'

'Well, here is the thing. I think Megan wants you to know she is asking questions. There is undeniably something odd about her. She creeped me out a lot when she questioned James, asking when he was coming back from his trip. The time of his arrival. If I was picking him up from the airport, that sort of thing.'

'That is weird. Do you think she's hitting on him?' I ask.

Ali shakes her head and picks up a pair of Katie's jeans, tucks them under her chin and folds them. 'No, I don't. I think she's playing a weird game, though.'

In my kitchen, I'm faced with a smiling Laura sitting next to her dad at the kitchen table having her nails painted by Megan. The three of them laughing.

CHAPTER SIXTEEN

I'm certain Glyn quickly fathoms what I'm thinking, so certain in fact that his cheeks blush. I imagine myself running over to the table. Grasping her ludicrous hair extensions, which would come out in my hand, of course. Then flinging her out of my house where she would land on the golden gravel, on her knees (and I've never behaved like that in my whole life).

Glyn shoots up from the table. 'Tina, there you are.'

Megan smiles, raises an eyebrow and extends a manicured hand with deep burgundy nails suggesting I sit and join them.

They're sharing a bottle of wine. I note the label — it's one of the more expensive Viogniers. That pisses me off. We keep those for auspicious occasions or so he informs me. Is this an auspicious fucking occasion? Is it?

I blow out a long breath and measure my response. I don't want Laura to pick up on my anger. Glyn and I have never argued in front of the children. Well, not much anyway.

Broadly speaking, I'm not confrontational. I'm more of a measured confrontationist, 'you need a bit of backbone', my mother used to say. In the newsagent when I was ten, a spotty teenager behind the counter gave me the wrong change after buying my *Look-in* magazine. I left the shop in tears. 'Go back in there and stand up for yourself, Tina,' my mother ordered. I did, but when he said no a second time I wept and ran all the way home. My best retorts are afterwards, when I've had time to reflect and plan my ripostes to do the most damage.

'What are you doing, Megan?' I ask, keeping myself calm by breathing, slowly.

The kitchen table is strewn with nail polishes.

'I'm painting Laura's nails,' she says as if it's the most routine thing in the world for her to be doing. They smile, sharing some sort of private joke. I see that Laura is happy and full of excitement, fluttering her fingers for me to see.

'They look nice, Laura.' My voice is taut like a violin string and unrecognisable to me. 'I can see that, but why?' Laura looks at me funny, her beaming smile freezing on her face, her fingers still in mid-air.

Megan sighs, but her voice is razor-sharp. 'You said you were going to and you haven't. Ergo, I thought I would volunteer in case you had forgotten, again. It's easy to forget. And you had promised, Laura, yesterday.' She reaches out and strokes her hair.

My anxiety right now feels like I'm hooked up to an electric fence. I want to say, 'Hey, Megan, you're clearly *deranged*, shall we take a drive and find the nearest looney hospital? Oh, and stop touching my daughter like that. You're not meant to touch kids without permission; it's inappropriate. You are inappropriate! As well as crazy.' But I don't say that, what I do say is, 'Why did you come here?'

'I wanted to see Laura's nails and ask you if you'd seen my purse. I asked everyone at the office. I left my handbag on Sally's desk after I had given her some money, she was popping out to Starbucks for us all. It was just before you left. Do you remember, Tina?'

I swallow, instantly suspicious. I don't recall anything of the kind. There was no *handbag* on Sally's desk because I placed my handbag on the floor by her desk. Sally's desk was covered with files. 'I didn't see your handbag on her desk. What is more, why not phone? There was no need to come over.'

Glyn keeps out of it, he's sat back down holding a bottle of shocking pink nail polish pretending to read the label. I try to make eye contact. It's no use he is reading, intently. As if.

Megan pouts. She stops painting Laura's nails and looks at Glyn apologetically, but she receives no support from him. Thank God. 'I'm sorry if I've misunderstood. I thought I would be welcome here, and, like I said, I wanted to see Laura's nails.'

'Right. That's enough,' Glyn says, putting the nail polish down and standing up. His eyes flick from Megan to me. 'The purse had her bank cards in, Tina, so understandably she was concerned. She thought you might have taken it by accident . . . because—'

'Because? Because what?' Why is he hostile with me?

With crazily trembling fingers I adjust the collar of my dress. A thought enters my head, *she's going to accuse me of stealing it.*

There's a slight quiver in my voice. 'We would have phoned you if we had it, Megan.'

She shrugs. 'I know, but I wanted Glyn's advice on what to do?' She sends him a fleeting glance before returning to look at me again.

'Apparently your scarf was inside her handbag, Tina.'

'What? What!'

'Yes, well on the top of my handbag, like it had fallen off.'

'Inside her handbag? No, it certainly wasn't. I left it in my office at lunchtime when you and I went out. I never touched it again. I didn't even bring it home.'

Glyn pulls the silk scarf from his pocket. 'Megan brought it with her when she came to visit Laura.'

'Evidently it was, Tina,' says Megan. 'I wasn't the only one to see it.'

I catch each word and try to understand the meaning. To absorb exactly what she is getting at. I watch their faces as they slowly start to fall into place. Horror grips me, tightly like watching a horror film and suddenly knowing what is coming next. I grip the back of the kitchen chair Laura is sat on. I suddenly realise that my life as I know it is about to disappear.

Laura stares at me, her eyes intense with bewilderment. 'Laura, will you take Matt and go watch TV in the lounge.'

'No! Mum. Did you take Megan's purse?'

'Of course not, now go, this is grown-up stuff.'

She's about to say no, when Glyn interrupts her, 'Go on, Laura, do as you are told or you won't get your nails done at the weekend.'

Bitch, cow, lying whore! I spit out the words in my head. She did that in front of my kids. *Bitch!*

'She could have taken that at any time! Do you seriously believe *her!* I demand.

'She found it on top of her handbag, all the other secretaries saw it,' Glyn says. His green eyes unable to look at me.

I say, 'Bollocks, it's not true.' I grip the chair, tighter, in a bid to stop myself from falling over. 'Search my handbag if you want, you won't find anything there.' And then I panic. There's a ringing in my ears so loud that I can't think straight. When I went out I took cash in my pocket. My handbag stayed here. I stand paralysed with fear. She was here. Oh shit. Shit. Shit.

Glyn lifts my handbag and looks inside.

Blinding fear grips my stomach. How is this even happening? I wipe a sweaty hand down the front of my dress.

'There's nothing in here, Megan. Tina must have dropped her scarf by accident. You've probably left your purse somewhere else. Just cancel your cards, it's all you can do.'

After a second I'm able to stand without the use of the chair. I'm awash with relief. So much so that I begin to tidy the table and place the bottles of nail polish in neat little rows. In precise, even groups. I place the homework sheets of paper together with the pens and pencils in height order. Megan watches. My behaviour could be seen by her as obsessive-compulsive, but she'd know this, right? Because she knows all about me. I know she does.

'It shows she was near my handbag,' Megan appeals to Glyn for back up.

'Look this is ridiculous, Megan, Tina would not steal your purse. We need to put a stop to this bickering between you both. Let's have a drink, together, all of us. I'm going to order a Chinese and call a truce. You both need to get on if you're going to work in the same office.'

'OK, Glyn, I'm happy to do that. Are you OK, Tina? Can I get you anything? Glass of water?' Megan says, looking at me, her face poker straight. Asking me if I want a drink in my own house.

I walk away. Go over to the kettle, fill it with water, bang it down on the worktop and switch it on. I stare at her house through the window. I don't want to drink with them. How can Glyn think this is going to blow away? Their chatter grates on my nerves.

That's when I catch a glimpse of it. I look at Megan's house. Then at Megan's handbag inches from me on the counter.

My hand reaches over and pulls out her house keys, my fingers curl round the cold metal.

CHAPTER SEVENTEEN

'I'm going to Ali's,' I say and hurry out of the house. Once on the pavement I look back at our house to make sure nobody is looking out and fall over our recycling bin, it rattles indiscreetly with bottles. I dart to Megan's front door. Shaking, I fit the key in the lock. It takes me three attempts before I'm in. Closing the door behind me, I lean against it. Christ, what the hell am I doing breaking and entering? Have I lost my effing mind? I'm furious at my stupidity. The injustice of the situation I've just put myself in hits me broadside.

The light outside is fading rapidly, and I haven't brought a light, not even my phone. How stupid! The silence inside roars in my ears like the aftershock of a rock concert when you think you've gone deaf.

Ali mentioned papers on top of a packing crate in the lounge. It is a shabby room, and there's a bad smell of damp everywhere. The boxes are situated exactly where Ali said they were. I trip over a small box.

A file sits at an angle on the top corner of the crate furthest away. I carry it over to the window. On the other side of the road my house is lit up like Blackpool illuminations, no wonder we have such a high electricity bill. I can see Megan wandering round my kitchen and settling at the window looking over. She opens the blinds. My stomach muscles tense as if I'm doing a Pilates crunch. I crouch down.

Knowing I probably don't have much time, I open the file and pull some of the papers out. The daylight has virtually disappeared. Picking up the file I make my way upstairs to the back bedroom where I won't be seen if I flick on the light. I stiffen. Something is in the room with me. A rustling sound comes from behind one of the boxes. I stand still holding my breath. I am being watched. All my senses tune in to the silence. My muscles tense. Rats? I hate rats. The rustling gradually grows louder. Out of nowhere something leaps towards me, I step back and two green eyes focus on me as they fly in my direction. I scream and lurch backwards catching my heel against a crate, sending me crashing down on top of another one. My bottom drops though the opening. I grip the edge with one hand before I fall in further and get jammed. It's a cat. A bloody cat. It lands on my lap, knocks the file clean out of my hands and jumps off darting out of the room. Its demonic shriek piercing through the dark, empty house. Christ.

Did I let that cat in? I've never done anything as crazy as this in my life! I could be disbarred if I get caught. I did once steal a pair of boots from Tesco. Not intentionally of course. I forgot I had them in my trolley, took off my coat, flung it over the boots and clean forgot. Mercifully, they didn't have one of those security toggles on. I was mortified to find them. I didn't go back to that store for months.

The streetlight casts weird shapes in the hallway, I hurry towards the stairs through the blackness. I don't remember ever feeling as scared in my life, not even when I stole the boots. I place my foot on the first step, take hold of the banister and tuck the folder under my arm. This seemed such a simple thing to do moments ago. I start to climb, slowly. My eyes hopelessly penetrating the darkness up ahead. Have you ever listened to all the strange noises emanating from an empty house? And what are they? It almost sounds as if it's alive, stretching and groaning. Halfway up, those same green eyes appear before me at the top. I virtually lose my footing.

'Stupid, bloody cat, bugger off,' I shout. My voice eerily loud and out of place in the stillness surrounding me.

I switch the light on in the back bedroom, it blinds me for a few seconds. Inside I drop the file on the bed covered with a floral duvet and pillowslips to match. Scattered clothes litter the floor and a chair is propped in the corner with an open suitcase by the side. A vanity mirror sits on the dressing table with photos stuck to the edges. A photo of a man dressed in jeans and baggy green sweat top lying on a sofa, he doesn't look well. I don't recognise him. My hand hovers over another photograph, I pluck it from the mirror. It's me! Taken unawares, last spring. I'm wearing my new fawn coat that I bought last winter. There are several others of me. What the hell is going on?

Perched on the end of the bed I open the file. I pull one piece of paper towards me, then another, then another. The name I see sends my mind reluctantly and annoyingly back to what happened ten years ago. How the hell is Megan linked to it? I see an image in my mind, was she linked . . . maybe . . . to Megan? Really? Have I done something to her in the past? But I don't remember her? My head aches. I don't want to think about what happened ten years ago. Who is she? I look at a photo of a man. Who is *he*? Did I do something to *him?* I shove them all back inside the file and smack it closed. So it's not a coincidence.

Through the window I see the security light from next door come on. A dog races round looking for somewhere to pee. Her garden is overgrown. There's a surprise. A quick look in her wardrobe proves she is stalking me, it's full of similar clothes to mine. I rush out of the house and trip on an empty litre carton of milk near her recycling bin. Angrily I pick it up and lob it into her garden like I'm hurling a bloody grenade in a war zone.

CHAPTER EIGHTEEN

When I get back from Megan's, I'm anxious and can barely think coherently. The last thing I want is to be chitty chat with *her*. And say what, for God's sake? Why do you have photos of me in your house? In your spare room? 'How do you know I have photos of you, Tina? In *my* house. Have you been snooping? Have you *illegally* entered my home and snooped around?' She'd love saying that to me. I slip the key into her jacket pocket hanging in the hallway and go upstairs without saying a word to them.

That night when we are snuggled up in bed, there's so much I want to say to Glyn. Only I know he is upset with me because I didn't stay and hold out the olive branch to Megan. But I have invested hundreds of thousands of pounds in acquiring this perfect family home and creating this wonderful family, he wouldn't understand. He has morals. I do too! Don't get me wrong. Well, I did have. No, I still do. He might not think the same way. In fact, I know he won't. But . . . well . . . you had to be there to get it. To really . . . get it and to understand why and how it happened.

Lying on his chest and playing with the tufts of hair, I remember Laura's smiling face and how grateful she was to Megan for doing her nails. And that jabs me in the heart. I almost feel annoyance towards Laura for betraying me with her. I know it's not her fault. She just wanted them doing. It didn't matter to her who painted them.

'Tina?' he says. 'What are you thinking about?'

I stop twirling my fingers in his chest hair. I thought he was asleep. 'Nothing. Sorry, I don't mean to be vague. I wasn't thinking about anything.' I'm not sure I want to talk to him about how I am feeling and certainly not about what I did tonight.

'I don't believe you. Tina, please don't take this the wrong way, but I've noticed you're starting to have a few bouts of your obsessive compulsion again.'

'What! I haven't. What makes you to say that?' I remember the way I tidied away the nail polishes and the homework papers. But that was *nothing*. I don't want to talk about it. I don't want to *discuss* it with him. I don't want to *think* about it. I want to talk about other stuff. I want to talk about stuff that isn't related to bloody Megan. Because this is. I know it is. I know he is looking for a smooth entry to talk about her.

'Megan said she noticed you at work, you know, having a few . . . tendencies.'

I recoil. Tendencies? Tendencies! I can't go there, not now, not after tonight and what I found. If only he knew! But he doesn't. And I can't reveal it to him. I can't allow myself to feel safe enough to confide in him. Not yet, because if he doesn't *understand*, who knows what might happen between us. He might believe I have really gone mad. Who wouldn't? I desperately want to mention something to him, even just a little bit, only a little bit won't be enough. It would be like unscrewing a bottle of pop that has been shaken. It would all come out and make no sense, because when I voice out loud what is in my head — it makes no sense. And yet, it's how it happened. My therapist said I need to keep my mind in order. If I keep my mind in order, I can control my *tendencies*.

He shifts positions; I don't move but stay lying on his chest, my finger entwined in his chest hair. 'Look, Tina, Megan is terribly upset. You were rude to her. She was simply

123

being helpful. I don't understand why you can't see that . . . she only has to tell Howard how weird you're being and—'

'I might have guessed you'd see it her way.' I shoot off the bed yanking the hair I have wrapped round my finger, hard. I grab a tissue from my bedside table and dab the corner of my eyes. Unsure how to behave right now, I stand and wait. When he says nothing but scowls and rubs his chest, I burst out with, 'You need to be aware of something I've discovered about . . .' I stop. An invisible hand clasps itself over my mouth. I need shutting up, because if I don't there is no way I'm coming out of this as the innocent party. I want to tell him everything. But he's the one person I can't tell. And the one person I desperately want to tell. I don't know who to trust. I can't even trust my own memory right now.

'For Christ's sake, Tina, don't launch into another attack on the woman,' he says, sitting on the edge of the bed, his back towards me, his head dropped into his hands.

I almost laugh out loud at the stupidity of my situation with my husband. The one man I love and would lay my life down for. 'No, no, listen to me. You don't get what she's like with me. You merely witness what she wants you to see. Don't you think it's a bit odd that Megan came here tonight?' I clench my fists with the sudden urge to shake him. Why is he not getting this? I stand very still watching the back of him not knowing what to do or say next.

'Look. Let's not argue over this again, please. Come here,' he says, and reaches over, grabbing me and pulling me across the bed to him, wrapping his arms round me. It's a sensation I adore, normally. It used to make me feel safe and secure, now I'm not so certain. 'You know when Megan came over she was upset, Tina. In a panic. She did not have a clue what to do? I do believe you think she's out to hurt you, but I can't understand why you feel that way. All I see is her trying to help you. If you had proof of something then I might think differently. I'm getting worried about you. You're acting so erratic. If it was up to me, I'd ask her to leave the firm. But it's not up to me, is it.'

'Why not? She's an adult. It is blindingly obvious you ring your bank to cancel your cards if you've lost them.' I stare at a spot on the duvet trying to stay focused and not lose it. No, it's not up to anyone but Howard and now he's getting his leg over he won't believe anything I say against her.

'I don't know why you're so averse to helping her settle in. It's not like you at all. She was kind enough to do Laura's nails.'

I scoff. 'Don't you recognise what she is doing? She's worming her way into our family. Don't you see it is not typical behaviour? And besides, don't you think it's odd that she had no idea what to do? A grown woman! Come on, Glyn, please. I for one do not buy it; she wanted an excuse to come over.' I pull away suddenly feeling claustrophobic. 'Why did she wait for me to leave the house?' I snap, annoyed that once again he's taken her side.

'I think she panicked, Tina, that's all. She didn't know you weren't home. In fact, she asked to speak with you first. She didn't want to see me. She wanted to talk with you.'

'That's pathetic, Glyn. She came round knowing I wasn't here. To spend time with you and Laura.'

'Tina,' his voice is gentle and calm, 'you're worrying me. How would she know you weren't here?'

'My car? It wasn't in the drive?'

'Right, so what you're saying is that she waited for you to go out. She staked out our house and waited. Then she sneaked over to *worm* her way in with us. For what reason? What possible reason would she have for doing that?'

I want so badly to divulge what I found in her house. But I can't. 'Oh, yeah, say it like that. Go on, carry on saying it like that, as if I am being unreasonable, making it all up. It is all in my *imagination*.' I twirl my fingers against my temples. But it does sound exactly like that. He only sees one side of this. To him I am nuts.

'Well, darling, unfortunately that's what this sounds like. Look, this case and that accident are clearly affecting you. Maybe you should ring that therapist you used years ago and get some diazepam. The doctor gave you the all clear but maybe it's stress.'

'What! Are you for real? My therapist? I haven't seen her in years. I don't need diazepam . . . wait, how do you know I took diazepam? That was before we met. I never told you I took medication.' Sure, I saw a therapist at the time. But it was only for a few months and I only took the meds for a month, no longer.

He shrugs.

'What? A shrug? A fucking shrug, Glyn? You give me a fucking shrug as an answer? Tell me how you know.' I want to hurl myself at him and pummel him for discussing me with her. I know it's her who's told him. Nobody else knows.

'Look, calm down. This is what I mean, listen to yourself. I don't know how I know, maybe you *did* tell me. Maybe you forgot and I've just remembered. I don't know. But it might improve your anxiety. You can't say you're not anxious; you've started forgetting. I witnessed you today tidying up the nail polish bottles and it's not the first time recently that I've noticed you being a little odd.' He gets up and walks to the en suite.

'I haven't forgotten anything! She moved all that stuff. She took my scarf earlier. It's all her, why can't you see that? When she was over here, did she stay with you the whole time?'

'She couldn't find the number for the bank, so we had to go into the study and use your laptop.' He flushes the loo and wanders back in.

Sometimes Glyn's inability to see the bad in people pisses me off. 'Did she see you use my password?'

'Tina! No, she was searching inside her handbag for a tissue. Dammit, she was genuinely upset and worried.'

'Worried. Why? You call the bank and cancel the cards. Big, deal.'

'Don't be like this, please. It's OK for you, you have money, but she was frightened they would empty her account and she didn't know how she'd manage without any money.'

I narrow my eyes and virtually spit out the words. 'I am sure, *Howard would lend her some money.*' Sarcasm drips from each word.

He turns away from me.

'What's wrong now?' I ask, sensing him tensing up.

'She said something strange. I didn't think a great deal about it at the time but seeing you like this . . . I thought she was exaggerating . . . I need to ask you.'

'What?'

'That cut on your leg.'

My hand drops to my thigh and I feel the crust of the cut beneath my pyjamas. 'What about it?' I say defensively. Where is this going?

'She's extremely concerned about you, Tina, despite what you think. She thinks you are suffering from stress and doing irrational things, which—'

I jump in before he's finished, 'Irrational things? Like what?' I turn to confront him. I stand in front of him. A tightness bands itself across my chest. She can't know about tonight, she can't. I can't think of any excuse for being there. Suddenly the room feels too small and airless. What if she caught sight of me coming out of her house? What if she took a picture on her phone? Oh, shit.

'Look, the truth is, Megan says she saw you touching her purse today.' I can hear the accusation wrapped up in the velvet tones.

My mouth drops open. Like a cat dancing on hot coals I move about the room. 'What! I never saw her purse, I've already told you this . . . is that why she came over tonight to tell you that she *saw* me?' An expression of pained incredulity covers his face.

Icy tentacles wrap round me, not just for what I'm hearing but what I see on Glyn's face. This could escalate very badly if Howard finds out. Oh, God! And if she finds out about tonight. That's it for me.

'No, she's worried about you and wanted you to own up. She isn't telling Howard. She doesn't want you to get into trouble.'

'What!' I am monosyllabic.

'Or get the police involved.'

'What!'

He comes over to me and lays his hand on my shoulder. Soothing as it normally is, tonight it's not. I shrug it off.

I stare at his face and see doubt there. 'I can't believe you are siding with her? Glyn, what's happening here? Why aren't you on my side?' The pain of disloyalty hurts. Deep.

'Tina, Christ, Rachel saw you, too! It's not me saying this. You were seen. And your leg. Look at it.'

I look down and touch the scab, again. 'What about my leg? I fell on Matt's truck the other day when you and he were playing in here. Remember?'

'I didn't see you fall?'

'I know. You'd gone. But all the trucks were on the floor and I tripped.'

'Megan said you would say that.'

'Megan said! Megan said! What is this? Is she the bloody oracle suddenly?'

He blows out a long breath. 'Darling, I'm really worried about you. I believe that you believe all these things, but now there's a witness who saw you with her purse.'

'Glyn, I can't believe we're having a row over this! You should believe me, not some secretary that's just walked into our lives. What the fuck is going on!' I start crying. 'Why do you protect her so much?' I don't want to say it. No, I don't want to say it. I mustn't say it. 'Are you sleeping with her?' Christ, I can't stop myself.

'Are you crazy!' He looks genuinely insulted and I feel rotten for asking.

If I wasn't crazy before, I am getting there fast. 'I don't want her in my home any more or near our children.'

'I'm ignoring what you just asked me.' He moves towards me. Is that pity I see in his eyes? 'Tina, she's a nice girl, everyone at the office likes her. James and Ali like her. Give her a chance. Stop being so testy, you don't need this hassle now. Look, just tell me the truth, did you take her purse? I'll support you, you know I will.'

I want to shove him so hard that it will hurt. I push him in the chest and he grabs my wrists. 'No. I. Did. Not,' I yell. 'Ali doesn't like her!' I say horrified he thinks so. 'She thinks she's weird too. It's not just me.'

'Are you self-harming? Tina tell me the truth. We have children. I need to know they are safe.' He pulls me close and I fight to pull away.

'What are you saying? Glyn, this is me. I don't self-harm. I wouldn't. And I would never harm my children.' My words sound as empty as that stupid bitch's house.

CHAPTER NINETEEN

The walk back to the office from the courts practically finishes me off. This weather is so oppressive. I've taken a pill for
my headache but it hasn't helped. Each step along Deansgate
in my heels compounds the banging in my head. Glyn and
I are not on great terms after the other night. I am keeping
my head down and remaining uninvolved with any office
politics.

I buy a sandwich and a coffee with vanilla syrup from
Starbucks across from the office, hoping the sugar rush will
revitalise me. I'm getting to a point where coming in to the
office makes me anxious all the time.

Cheryl, the receptionist smiles at me when I step through
the glass doors, it's one of those pitying kind of smiles, which
I have endured from the staff for the last couple of days. I
know nothing about what's been said about me. I won't ask.
But I'm clinging on to the fact that Glyn hasn't spoken out
of turn. He wouldn't.

I walk past Howard's office, his voice bellows out
through the open door, a couple of other office doors along
the corridor close discreetly.

The secretaries look my way as I pass. It's hushed in
there; the normal buzz of low-level conversation is not

130

present here today. A stillness fills the atmosphere so thick it's stifling.

Arriving at my office, I sigh with relief to be away from the spotlight. I sit down, kick off my shoes under the desk and open my sandwich then ask Sally to come in.

I turn on my computer and log in while taking off my jacket. The mayo oozes out of the side of the bacon, lettuce and tomato sandwich when I take a bite. I click the email icon. 'What?' I say out loud. I put the sandwich down and hit the refresh button and nothing changes. I check I've clicked 'Inbox,' but the screen stays the same, no new emails. 'That's weird.' I log out and back in.

My office door opens. 'Oh, hi, Sally.' It is great having her back. I click several buttons but nothing changes.

'Sally, is something wrong with our internet, I can't get my emails.'

'No, everything is working,' she says in a strangled voice as if she doesn't want to be in here.

'Really? Because I'm having trouble retrieving them. The, um, what-do-ya-call-it — little spinning wheel, it's spinning but nothing changes. My inbox is empty. Is everything OK, Sally?' I can see the strain it takes for her to talk to me. Why? What have I supposedly done now? I soften my words with a smile. 'Sally, what's wrong?' Then a thought hits me — the children. What if something's happened? I snatch my phone off my desk and check for missed calls. 'Has there been a call from school? Has something happened to the children? Is that it?'

Sally shakes her head.

'What is it, then?' My voice has a fish-wifey tone laced with prickly irritability to it. But who cares. What is wrong with the woman? I don't have time for this. Christ, I should not take it out on her. This bloody place is exhausting my patience. Why can't she just tell me what's wrong?

She clears her throat, 'Mrs Miller came in today,' begins Sally.

'Mrs Miller? Why did she come in?' I interrupt.

She looks feverishly at the door as if she's waiting for someone or something to happen 'She came to see you, Tina, she said you arranged an appointment. At the courts. With you.'

'With me? At the courts? She must have got confused. That is not for another two weeks. I told her I was in court today. In fact, I told her I was in court for the last few days and I would get in touch with her at the end of the week.' The raised voices from Howard's office are directly outside my door. What is going on?

'You sent her an email at the beginning of the week, Tina,' Sally says in such a faint voice I can barely hear her. Her eyes dart to the door and the approaching voices.

I'm pulled back to the conversation. 'I didn't, Sally. That's preposterous. Talking of which, I have no new emails, don't you think *that's* odd?'

Sally sits in my chair and plays with the computer and clicks a few icons. She brings up my sent emails. One addressed to Mrs Miller, requesting her to join me at the courts, today.

She waits for me to offer some explanation. When nothing is forthcoming, because I am looking steadily at the screen, Sally says, 'She was hopping mad when she came in. Demanded to see Howard. She really laid into him. Threatened to get a new lawyer. Threatened to sue us.' Tears well in her eyes. 'Howard questioned me as if I was lying to protect you.'

'Sue? What for?' I'm frozen to the spot and sit down again looking at the screen and reading the email one more time. I don't remember sending that email. I don't. Did I mix up the dates? I can't work out why I would have made such a stupid, unprofessional error. Worst of all the embarrassment of the whole office knowing about it.

I walk to the door barefoot and close it, gently. I notice the mirror that hangs on the back missing.

'Have you moved the mirror off the door?' It's not a question. I know it sounds like an accusation.

She shakes her head. 'Do you want me to get Howard?'

'Absolutely not.' I nearly laugh because it makes no sense. I know I didn't send that email and Howard is the last person I want to see right now.

I'm back at my desk when Howard bursts through the door like an avenging angel. I push back in my chair, instinctively. Sally steps back, too. Glyn follows in behind and closes the door. Sally makes to leave.

'No. You stay, please, Sally,' Howard says.

'Howard, I've just been told what's happened and we will discuss this, but I think Sally can leave. There's no need for her to be here.' If I could just think of a smart little phrase that would take the edge off what's to come, I might be able to save my reputation. But I can't.

Howard laughs, a deep baritone sort of laugh. 'There's every need, Tina.'

I respire deeply as my heart lurches. His face is florid, a vein in the side of his neck looks like a fat worm pulsating. I look at Glyn who is poised to do something. What that something is, I don't think either of us knows. He reminds me of a coiled snake, watching and waiting to pounce. I feel an unexpected jolt of love, but then I recall what he said the other night and it's gone.

Howard stands in front of my desk with his hands gripping the edge and leaning forward in an intimidating manner. His tone is resonant and full of accusations. 'Do you know what has happened?'

I cross my arms and nod. He battles with the words he wants to use and the ones he must use to not provoke a disciplinary action from Sally or me.

Before he can imply anything, I inform him, 'Howard, I take it as a personal insult that you will not believe me when I tell you that I did not send that email to Mrs Miller. I do not overlook important details. I do not send incorrect emails to my clients. I do not lose important paperwork. I have never done any of those things in all the time you have known me. I have an excellent memory and one which you have on numerous occasions commented on.'

Howard takes a deep breath, but without shifting his eyes off me he continues to lean forward. 'No. No, you haven't, I'll give you that. You did forget to pick up the kids, once.'

I think he's trying to be clever with that remark. I'd laugh, if it wasn't such a low-level punch. 'Howard,' I scold, 'that was one time, a long time ago, it has nothing to do with what is going on now.' We had a heavy client meeting that went on longer than anticipated. I was chairing the meeting and lost all track of time. I can hardly be charged with forgetting.

'Well, it brings me to the lost paperwork.'

My head jerks back. 'What lost paperwork? Is there any?' I demand. I press my hand to my throat, I think I might be having a heart attack. His words bring back the anxiety of that day.

'The originals for the Miller case? Don't *lie* to me,' he thunders. 'Megan told me about it after the rampaging and humiliated Mrs Miller launched herself at me after being sent on a wild goose chase to the courts.' He moves away from the desk, makes a deep growl sort of sound deep in his throat and paces the floor.

I'm close to tears. 'Megan told you, did she?' I say in a 'and you'd believe everything she would say, wouldn't you?' tone. I'm very aware my innocence remains an issue here and proving it is going to be difficult. 'Why did Megan tell you that? They were not lost, it was a case of not being able to find them on the system.' I am covering my arse here, technically he can't accuse me of losing anything when in fact they were never lost in the first place. I'm careful not to incriminate myself.

His mouth twists. 'That's as maybe. But you did send Mrs Miller to the courts today. What do you have to say about that?'

I'm conscious Sally is still here and in my professional opinion she should not be privy to any of this conversation. 'Howard, do you really need Sally here?'

'Yes, that is something else to do with your erratic behaviour of late.' I'm bemused to what he is referring to that would concern Sally. He leans over my desk once again in a form of intimidation. 'Megan tells me when Sally was off sick she phoned in and you refused to speak with her. This is another character behaviour I'm unhappy with, Tina. She also said you were hostile towards Sally and voiced your intent to fire her when she returned. This is not the way we work here.' His voice escalates, 'She also tells me you are taking diazepam for your anxiety!'

I can't bear it any more. Is this what Megan intended? To destroy me with false accusations that I am unable to disprove? It's just been a matter of fashioning the right allegations against me. Allegations I can't refute. I slip on my shoes to provide me with extra height and stand up to face him off. Leaning into the desk I am inches from his face and towering above him. He might be loud and bolshie, but he's short and acutely aware of his lack of inches. I exploit this to empower myself. I hiss my words so close to his face that I can smell the stale stench of his cigar breath. 'How bloody dare you believe that woman over me! I would never, ever, say any of those things about any member of staff to another staff member. Sally is my right hand; I would never fire her.' I catch Glyn from the corner of my eye looking at me wide eyed, mentally ordering me to cool down and back off.

The hell I will.

Howard says to Sally. 'Sally, did Tina say any of these things to you?' He doesn't back up and we stay locking horns.

I notice Sally stiffen beside me.

'I got an email, she didn't call me. But we've ironed out any issues there might have been.' She smiles at me cautiously, reassuring me that she doesn't blame me.

He grumbles some inaudible words under his breath. 'Are you taking diazepam?'

'No!' I say full of resentment that he even asks the question.

'I want to look in that locked drawer of yours.'

I pull a small key from beneath the phone and open the drawer. In front of me is a box of diazepam.

'That's not mine!'

I see Glyn flinch.

Colour rises in my face. 'That's not mine; I don't understand how it got there. But it's not MINE!'

'Tina, perhaps this is all getting a bit too much for you.' Irritation drips from his voice. He pulls back from the desk. I look at him astonished. 'The proof is in the emails you've sent. I can't allow this to make its way out of this office, ruining our reputation. Do you have any idea how much damage that can do to the firm?'

It is at this moment that Glyn makes his move. 'OK, listen, it seems to me that a lot of this is circumstantial. Howard, nothing was lost so you can't accuse Tina of losing anything. Just because Megan says it's so, does not mean it happened. The email she denies sending. I agree this is more difficult to deny, but somebody could have accessed her email account. Have you thought of that?'

Howard thrusts his hands up in the air and turns to face Glyn, his agitation now focused on him. 'What? You think this is a conspiracy against Tina? By whom? And the pills? What! Someone planted them in her drawer? Surely not Megan. She said Tina would accuse her. What would she have to gain by it? Moreover, you yourself were aware of her panic over the loss of those files, were you not? I know you've been concerned about her.'

Glyn looks at me directly. He will not want to incriminate himself by lying. 'Alleged, loss of files, Howard. Tina was unable to access some files from her laptop and she asked me to check when we came in on the Monday morning. They were all there and that was the end of it.' I want to cry, he's taken my back. I knew he would. I want to rush over and hug him. My face softens, and I hope he can see my appreciation, but his dark look tells me he's unhappy with me. 'The pills — I don't believe Tina is taking them. I have no explanation why they are in her drawer.'

Howard makes a grunting sound. He turns to face me, once again. This time his voice is sharp like a slap in the face. 'You still sent Mrs Miller the email. I won't believe somebody has tampered with your account. If you are taking pills how would you know you didn't?'

'They're mine,' Sally butts in.

We all look at her. 'Sorry, Howard, I was taking them for my own anxiety. I bought them on the internet and hid them inside Tina's drawer because I know she never goes in there. I'm sorry.'

You could hear a pin drop.

There's a beat.

He leans back across my desk and with a threatening tone and clipped words says, 'I don't want to lose this account, Tina. Do. You. Understand. What. I. Am. Saying?'

CHAPTER TWENTY

When Howard leaves the office, I stand up and look out of the window. The air conditioning maintains the office at a clement temperature, if I open the window hot, sticky air will rush in. I see Glyn's reflection; does he hate me? Does he actually hate me? I can't hear the street sounds below through the triple glazing; it's like a TV show with the volume turned off. People jostling on the pavement, rush, rush, rush. What for? Why? Where's the emergency? A woman in far too high shoes rushes along, carrying packages, trying to navigate the traffic. 'Do you think,' I say cautiously without turning round but watching his reflection, 'any of this would be happening if Megan hadn't started work here?'

There's a long pause.

My eyes stay with the crazy woman zig-zagging through the traffic, inside I feel bleak. Where is all this headed? And why have I little control over what is happening to me?

'But she did start,' his voice is stark.

What I want is support, but it looks like he is going to accept this situation as is.

'Megan didn't make you take the diazepam. You did that all by yourself.'

I flop into my chair suddenly exhausted, shaking my head. How can I make him believe me? It is as if my life is not my own but a puppet and someone else is pulling the strings.

'No, I didn't.'

He flinches.

'What can I say, Glyn. I can't explain any of this, I have no idea how, apart from what I've said about my account being hacked — you even told Howard the same.' While talking I go through the process of changing my password on my computer. I click confirm.

His thunderous scowl speaks volumes. 'I know you don't want to hear this, but I'm going to lend a hand with this case.'

'What? Definitely, not,' I say with conviction.

'It doesn't matter what you say, I outrank you here, Tina. And if it's not me, you can bet Howard is thinking the same thing. Would you prefer that? You need to get yourself together. I can't figure out what's going on with you. But seriously, get your shit together and throw those bloody pills away.'

'Just what do you mean by that?'

'You get the picture. You can probably kiss your partnership goodbye, that's for sure. And if you're not mindful your career too. You're a mess. I can't believe you are taking those pills again.' He stands up to leave. 'I don't know what the fuck is going on with you but sort it out because from where I'm standing it's a mess.'

'OK! OK!' I want him to shut up. 'But—'

Glyn holds up his hand. 'Stop right there. Remember the email came from your account. There's no altering that. You've changed the password now. Good. There shouldn't be any more emails incorrectly sent out unless sent by you. Should there?'

I snort. 'Unless somebody,' and by somebody I clearly mean Megan and he knows it, 'jumps on while I am away from my desk.'

'Dammit, Tina.' He slams his palm down on my desk. It makes me jump. Glyn has never spoken to me like this. Not my Glyn. What's happening? 'Then don't leave your laptop exposed. If you need to leave your desk, log out. Have you considered that Megan might be trying a little too hard to be accepted and you are misinterpreting everything she does? Some people are not as self-confident as you.'

'I'm not cracking up you know. No matter how things look.'

'It looks bad, Tina. It's stress, like the last time.'

I glance at him. 'It's not the same and you know it.'

He looks at me passively as if we are strangers.

'Do you remember when Matt was born? We had all that worry because he wasn't feeding and the health visitor and doctor told you there was nothing wrong with him. But you knew there was something wrong. He kept throwing up after each feed. Wouldn't stop crying, slept a couple of hours at a time. You had no sleep for nearly four weeks and all the time you were battling for somebody to believe you.'

I do remember. How could I forget? Each day was like walking through fog. I was drained and would fall asleep at the sink while washing-up, or on the loo. The tiredness consumed me. Hauled me down like an anchor tied to my legs. But I couldn't sleep because I had Matt and Laura to look after. Until that awful morning when he didn't wake me with his crying. When he came round, I called the doctors. Unable to speak, because panic had taken my voice, I cried and the more I tried getting out my words the more choked I became.

In the practice the absurd doctor told me nothing was wrong with my baby. I experienced one of those out of body moments; I saw myself get out of my chair, take off my shoe and calmly slam the heel into his head. He patronised me when I insisted he contact the hospital. He told them I was a hysterical mother. Turns out that Matt had pyloric stenosis. Pylorus is the valve that allows food to pass from the stomach into the intestine. Pyloric stenosis is when this muscle thickens and stops milk from leaving the stomach causing forceful projectile vomiting after feeding. He asked me if the vomit was really projectile and if it was hitting the wall. I wanted to reply — that if it was hitting the wall, I would be calling a priest not the doctor.

'You suffered from headaches, irritability, the shakes, loss of memory, you even stopped halfway through a conversation because you'd lost the thread of what you were talking about. You had all of that because of the stress you were going through with Matt.'

Megan chooses that moment to walk in on us. 'Sorry, Glyn, your client has arrived. I've taken them to your office.'

My hackles rise at the way Glyn smiles back.

'Sorry, I didn't mean to interrupt.' She looks at me. 'But he's been waiting ten minutes. I thought I'd best come and remind you he was here. Oh, and we could hear you both shouting,' she says with an apologetic expression, using that breathy voice which irritates the hell out of me.

'Yes, excellent, Megan, I will be right there, thank you.'

'I'll leave you with those thoughts, Tina,' he says and waves it away as if we've been having a pow-wow about what we are having for dinner tonight.

I file some court papers and catch up on correspondence, email Sally with instructions and let her know I will be leaving the office shortly. I cannot stay here a moment longer than I need to. This whole thing has me wound up.

Focusing on my email responses, I double blink — my screen changes, darkens for a second and then my cursor shoots across the screen, then it's all back to normal. Maybe I nudged it with my hand without realising. I frown looking at my hands still on my keyboard. Did I move my hand onto the mouse? I must have done. Christ, I don't even remember doing it.

I pull out my heavy bottom drawer for some hand cream before leaving and find the mirror from the back of my door stowed right at the back. Shit. Did I put it in there?

CHAPTER TWENTY-ONE

I grab my handbag, my briefcase and my phone and leave the office without a goodbye to either Glyn or Sally, eyes forward and head held high. I walk down the corridor, past the secretaries and into reception towards the glass doors. A journey that seems a short distance every day, feels like a walk of shame right now.

On my way down in the elevator I check the time — two hours before school's out. Maybe I will pop over to see Ali and fill her in on the latest. The elevator pings and the doors slide open. I shoot out of our building onto Deansgate, one of the busiest thoroughfares that runs through Manchester city centre. I am pulled along with the crowd in the direction of the car park. I'm not paying much attention to my surroundings. It's a humid kind of day, with clouds threatening rain, we could do with some rain, it hasn't rained in weeks. I wouldn't be surprised if there was a hosepipe ban soon. Alone inside my head with only my thoughts for company, I find it's not very congenial in there right now. I'm confused and worried. It bothers me I'm clearly having problems remembering and breaking the law.

My phone pings with a text message. It's Ali. How fortuitous. I move to the inside of the pavement away from the crowds and lean against Waterstones' window. She leaves me a voicemail, I call it and listen. The window display is colourful with cardboard cut-out trees and shredded green paper on the floor pretending to be grass and pretty little dolls sat in a circle playing at reading a book. Howard and Megan stand together, inside, talking. Intimately. They laugh together. My shoulders sag. 'Oh, God,' I say out loud, 'he's so bloody smitten with her.' The man standing next to me looks at me quizzically and moves away. I turn round and lean against the window. *That* fiasco earlier keeps replaying in my head. I looked so guilty! I acted guilty! My denials sounded guilty! If I had been on the other side, *I* would have thought I was guilty.

Hastily walking to my car in the underground car park, a few feet from Waterstones, I'm assailed by a stench of urine that fills my nostrils as I climb the stairs to the fourth floor. I throw a pound coin into the empty cup of a homeless man sitting by the elevator as I rush by.

Inside my car the lingering memory of those accusations and Glyn's face when the diazepam appeared overwhelm me. How clever Megan is to find the key to my drawer. And she knows my history. I toss the box of pills from one hand to the other. There's a feeling of distaste and violation that she has dug into my life. As if she's reached into my personal memories and poked around like Pandora opening the box and is thrilled to find so much to play with.

I turn the car on to start the air conditioning. I can feel a rising level of fury. I picture my mother. Confident. Strong. Never one for moral dilemmas. 'You need to stop overthinking things, Tina. Guilt will prevent you from achieving what you want.' That's what she told me so many times as a child when I felt badly done by. My mother wasn't the sort of person you challenged. She never doubted herself. So I usually went back out and dealt with whatever was causing me grief. 'There,' she'd say later, 'don't you feel better now you've stood up for yourself?' I had and I hadn't. I faked it. I'd been terrified. I got better at it as time went on. A lot better. I didn't want my mother to think I was weak. She stood up to anyone who dared push her down and she tried instilling that ideology in me. That is why it is so tragic how she imploded when my father left her for another woman. I pull out my phone, but there's no signal in here.

How the hell has Megan managed to make her way into Howard's affections so quickly? Granted he's a good catch. Divorced. Charming house in the suburbs. Grown-up children. Holiday home in Majorca. I think this is a ploy to get at me and gain power to undermine me by sugar-coating his brain. I have noticed she notches up a gear or two when talking to Glyn and Howard. I punch the steering wheel and accidentally hit the horn startling a couple walking past. I raise a hand in apology and slowly pull out of the parking bay.

When I reach the exit and join a queue, I scroll through the list of calls on my phone until I get to the private investigator. I need to wait until I'm out of the car park to receive a signal. He answers after three rings, his heavy Irish accent difficult to understand. We haven't met; we've corresponded by email and phone. I chose him because he was the only one of three that answered the phone. We chat for a few minutes and to my surprise he tells me he has plenty of information on Megan. 'Oh! Right. Really? That's excellent, isn't it?' I hadn't expected much. 'That's great. Yeah, good. We'll meet. Let's meet. Soon. Can you meet soon? I'd like to meet right now. How are you fixed to meet? Tomorrow? OK. Braitling? Can't you come here? Oh, OK, yeah.'

I thought I'd never feel that awful sense of shame again. The more I hear the word 'Braitling' the stronger the feeling grows. I believed I was done with those feelings. My therapist told me I had closure and was in a 'good place'. That I had come to terms with what had happened, none of which was my fault.

My phone pings with an email alert and then rings, *Alexander Bamfield* flashes up on the screen. Shit. I wondered how long it would be before he called. Luckily my voicemail is a generic one.

Pulling up outside Ali's house I notice it has rained here. Seeing her smiling face at the window, warm and friendly, I begin to relax for the first time today. Walking through her garden gate, I sidestep a toy pram and a dolly minus a head and a leg. I'd like to see a certain person in that state.

I smile, reassuring her that I'm not judging and laugh, because I know she knows I am. My high-pitched laugh verges on the hysterical inside my head. The audible sound comes from a strange place in the back of my throat, almost by its own volition and sounds nothing like a laugh at all. Ali clasps my hand as I reach the glossy red front door. I'm delighted she isn't privy to my miasma of tangled thoughts right now.

As children, Ali always stuck up for me and managed to get hurt on my behalf. I would stand up for myself, as Mum wanted me to, which predictably led to a fight. And I was hopeless at fighting. Ali, she was like an alley cat. She jumped in and annihilated them.

Ali's family wasn't particularly wealthy or privileged, they were comfortable. We grew up together, we came from similar backgrounds, until my father legged it and then Mum had to sell the house and start again. All with backbone, though. She never let anyone see how hard it was for her to deal with the fall from grace. Ali's family were good people; they never spoke about it, but suddenly I was taken on holidays and invited to parties and barbecues. Her mother was one of those floaty types; she was kind to everyone, from shop assistants to waiters to traffic wardens, yes, even traffic wardens. I wonder if Dad hadn't left, would we have become such good friends.

'Are you OK, hun? The last time you laughed like that there was trouble at mill.' She tries lightening my mood. 'Has something else happened?' I brush away her concern with a flap of my hand and roll of my eyes in a vain attempt to blink back the tears bubbling on the surface.

I haven't bothered Ali with all the events that have happened since we had lunch in the garden. I don't want her to think I'm nuts like everyone else. And she will do when I tell her I broke into Megan's house. It just sounds so crazy when you say it out loud.

'I've prepared iced tea.' She looks at me with curiosity. 'Do you want a glass or would you prefer traditional tea? Sorry, I forgot you're not a tea drinker. Coffee?'

'I will have an iced tea if it's heavily sweetened.'

'It's close today, don't you think? I thought that storm might have brought some relief but it doesn't seem to have accomplished anything.' She pulls the jug from the fridge and fills two glasses, handing me one. 'It's watered the gardens if nothing else.'

I perch on the stool tucked beneath the work island and wipe the condensation from the glass with my index finger. I tell her an abridged version of what's gone on, keeping my eyes downcast. I am about to tell her I'm going to Braitling tomorrow to meet the private investigator but decide against it. Too much information. Even to me it sounds bonkers. She doesn't miss my hesitation, though. But she says nothing. I think she is giving me space, like the therapist did. In the hopes I will open up.

Ali looks at me with wide eyes. 'Christ, Tina, how can you prove it's her? She seems to cover all the bases. Are you certain it's her?' She reaches out and covers my hand with her own.

'What? Are you kidding me, Ali? You too?' I pull away but she hangs on.

She shakes her head vehemently. 'No, not at all. It's so hard to believe that's all. I'm not saying it's untrue. I am trying to say it's like one of those bloody movies we like to watch. I just don't understand why she is doing it? Have you heard back from that private investigator you were going to call?'

She's right, of course. To anyone on the outside it does sound mad. But I can't bloody prove any of it. And yet, I thought Ali would be one hundred per cent behind me. So why do I feel she doubts me?

'Why are you questioning me? What's bothering me is you don't believe me either.' I say. 'The office I can get over.

146

I can deal with them, eventually.' The last word fading out but clearly audible. I stall for a second or two before continuing. 'But you and Glyn . . .' I sip my tea. 'I want you both to believe in me. Believe I am not crazy or under stress or suffering from some sort of bang to the head delayed reaction. Everything has got out of hand. It seems as if it has all blown out of proportion. But it's not, is it, because at the end of the day all these things have happened.' My agitation is clear in my tone.

'Tina, I do believe you. And I agree that there is something not right about her. But I just can't understand why, without a motive, she would do these things. That's what is so hard to get my head round. Are you telling me everything?'

I struggle to look at her. I use the silence that has fallen between us to wipe all the condensation from my glass; I stir the ice cubes with my finger.

'Ali, it's like she is trying to destroy me and wedge herself into my place. Despite everything I do to stop her, she is one step ahead and I am plunging deeper into the hole she has prepared for me.'

'You haven't answered my question. Have you told me everything, Tina?'

We sit in silence, Ali isn't going to say another thing until I answer her question. I know her.

I grope round for something to say. The right thing to say would be, 'Yes, actually there is something I forgot to mention.' But admitting to breaking and entering doesn't come naturally.

I glance at Ali from beneath my eyelashes. She's swirling her drink, watching the ice cubes clashing in her glass.

I look round the comfortable house. The kids and I have spent so much time in here over the years, putting up tents in the lounge for the girls. Sitting in front of the fire on a cold winter's night after school and toasting marshmallows over the open fire. I'd ring Glyn and tell him where we were. He was amazing. He'd get home and prepare tea for us. Then come over and pretend he'd just got home and there was no

147

food in the fridge and we'd have to go shopping. I'd coast along with the pretence, secretly knowing some amazing food waited for us back home. The kids always fell for it with Laura being the dramatic one, crying, 'Oh Mum! There's no tea? Do we have to wait? I'm *so* hungry I could eat my hand!' Then started mock gnawing at her hand. Why did she never work it out? Was she slow? It hadn't ever occurred to me she might be.

'I saw Megan at school,' Ali says and picks up her drink taking a sip. I guess she has given up waiting for me to reveal.

'What day?'

'The thing is, Tina, I am not sure how to tell you, which is why I haven't . . . yet. I didn't want to worry you even more. That doesn't mean I wasn't going to. I just wanted Glyn to tell you.'

'Glyn? Tell me what? What are you talking about?' My body stiffens, preparing for some dreadful news. I watch her face and a raw sensation descends over me as if a layer of skin has been removed. I undo the buttons on my blouse and fan myself with my hand. Grabbing the tea towel, I dab at my temples, sweat runs down my back and between my breasts.

She leans forward and grabs my hands, holding them firmly. 'This is why I think you are holding back and not telling me everything. It happened yesterday. At first, I only saw Glyn walking up to the gates. It surprised me because you said you were picking them up. I wondered if you were ill and thought of taking Laura back with me for tea if that was the case. Give you some peace.'

'I wasn't ill.'

'I know that.'

'Did you speak to him?'

'Yeah, I did. He told me you'd been held up in court and so he'd come to pick up the kids.'

'I had. What has any of this got to do with Megan? Was she there yesterday?' Panic begins deep in my belly. What is going on? Is Glyn *seeing* Megan on the side? God, I've been so cocooned in the snugness of my marriage. I thought it was forever. And I thought it was snug. OK, so we are battling through stuff right now. Have I missed some colossal warning sign?

'I'm coming to that. She was with Glyn, wearing a suit like yours. You know the pinstripe one you have from Hobbs with the pink stripe running through. She even wore nude stilettos and her handbag was identical to yours, too.' She nods towards my oversized neutral handbag dumped on the chair.

I pull my hands away and quite suddenly I need air and I can't get any. I struggle to take a lungful; my chest won't expand. Ali rushes over to me and steers me to the back door. Outside, I inhale and inhale, but I can't take in any air. I begin to feel light-headed. My legs wobble. Ali rams a brown paper bag over my nose and mouth that smells of pear drops and orders me to breath deep. I do and it starts to help straight away.

'Look, Tina, I didn't say anything because I thought Glyn would. I didn't want to stir up any more trouble. But when you didn't mention it, and I'm pretty sure you would have if you had known. As your friend I felt I had to tell you.'

I breathe out into the bag and in again. 'I don't understand what she was doing there with him. Why would she be there? Did you speak to her? Did you ask her why she was there with Glyn? Did you question Glyn? Did you do anything for fuck's sake?' I squeeze my eyes shut and clamp my lips tight regretting my outburst. Then use the bag again.

'You have every right to be cross with me for not telling you, but please don't shed your anger at me. I did fucking question her, and Glyn too for that matter. In my most commanding telling off voice I use for the children. I was by no means polite. It came out in a rush of uncontrolled words and emotions. When I saw her dressed like you it really got to me.'

I laugh, imagining Ali having a go at Glyn in that posh high pitch, Jean Brodie voice she has when she's cross. I breathe into the bag again.

Ashamed by my outburst and feeling wobbly like I'd just stepped off an amusement park ride, I say in a more measured tone, 'But she wasn't wearing that suit at the office.' I would have noticed. 'Why would she get changed? What did you say to her?' I'm firing questions at her at the rate an M60 machine gun fires a round.

'Well, I asked her. I said, "What are you doing here, Megan? Does Tina know you are here? Glyn, does Tina know *you're* here with Megan picking up *your kids*?" I kind of spat the words out, and she just kind of looked at me? Like, I am the crazy one. I think she wanted to tell me to fuck off. She wasn't happy I was there. Tina, something is very wrong with her. She looked as though she was plotting something heinous to do to me. She scared me. That is why I'm asking if you're telling me everything. She's got it in for you and maybe for me now by association. There has to be more to her just showing up unexpectedly like this.'

'Why was she there?' A huge tidal wave of fear clings to me like a damp cloak. I carry on breathing into the bag. We walk back inside and I take my seat again. I put the bag down and take a sip of cold tea.

Ali looks at the table. 'She leaned into Glyn, telling me that Glyn had asked her to accompany him.'

'What!' I almost fall of my stool. The glass in my hand shatters.

'Jesus, Tina.' She leaps up, 'Are you alright?'

'I feel dizzy.' I see blood on my hand but it doesn't register any pain.

'Shall I take you to the hospital?'

'No, no, I'll be fine.' I wash my hand under the tap and wrap some kitchen paper round it. 'It'll be OK.'

Ali mops up the spilt tea. A strange expression crosses her face. 'Well, anyway, as I was saying. I gave him the death stare but he wasn't touched by it. He smiled easily and told me he'd given her a lift home. She had a flat tyre in the car park, she was leaving work early for an appointment or something, I can't remember what she said. Glyn was on his way to pick up the kids, remember I told you I had to take Katie to the dentist? He simply asked if she wanted a lift and she tagged along.' She throws the wet paper towel in the waste bin. I sit half on and half off the stool. 'He made it sound innocent and you know what, Tina? I think it was in his eyes. I really do. But her! Oh, no. She was milking it so that I would go running to you. I could see it in her eyes.'

I pull my hand away and flex my fingers. There's a quiver in my voice, 'Do you think there might be something going on with them? Christ, I can't believe I said that aloud.'

'No way! No, I told you, I believe it was all innocent on Glyn's side anyway.' She makes me look at her.

'Why would he do that? I need to speak to him about this. We were happy, weren't we? You remember us being happy, don't you? Before . . . before she came along. I am not imagining that, am I?' I ramble on. 'I can't phone him at work. I'll have to wait until he gets home.'

Ali smiles, tiredly. 'Stop it. Now you're imagining things that are not there. Of course, you were happy. Aren't you happy now? Glyn is friendly. He is kind and likes to help people. As you do. I genuinely don't think anything is going on.'

'They found diazepam in my drawer at work. She told Howard I was taking it for my anxiety! I don't even have anxiety! Suggesting that was why I forgot stuff. Made mistakes. She made it look so real.'

'Shit. And it's not yours? I mean, I know it's not . . . is it?' She says in a dealing-with-a-possible-crazy-person kind of voice.

'No! It isn't, Ali. Christ, Glyn said the same thing. Why would I take that?'

'You took it once before.'

'Yes, but that was a long time ago. My mother died, for chrissakes; I was in a mess. I was screwed up. I was in therapy, but that was then.' I'm so confused right now. I didn't think Ali knew about that. I'm sure I never told anyone. Did I?

'OK. OK, sorry I doubted you. You never did tell me what happened with your mum. You disappeared for a year.

Did something happen there? Apart from your mum dying, I mean.'

She knows we moved away, everyone thought me crazy to move her at that time, but it was what she wanted. It was the only thing I could do for her. I couldn't save her. I knew she wouldn't really know where she was, but just in case, I had to do it for her. It holds so many bad memories for me. I know I did something bad there, but I can't remember. We moved to Braitling after Mum was diagnosed with stage five pancreatic cancer. She wasn't mentally present any more, but she'd been banging on about going there for a long while before the cancer. When she was lucid, she told me she and Dad had often gone there for long weekends before they had me. I found photographs of the place and it really was idyllic looking. In her lucid moments she wouldn't talk about much else. After the diagnosis, I moved there with her. There was no more treatment and I wasn't going to let her die in a hospital, she would have hated that. I wanted to give her what she wanted. There wasn't anything else I could do for her. I knew it would only be temporary. It wasn't until after she died that I found out that was where Dad had been living with his new wife. I never knew if Mum knew that. Maybe she did. Maybe in her crazy, mixed up world she thought she'd see him again. She'd never got over him. I've never told anyone; my mum's death was too painful.

'You just thought, like Glyn, that I would simply take drugs because I was anxious? Only I am not anxious, am I? I'm only anxious because of what she's doing to me.' I shake my head. 'That doesn't sound right, does it?'

Ali lowers her eyes. 'Tina, why won't you open up to me? Why did you need to go to therapy? I know it wasn't just because of your mum. You are one of the strongest women I know.'

I am flattered she thinks so. I do not feel strong, however. 'Ali, what if she tries it on with him. What if he sleeps with her because she comes on strong and he can't refuse? Men are weak. Look how she's wrapped Howard round her finger.'

'You're not going to tell me, are you?'

'I don't remember anything. That's the truth. Losing my mum threw me off the rails. Nothing else. Right now, I am worried she's going to fuck my husband just to provoke me.' A headache starts deep in the back of my skull, and I know it will turn into a migraine if I'm not careful. I swallow two paracetamols.

'Tina . . .'

'Just stop. Please. There is nothing to say. Just answer me. Do you think Glyn will . . . sleep with her?'

'No. That's Howard, not Glyn. Have you said any of this to Glyn?'

I'm embarrassed. 'I asked him, yes. When we had that row.'

'And what did he say?'

'No, of course.' I take a deep breath.

'Well, then. Did you believe him?'

'Yes, I did, yes. I think so.'

'You think so? Are you delirious? He loves you. He's besotted with you, and he wouldn't do that. Not Glyn. He wouldn't.'

I don't tell her about the horrible row we had and the way he spoke to me or the doubt I heard in his voice. Maybe our perfect marriage isn't so perfect after all if something like this can cause cracks in it.

Her phone rings and we're both momentarily distracted. Then I remember I'm going to Braitling tomorrow. Leaving Glyn alone isn't my preference. Ali finishes her call and checks her watch. 'Sorry, but if we don't leave now we will be late for the kids.'

'I'll give you a lift to the school, shall I?'

'Leave your car here and let's walk,' Ali says giving me a hug. 'I'm your best friend, remember that, Tina. You can say anything to me and I'll support you.'

I'm not so sure about *anything*.

CHAPTER TWENTY-TWO

Before we leave for the school, I nip to the loo. I hear the clatter of something falling on the tiled floor. A debit card lies face down next to the toilet. Hesitantly, I pick it up and see it's Megan's debit card. I drop it as if I've been scalded.

As we leave, I'm in shock. I put one foot in front of the other waiting for a reaction from my body. I know I should be feeling something. Anything. As Ali locks the front door, I say, not really in the moment, and feeling apathetic, 'I have to go to Braitling tomorrow to meet that private investigator, but I'm scared to go after what you've just told me . . .' I need time to process what's just happened and what Ali has said.

Ali doesn't bat an eyelid. She turns round, smiles, loops my arm and pulls me along the road towards the school. 'OK, that's great. The sooner you find out about her the sooner this will all be over. Have you told Glyn? I have an idea, why don't I collect the kids from school and keep them here until you get home? Tell Glyn tonight, so he doesn't override me. What will you tell him about the trip?'

'I don't know, if I say I'm going to Braitling he'll know it's something to do with Megan and then we'll have another row.' I'm too hot. I take off my jacket and fling it over my shoulder. I'm surprised I'm able to talk so calmly.

'Mmm,' Ali says, chewing her bottom lip. 'It's a tricky one, for sure.'

I finger the debit card in my pocket. It fails to elicit the reaction I feel it should.

'Now, this is just a thought, but have you emailed this private detective? If Megan hacked your emails, she could very well know about it.'

'I did. But I deleted it immediately and his reply,' I say in a hushed voice, virtually inaudible. I realise how unprepared I am to face what I need to do or worse what might be happening to me. Maybe if I told Ali it would make it clear in my mind. Make what clear? That I stole the card after all? That I am having blackouts as Megan insinuated? My personality is to keep things to myself. I am not a *share all* type of person. I learned this from telling my mum too much over the years. Her favourite saying was, 'People with too much ammunition will mould their bullets accordingly, Tina, to hurt you.' Ali isn't like that. But this is big. This is bloody huge. My cheeks burn with the guilt that I might be a thief as well as a cat burglar.

'Tina? What's wrong? What have you thought of?' She tilts her head down to see my face from over her sunglasses.

I reach out and grab her hand, squeezing it and fearful of confessing. 'I've just found Megan's debit card in my trouser pocket,' I say quickly and scrunch up my eyes. Like tearing off a plaster I want to get it out there as quick as possible.

'What?' Her tone is harsh with shock.

I can't look at her. 'It fell out when I went to the loo. Honestly, Ali, I don't know how it got there. I really don't. I'm sure it wasn't there earlier. She must have planted it on me.'

'Tina. How . . . I mean . . . where . . .'

'I don't know.' I feel light-headed.

Ali grabs me and gives me a hug. 'Tina, I'm worried about you. Glyn is worried about you. I have to tell you that he's been texting me. He's worried to death. He doesn't know what to do. He's at his wits end. He's firefighting at the office with Howard. I know you think he's pulled away, but I think he's terrified. And now so am I.'

I stand wrapped in her arms, my own limp against my sides and remember her horrified face just seconds ago. 'Because you think I took it?' I carefully release the breath I'd sucked in and wait for her answer. My heart thumps against my ribcage.

She pulls away and looks clearly terrified that I might have really taken it. 'No, no, because she's so clever and manipulative. Get rid of the card,' she says with affirmation.

'What? No!' Rage and pain race through me like a poison. Rage and pain for Glyn who will never recover from this if he finds out. For how she is setting me up. For how everyone will believe I took it if they find out. 'I need to give it back to her, don't I?'

'You idiot. Who do you think is going to believe you when you tell them that you happened to find her card in your pocket? Think about it.'

'I am.' I stand by the wall beginning to crumble. My life fragmenting into tiny pieces round me. I silently scream, *I'm not losing my mind.* But what if I am! What if there is something wrong with me?

'Nobody knows you have it. Apart from me and I'm not going to reveal anything. So, it's her accusation that you took it. Without evidence she can't make it stick.'

'Yes, you're right. Unless—' I say lamely.

'Unless nothing, Tina, I know you didn't take this. I believe you. Stop looking like that.' From her face she is clearly terrified. Should I be as terrified as she looks?

I don't want to go home when we pick up the kids. We decide to go to the park instead and grab an early tea of fish and chips.

A bit of a breeze picks up while we sit on the park benches, it cools us a little but it's short-lived. The dense air clings like a blanket. Fish and chips probably wasn't the best idea.

I chew on a salty chip, pondering how well I know my friend.

Ali stops chewing and looks at me. She doesn't speak. She lays a comforting hand on mine. 'I'll never judge you. You know that, right? I haven't forgotten what you did for me with my divorce.' I know that Ali feels she can never repay me for helping her through her horrific divorce. It's her own way of showing her gratitude and I love her dearly for it.

If I hadn't helped Ali with her divorce she would have been left with zilch and on the street. Her ex-husband lied and manipulated the system. The law is a wonderful thing. I believe in it wholeheartedly, but I also recognise that if you understand how to play the system you hold all the cards.

If it hadn't been for Ali's family, I would have grown up in a world of silence and anxiety. I owe her. When Mum died, I was and wasn't surprised I had a to go into therapy. The huge responsibility of looking after her and the shame. I never told anyone about Mum — obviously Ali and her family knew, and now Glyn. I was embarrassed and to a degree disgusted she had a mental illness.

So I tell Ali, because I'm scared of the madness haunting me and remembering more and more if it might be hereditary. Afraid I might be going nuts like Mum. 'I broke into Megan's house.' The words blurt out. If I don't conceal the secrets then by default I can't be following in my mother's footsteps. Right? That's my logic, anyway. There's one secret I won't be able to tell. And as the shock registers on her face I know how crazy I sound right now. Muscles ache from being clenched in fear and I slump back onto the bench.

'What?' Her face falls. 'Oh my God, how did you manage that? Jesus, where was she?' I know it's pointless evading so I tell her how I got in.

I push my sunglasses up on my head catching my hair, which sticks out at angles giving the impression of an unbalanced businesswoman. 'Painting Laura's nails. Like I said before, it just got to me and without thinking I lifted her house key from her bag and raced over there. I can't believe I did it without thinking it through. How stupid was I? It was nearly dark when I went round and I forgot my phone

157

so I had no light. Obviously, I couldn't switch on the lights, for obvious reasons. Jesus, Ali, I could get struck off for this.'

Ali's reaction isn't what I expected. She starts to laugh then places her hand over her mouth staring at me and shaking her head. 'Tina, I'm shocked that you had the bottle to do it. I was contemplating it, but I thought you'd say no, you being a lawyer and all.'

'Are you serious? It was foolish and could have gone horribly wrong for me if she had come home. I was terrified.' Her laughter infects me and I chuckle too, but mine is of the nervous kind. 'The house was eerie, I was petrified. A bloody cat leapt out of the darkness landing on me and scared me half to death.'

'Did you find anything?'

I finish my last few chips. 'Yes, I found a lot of photos of me taken a while back, and some of a man I didn't recognise.'

'Pictures of you? Are you joking? Seriously? That's creepy. Did you find anything else?'

I shrug. 'She's been stalking me for a while.' I shake my head in disbelief. 'How have I not noticed this woman, Ali, she's hardly blend in the crowd material, is she?'

'No, definitely not. I think you need to go to the police.'

'What? Are you kidding?' I say midway through scrunching up my fish and chip bag. 'I can't go to the police.'

'Why not? Look, she's stalking you and has been for a while you say.' Her tone is jagged, all the laughter gone now. 'She could be dangerous. Maybe a psycho. How do you know it's been a while?' She looks over at the kids, Matt is inside the tunnel in the playground and she launches herself off the bench to check he's OK before I even notice. Am I becoming a bad mother? 'Katie, Laura, don't leave Matt out of your sight. How many times have I told you, you must keep an eye on him when you are playing together.'

'Why? We're playing, and he's in the way,' says Laura.

I move and stand by Ali. 'Just do it, Laura. Remember what they tell you at school — keep vigilant.'

'He'll spoil everything.'

'That's tough.' My tone loses all its muminess.

'How do you know it's been a while?' Ali asks again as we move back to the benches.

'The photos she has. I'm wearing a woolly hat and scarf; she probably took them in the winter.'

'But what winter? This one or last year or before? How do you know she hasn't been stalking you for years? No, you need to go to the police.' She purses her lips. 'I don't like this, Tina, I have a horrible gut feeling.'

'No,' I say bluntly. Grabbing all our rubbish, I throw it in the bin. 'I can't.'

'Have you forgotten the films we watch and what these sick people end up doing? Think about your family. Have you considered she might harm them?'

'That's a bit melodramatic, don't you think?'

'No, I don't,' Ali yells so compellingly that I drop onto the bench. The kids stop playing and look over. 'It's OK, guys, carry on playing.'

'And say what? What do I tell them when they inquire how I know this? Do I casually drop it in that I broke into her house?'

'Shit, you're right.' She plonks herself down next to me. 'I'll tell them I did it.' Ali volunteers as if suddenly her breaking and entry is OK, not punishable by the law.

'What! Certainly not. Besides, you, me, it makes no difference, it's against the law. What? Do you think you're beyond prosecution? Listen to me, Ali, I. Broke. The. Law. No, you stay out of it.'

'Right. You're right. Jesus what will you do?' Ali puffs out her cheeks and exhales though her mouth making a sound like a deflating balloon. 'Look, Tina, we might be getting a teeny bit paranoid. I mean, she's probably not a psycho.'

'No, you were right the first time; she is a psycho. Look at everything she's done? Is doing? Let me see what I find out tomorrow. I'm not naïve, but I do need to know why, and right now she is backing me into a corner.'

A bit later, I twist the key in the lock, push open our Victorian stained-glass front door and hear *that* familiar voice coming from the kitchen. The children run in ahead of me.

CHAPTER TWENTY-THREE

I hear Laura giggling in the kitchen from the hallway.

In the kitchen, I'm faced with Megan holding Laura in her arms, her long legs nearly touching the floor. I am speechless. I didn't know it was possible to have so much tension spring back into my body when it is already so full. I refuse to allow this to take control of me. Where is Glyn? Didn't I tell him I didn't want her in our house? Laura giggles some more. Sensing me, she turns round, wriggling to be released and runs over to me grabbing my hand. I grind my teeth so hard my jaw aches. She takes my limp hand pulling me towards Megan who wears the most unsettling look I have ever seen on anyone's face. I can't believe what I'm seeing. I feel as if I've walked into a nightmare.

'Mum, don't you think it's funny? She looks just like you!' Laura squeals.

'Laura go to your room and take Matt with you,' I shout at her, I don't mean to raise my voice. She looks at me, defiant. I give her *the look* and she stomps out of the room with a painful throwaway remark, 'Her hair is nicer than yours.' The dagger strikes me right in the heart.

I turn to Megan. I waste no time on civilities and lash out. 'Just what the hell do you think you're doing? Are you completely mad?'

Megan walks towards the basement and flashes me a smile. 'Is that anyway to greet your neighbour, Tina, and all that coarseness in front of the children.' She tuts. By her raised voice I take it Glyn is in the basement and this spectacle is for his benefit.

Footsteps race up the stairs. Just before he arrives, I catch a glimpse of a smile tugging at the corners of her mouth. 'They say imitation is the highest form of flattery, don't they? And besides, I think Glyn likes it.' This bit she says so only I hear.

I meet Glyn's gaze at the top of the stairs. Just what the hell is he playing at allowing her back in our home and why is he looking so dishevelled?

'Do you think this is normal?' I point at Megan. Without waiting for a reply, I continue, 'The woman has dyed her hair the same colour as mine and had extensions! She looks like me! She's dressed like me! Don't,' I say to Glyn as he attempts to speak. I can't get over how ruffled his hair looks as if somebody has messed it up. 'How can you say this is normal or acceptable? She comes here to our house when she likes, she even went to the bloody school to pick up the kids as if she was me!' I'm yelling, I know, and I want to bring my voice level down but I can't.

Megan moves to the basement door and leans against it. Glyn looks her over. 'I agree it is a bit weird, Megan. Why?'

She purses her lips. I don't think she was expecting that from Glyn. Frankly, what the hell did she think he would say? *Oh, grand, now I have two of you?*

Before she can reply, I jump in and cut her off, 'And what were you doing with Howard in Waterstones today? Cosying up? Trying to twist things in his head to satisfy you?' I can't stop yelling. I'm aware I am the only one with a raised voice.

'Howard? Today? Don't be ridiculous. Oh, Tina, we both know that's a lie,' she says in a resigned voice. She immediately turns to Glyn and shrugs her shoulders as if stating the obvious, that I am nuts, just like she's been saying all along.

I step towards her. 'Do you deny it?' What had I been expecting? Honesty? Congratulations on discovering she's

161

a manipulative bitch after all? '*Marvellous, Tina, well done for finally discovering what I'm about.*'

'I haven't left the office today except at lunchtime and then only to the sandwich shop.'

'Via Waterstones,' I snap.

'Tina!' Glyn gives me a censorious look followed by a roll of the eyes, as if I've announced something so inane it's ridiculous or worse, as if I'm embarrassing him. It hurts and stings like salt on a wound. 'You're making a rather hefty accusation here. Have you any proof? Don't forget Howard may have asked her to go there and they have been out as a couple.'

I haven't, of course I haven't.

'Mummy, I'm tired,' says Matt walking into the kitchen, rubbing his eyes. I bundle him up in my arms. My eyes flick to the overly large clock on the kitchen wall. It is far too early for bedtime. I am becoming neglectful of my children and this is not how I want to behave. If anyone had ever told me that I would feel annoyed about my children stopping me doing something, I would have laughed in their face. To me they are my life, my centre of gravity. Yet, right now, I cannot see beyond stopping Megan destroying me. There is an irony here, whilst I am saving myself, I can see I am damaging my most precious treasure.

'Sorry, darling. I know you're exhausted.' I smother him with kisses and breathe in that smell that is all his own, taking it deep into my lungs. I move to the fridge, pull out the milk, pour some into a cup and heat it gently in the microwave, all the time trying to calm down. My hand shakes. The last thing I need to do is lose my control. I'm frustrated at Glyn's lack of empathy with me. Either I am really imagining all this or none of it bothers him. But of course it must bother him. The microwave pings, I pull out the milk and slam the door. 'Here, go and sit down for five minutes with your picture book and drink this and Mummy will take you to bed when it's all gone.' My chest constricts at the sharpness of my voice. It's no good, I can do nothing about it right now.

I look at Glyn to gauge his thoughts. I can't help feeling disappointed that he's not more annoyed with Megan than he appears, and because of this, my thoughts run wild.

Glyn's cold voice when he does speak cuts right through me. 'Well? Do you have any proof?'

'No, I didn't stop to take a photo,' I snap. 'Just hang on a second here, what the hell does she think she is doing trying to look like me.' I am offering Glyn the opportunity of giving me some sympathy and a little bloody support, which I feel is sadly lacking. I don't want to argue with him in front of Megan, but that is exactly what is happening. What is that feeling I'm having? Envy? Am I envious? I am. I am envious of what appears to be his support for Megan instead of me. Does he not care about me any more? Is that what is happening here? Is that why his hair is ruffled? I can't bear thinking of that.

I try to act cool and in control, even as my heart is racing and my anger with Glyn raging.

His voice is monotone. 'We'll get to that in a moment. You can't go round accusing people of having a relationship without proof, you of all people should know that.'

'Relationship? I never mentioned a relationship. I thought they were just going out!' I shift my look from Glyn to Megan. 'Are you having a relationship with Howard, Megan?' Wasn't it he who first mentioned they were having *a thing?* I am so confused.

'Tina!' Glyn snaps again. 'Why are you persisting with this? She has denied it once and God almighty, if Howard should hear of this.'

The air between us is thick with animosity.

'What? Will he be outraged and sack me? Well, he bloody well can't and you know it.'

I'm aware that Megan is observing us, intently. Judging. Enjoying the friction between us.

'No, maybe not, but you can kiss your partnership goodbye, for sure.'

I push on, 'Right now I'm not interested. I do want to know why she is dressed and looking like me, though? I bet if we go over to her house she will have a wardrobe full of clothes identical to mine.' I stand in front of her waiting for a reaction. I defy her to deny it.

'Yes, well, I'd like to know why you've done this too, Megan. To be honest it is a little odd,' Glyn says, finally. I scoff at his choice of adjective.

I jump in, unable to keep silent. 'And why were you at the school picking up *my* children, dressed in a suit identical to mine? And making out to Ali that Glyn wanted you to pick up the kids with him?'

'Glyn gave me a lift home, my car had a flat tyre and he was leaving to pick up the kids, so he offered me a ride. He was late and said he had to pick up the kids first before dropping me off, so I went with him. No big deal, Tina, it was too hot to wait in the car.'

'The funny thing is Ali thought you were coming on to Glyn in front of her. Isn't that funny. Of course, you wouldn't be doing that and trying it on with Howard. Would you? Or would you? Oh, and your car problem, bit of a coincidence Glyn was around, wasn't it?'

Megan looks a tad thrown for a moment. And I can't help but feel slightly elated. Finally, I'm bringing her down and will prove to Glyn what a conniving liar she is.

I edge closer to Glyn hoping our bond is once again gluing together, but he sidesteps me without looking in my direction, causing me to falter. The disappointment from his actions momentarily flaws me. There comes a point when two people have pulled apart too much and the distance is too great to cross back. Has that happened to us?

Glyn watches the scenario and I can see he is waiting for Megan to speak without interjecting. His usual tactic to get someone to talk. It would go some way towards me believing he is on my side right now. Even if just a bit.

'Err, I don't think I was coming on to Glyn like you suggest,' she says. 'And Glyn asked if me if it would be OK going to the school before he dropped me off, otherwise he would be late in picking up the kids. Of course, I didn't want that, did I? And neither would you, I imagine. So, I went to school.'

'I don't think Ali would have conveyed what she did if you hadn't given that impression. You deliberately implied by your actions something was going on,' I say. 'And why get changed? You were wearing an identical suit to one of mine at school which you weren't wearing in the office that day.'

'Tina, I think you're really going off topic. Firstly, at the office I wore a white dress if you recall. I spilt coffee over it, a lot of coffee. Glyn offered to take me home via the school, I couldn't show up with a big splodge of coffee all down my dress. So, I changed. I had the suit in the boot of my car,' she says. 'I honestly didn't know it was a copy of one of yours. It's just off the peg; anyone can buy it.' She looks at Glyn. 'It was a coincidence. I don't know what all the fuss is about. It's a suit, hundreds of women have that suit.'

'Tina, I do think you're blowing this out of proportion. I did ask her to the school. Everything she says is accurate. There's no ulterior motive here, Ali just misread the situation.' He looks sad and uncomfortable.

'Really? A coincidence? Happened to have a suit already in the boot? Who does that? A happy coincidence, don't you think? I think we need to go look in your wardrobe.'

'If you want to go to mine, I don't have a problem. You know the way, don't you?'

I scoff at her barb. 'Sure, you don't. And why didn't you call the rescue services? Why ask Glyn?'

'I'm not a member of any and the local garage I found on Google said they were too busy.'

'And that's when Glyn happened to come by and rescued you, is it?' Something comes to mind. 'Did you google them from the car park?'

Glyn protests but I stop him by holding up my hand. 'Just a second, Glyn. Please, let her answer.'

He doesn't wait. 'I don't think it is necessary to know where she googled from, Tina. It's hardly relevant.' He looks contritely at Megan.

'Just let her answer, please.'

'It's OK, Glyn.' She stands away from the door frame. 'I did, yes. It was hot and my car was stuffy, I got out and googled and that's when Glyn turned up, midway through my conversation with the garage.'

'Which garage was it? Do you remember?'

'Take it easy, Tina, this is not a court room.'

She narrows her eyes and a smile twitches on her lips. 'I do. Yes. It was Fraser's.'

'Well, I know for a fact there is no signal in that part of the car park, the only place there is signal is near the exit. Therefore, you're lying. You planned to have Glyn rescue you.'

'Oh my God, Tina, this is preposterous,' Glyn says. He looks alarmed as though I'm about to jump off a cliff.

I pay no attention to him and carry on. 'Show me your phone and your history. Show me where you googled.' I'm praying she hasn't cleared her history.

She opens her phone and shows me the page and then she shows me the dialled number for Fraser's Garage.

I grab her phone and look at the page and check the timeline. It's all as she says. 'But there isn't any signal there. I know there isn't. You must have gone down to the exit then back up to the car. Just so you would have proof of your lies.'

'Tina, I think you need to back off. Stop this right now. She broke down. I helped.' He snatches my hand just as I'm about to fling the phone at her. 'Tina! What's got into you?' Keeping hold of my hand he looks at Megan and I see some private mental communication going on between them.

I shriek, 'Get out of my house right now and don't you dare turn up at work again. No, first let's go to yours and look in your wardrobe.'

Megan sobs and says, 'I can't lose my job. You can't sack me. Can she, Glyn?' She rests her hand on his arm.

Oh, Please. Spare me the drama. Standing between them, I say again, 'Let's see your wardrobe.'

'No, she can't sack you,' Glyn says. 'Tina this has gone on long enough.'

'Ask her why she has changed her hair, that's weird, at least ask her that!' My mind is racing, and I can't comprehend how this has flipped over. Again.

She hands over her keys and I stride out of the house.

'I wanted strawberry blonde,' she says. 'But the colour reacted and it turned auburn. I didn't plan it, Tina, how weird do you think I am? So I had the same colour extensions put in. I didn't think it was as close a match to your colour. I didn't even realise.'

'Right, she's explained why her hair is like it is. You'd better go home, Megan. Tina, we are not going to Megan's to snoop. Come back.'

'Yes, we are. Oh, come on, Glyn that's a lame excuse. And not true!' I want to pull out her extensions. I want to punch her. Swat her like a fly. I want to do something hurtful like she is doing to me.

'No, I'm not going over there. Somebody needs to stay with the kids. I'm asking you not to go, Tina. Please leave this alone.'

I can't, though. The law is on her side. In the eyes of the law she has done nothing wrong. But I could be in serious trouble for my aggressive behaviour towards her and if she finds out about breaking into her house. Well, I can't bear thinking about that one. I ignore Glyn. I'm going to take photos and then I'll have bloody proof. He'll believe me then.

I open her front door.

She lets out a deep sigh. I stride in confidently, straight to the stairs, climbing them two at a time. Over my shoulder I shout, 'Come on, I'd like you to witness me taking photos as evidence that will once and for all put you in your place. Mind the cat doesn't get out.' Megan looks at me questioningly; realising my error, I carry on to the top. I stride to her bedroom and pull open the wardrobe. Nothing. Nothing resembling my clothes are inside, not even the pinstripe suit. I push all the clothes hanging to one side and search at the back of the wardrobe, pulling boxes and shoes out. But there must be. I know she has outfits like mine. I know it. I've seen them. I run to the other room and search but discover nothing. I feel such a fool. I want to show Glyn what a liar and manipulator she is, and now I look like the crazy one.

I stand in silence.

Megan moves in front of me with a smug look on her face. 'Did you find anything, Tina?'

'You know I didn't,' I snap.

'Aren't you going to apologise? You really have gone over the top with this behaviour,' Megan says nastily.

'I know you've moved them. Hidden them somewhere,' I say tersely.

I catch a glimpse of a smile tugging at her lips. 'If you want to search the whole house, Tina, go ahead.'

I can't read her expression. But I don't need to, I already know she is joyful at my outlandish behaviour. I couldn't have performed better if she had written the script for me.

'Incidentally, how did you know I have a cat and which room is my bedroom?'

'I took *a guess*, and the cat was in the hallway, Sherlock.'

She plays with her phone. 'I videoed you, by the way. My, my, you look totally la, la.' She laughs.

I storm downstairs. She follows. 'I know you've moved everything. But I know you have them somewhere. You can't wear them now though, not now I have brought to light that you are imitating me.'

'I think you need to go. Now.'

I leave catching a glimpse of the tidy lounge now devoid of packing cases. It looks normal and ordinary. 'You've moved *everything*, pictures, papers, the lot, haven't you?' I demand, suddenly realising my mistake, she knows I have been in her house and that was the reason for her coolness when I demanded to come over.

'How would you know? Did you break into my house, Tina? That is against the law.' She wiggles her phone in my face.

* * *

168

'What!' Glyn nearly blows a fuse when I tell him. His face reddens. 'For fuck's sake! Tina! When did you break into her house?' His grip on me is firm. He looks at me with incredulity stretched out across his face. He looks pained and scared. 'I never thought you would ever do anything so *stupid*,' he hisses. 'I'm sorry but I think the bang to the head has really affected you.'

'Why don't you believe me? She has hidden everything away,' I insist.

'Shut up about it, Tina.' He breathes in deeply. 'Darling.' His hold on me relaxes as does his face. I see worry and pity mixed together in his eyes. I must sound crazy to him. I sound crazy to myself. 'Let's not dig ourselves in any deeper, babe. I want to support you, really I do, but you have to admit that you have no proof and all this has started since that bang on the head.'

'She videoed me tonight.' I nod my head in the direction of her house.

He looks at me as if I've sprouted another head. 'Fuck. She'll tell Howard or go to the police. Oh my God, do you realise what this means? You broke into her house. You're a fucking lawyer.'

I jostle him away from me full of frustration at my situation.

'You're a lawyer. Do you understand what she can do to you?'

I nod my head but stand my ground. I must get him to believe I did this because she is stalking me; trying to take my family from me.

'You need to apologise to her. Tonight!'

'I will not! Look, Glyn, you don't see it, but she's trying to take over my life, she has bought clothes like mine—'

'It's not a crime to copy somebody's clothes.'

'It's not, but look at her hair, she has replicated that too. She's wormed her way in at the office; my files have disappeared then re-appeared . . .'

'So you say, but all I see is you misplacing them.'

169

'What about her hair!'

'She bloody explained that, Tina, it was an accident it could happen to anyone.'

I start to cry because I can see he doesn't hear me and frankly I don't have a clue what else to do. I am backed so far into a corner it's paralysing me. I give it one more go, 'Glyn, look what she did with Laura. I was going to paint her nails. She's my daughter that's my job.' Even to me that sounds pathetic and whiney.

'Get a bloody grip, Tina,' he yells. 'Do you have any idea how this sounds? Do you? It's pathetic. It's trivial. Except your breaking in to her house. That's just ridiculously irrational!'

'Why don't you see what I see? Why don't you believe me, Glyn? You seem so cosy with her; she's come between us, don't you see? Look at us yelling. We don't behave like this.' There comes a point in an argument when you recognise you are losing and you need to cut your losses and back down. That's me right now. Except I cannot back down and I will not walk away. I am the only one who knows I am not crazy. But doesn't every lunatic believe that?

'No, we don't, but then again you haven't lost the plot like this before or broken into somebody's house! And you require evidence, Tina. EVIDENCE! You're the lawyer you should know that.' He rubs his hands over his face as if to try and clear his head. 'Do you realise what she can do to you? If it is true what you say, and I don't for one second believe it is, then you have played right into her hands. She controls us. US! I have to go over there and try to convince her to keep her mouth shut and not show that damned video.' He turns round and strikes his fist into the wall then grimaces with pain. 'Bloody hell, Tina, if she takes up with Howard, she has a hold over us.'

I hiss at him, 'She has no evidence I was in her house or that I broke in. It's heresy. Crap. She has no EVIDENCE! Stop stressing. She can't accomplish anything without proof. That video proves nothing.'

He sighs. 'I hope so, Tina, I bloody hope so. But something tells me this isn't going to go away that easily.' He flings open the door, hesitates and turns back to me. 'Have you thought about the kids in all of this? Have you? Get a grip, before you destroy all we have.'

'I . . .'

'Don't say any more. When I return you will go round and apologise.'

'I will not.' I don't care if I sound like a petulant child. I will not apologies to her — EVER.

Glyn slams the door. I watch him walk down the path towards Megan's house, knock on the door then disappear inside. When the door closes I experience a pain, deep, way down inside my soul in a part of me I have never felt agony before. I can't explain it; it's a profound ache that shakes the very essence of who I am. Then I swipe the surfaces of the kitchen clean. Kicking everything that falls in front of me. Turning round and round and gripping my hair in deep frustration at the lack of control I have over my life right now. Then, incapable of holding myself upright any longer, I slide down the kitchen unit and hug my knees close, rocking back and forth. I stay like this for ages staring at the door until a shrill noise focuses my attention and after a moment of confusion I see my phone light up. A text message from an unknown number. Hesitantly I open it. *How would social services view your behaviour?* The words come in and out of focus making me giddy.

CHAPTER TWENTY-FOUR

My eyelids are heavy and as much as I force them to stay open they close.

The clock says just after midnight when he climbs into bed and immediately my hackles are up. I pretend to sleep when he rolls over and pulls me towards him so we are spooned. I concentrate on my breathing and keep my eyes closed.

'I wasn't sure you were awake, were you or did I wake you?'

I don't reply. In fact, if I am honest, I'm not sure what to say or how to initiate a conversation with my husband. There seems such a big chasm between us right now and I don't know how to bridge it. Or worse, if I even want to. I am so clouded. I love him, but I don't like him right now. I want us to mend, but I'm unsure if I really do. I want us to get back to how things were between us, but how can they with the mistrust swirling round us? He spoons with me and I silently weep into my pillow.

The following morning, I feel no better. I've had a rotten night, but I've tried putting it all in some sort of perspective. The problem is, I can't seem to figure out what is going on with Glyn and Megan. I don't want to believe what looks like the obvious, because it may only look obvious because she is manipulating it that way. Unable to cope any longer with my thoughts I push back the covers and begin to climb out of bed.

'Tina, what is going on with you right now?' Glyn asks, and I am sick of hearing this damned question. He pulls me back in, closer to him and nuzzles my neck. This is not going to happen. How can he even think that I could? I can hear in his voice he has calmed down, but I can't help wondering how? Was it her? Did he have a lot to drink with her? Shit. I must stop thinking like this. 'You scared me earlier. It's as if you're losing your mind. I didn't know who you were last night, you frightened me. I thought you were going to have a meltdown. I love you, you know, I haven't stopped loving you. Please let me help you.' His hands begin to roam my body, following the contours of my shape.

I sigh. I love him too; it's just that he is driving me insane, quite literally with his allegiance to *her*. I am not going to say it though, it will only stir things up. I do want to hurt him for it. He should be on my side, and I certainly should not be pussyfooting around him. I know this. Except, I'm scared it will go the wrong way for me. I almost lose my resolve and fire a bullet. I don't. I'm a coward and I'm scared of losing him. I grab a hold of his hand round my waist and squeeze it tight and stop it moving further. 'She is trying to destroy me, and I have no idea why. She even has you believing her.'

'Tina, she is trying to settle in, new job, new neighbourhood. She has no friends here apart from Rachel and she has enough to keep her occupied. She won't want to spend time away from home with Megan. Besides, Howard won't get rid of her. She's lonely, that's all, and maybe she is trying too hard. I think you are reading far too much into what isn't there. Why is it so difficult for you to be nice to her? This isn't like you. You need to get a hold of yourself and apologise to her.'

I snort. 'God, she has unarguably taken you in, big time. Why can't you see it? Why can't any of you see she is manipulating this whole charade?' Then I remember something Ali said to me. 'You know the other day when we went out with the kids on the bikes? She came over here and sunbathed in our garden. Ali saw her. She was dressed like me and wore a large sun hat identical to mine. Ali even thought it was me until she took off the hat. That is not normal. And we should get that bloody fence fixed. That day you said I left the French windows open overnight? I didn't. So, tell me what the chances are of our neighbour having the same sun hat as me? I bought it in New York on one of our trips before we had kids.'

'Why didn't you tell me this before? Have you checked your hat is still here?'

I go to the wardrobe and open my hatbox at the back. It's empty. It's gone. 'No, it's gone. But as you say, I can't prove that, can I? Next you'll tell me I probably gave it to charity or something as stupid as that because how would she have taken it.'

I grab my dressing gown and stomp downstairs. It's early but it's light. I fling open the curtains and blinds in the kitchen. Open the bi-folding doors, I drag a coffee pod from the box and fling it into the coffee machine. While the water heats up, I stare at her house. Christ, I want to rush over and . . . and . . . and . . . I don't know what I want to do to her, but whatever it is, it will be jail time.

The coffee machine pings and I stuff my cup under the spout. Glyn is unwilling to even consider that what I am saying has any truth. Which to me appears totally illogical for a lawyer. I doubt myself and second-guess everything I do, too fearful of making a mistake or forgetting some important piece of information. If the truth be told, I am scared I might have my mother's mental illness. They say some things are hereditary, like height, colour of eyes, hair and skin type. Some mental illnesses are known to have passed down the genetic line. What my mother had was caused by trauma, or so we were told. I never delved too much into it, afraid of the answers. I drink my shot of espresso in two gulps.

Howard is taken by her and I can see why, that is pretty obvious. The secretaries, apart from Sally, love her. I guess they have no reason not to like her it isn't them she is firing bullets at. Nevertheless, it is happening so why can't anybody apart from Ali see it?

Suddenly I think of them both at her house last night, drinking, laughing and Glyn agreeing with her that I am losing my mind. Together. Alone in her house with her crying and feeling sorry for herself and Glyn consoling her. My head throbs. My chest burns from all the tension. *Is he fucking her? Is he?*

I sit brooding for what feels like ages and watching her house for signs of life, my anger colouring my thoughts. I remove one of my protein drinks from the fridge; I've started buying these, they're crammed with vitamins and all sorts of miracle wonder herbs to help with memory loss and energy. I drink it quickly; it's vile, I shiver at the acrid taste and bin the empty bottle. How dare he side with her. He likes living here. In this spacious house. In the most valuable part of Knutsford. He wouldn't live here if it wasn't for my inheritance and me. Ha, funny how he seems to have overlooked that already. I am not letting her ruin my life and what we have. And he certainly is not going to take all this away from me if that is what he is thinking. What! And shack up with her? Is that his plan? Has he got bored with me now and taken a fancy to a bit of totty. Well, I am the divorce lawyer, and he is not receiving a penny from me if he tries to play that trick.

I lob some empty crockery left by the sink from last night into the dishwasher and slam the door; I hear crockery hitting crockery and wince. Christ, I must be having a caffeine rush, my heart races. I feel a little faint and grip the edge of the worktop.

A car comes up the drive. I watch and I'm shocked when Glyn's parents climb out of the taxi. Great. How has their trip come round so quickly? I thought it was still a while off, but what would I know right now? I don't need this.

I race upstairs and get ready for work.

The doorbell chimes.

'Your parents are here; you'd better get up and let them in. Did you know they were arriving today?'

Half asleep he mumbles some obscenity; he gets up and sees me getting dressed, without saying a word he pulls on his dressing gown and leaves the room. I hear him welcoming in his parents, the kettle going on, lots of noise and laughter.

I don't want to see his parents or talk to them. How can I? I don't want to be civil with them, not that any of it is their fault, but he is their son and they will side with him. If I'm honest, I do not want to have to explain my mad rantings to them. I do not want another person to think I'm crazy.

Five minutes later, I am sitting in my car and switching on the engine.

I pull up outside Ali's house. I knock, gently, not wanting to wake up Katie as it's only 6.30 a.m. She opens the door, half asleep, takes one look at me and drags me in.

'What's happened?'

There's a pause before she ushers me into the lounge and closes the door. 'Can I get you a drink? Coffee? Something stronger?'

Yes, a bottle of vodka would do nicely, thank you, I want to say. She looks edgy, I hope she isn't annoyed with me for waking her up. 'No, nothing, thanks. I'm not sure why I am here.' I wobble unsteadily and sit on the nearest chair. I relay the events of last evening, mindful to include all of Megan's actions and her fawning over Glyn. I'm struggling to remember, everything seems fuzzy. 'And to top it off, his parents have arrived. Why didn't he tell me they were due today? I know he didn't. He'll probably say he did and that I've forgotten.' I rub my temples.

'My God, she is clever, I hadn't realised how smart she is. She seems to have manipulated you into breaking into her house. Tina, you don't look well, are you OK?'

'I feel a little weird, I've not eaten yet, I think my coffee was extremely strong. I've fallen straight into her hands, haven't I? You are the only one that sees her for what she is truly

176

like, everyone else thinks she is so bloody marvellous and I have become the ogre.'

'Including Glyn.'

'Most of all, Glyn. Can I have some cereal, please, I need to eat something.' Ali brings me a bowl of granola with lots of milk. 'Were you up when I knocked?'

'Oh, yes, only by five minutes. I was talking to James. Time difference, you know. I speak to him most mornings at around this time.'

I have been so centred on my own issues I haven't even asked her how he's getting on. 'Shit, Ali, sorry. I'm so rude, I haven't asked you how he's doing?'

'Oh, that's OK. He's good though. He's managed to secure the funding he went out there for. So, of course, he's delighted with himself. He's back in a few days and I can't deny it. I am desperate to see him again.'

I smile my understanding, remembering how I felt the same way about Glyn not so long ago. 'Glyn thinks I've lost it. He believes her version of things.'

'That is weird, who is she to cloud his judgement like this? What is he going to tell his parents?'

I shrug. 'I can't think about them right now. I'm going to work.' I get up and grab my bag and the room spins. 'I can't think clearly right now, Ali.'

'Remember I'm picking up the kids and bringing them home. Have you told Glyn?'

'Oh, Ali, sorry, the private detective called, he's postponed. I'm now meeting him tonight in a pub in Wigan. I forgot to text you what with all that crap going on last night. Sorry, it clean went out of my head. So, as I've blocked my time out at the office, I thought I'd pick the kids up today, I think they sense something going on between Glyn and I. I just want to be close to them.'

Ali says nothing.

'I accused him of sleeping with her? Mental, huh? I don't think he is, but I don't get what's going on with him. You don't think he would, do you?'

'It doesn't matter what I think, Tina, Glyn can be trusted.'

I narrow my eyes. 'What does that mean? Have you witnessed something? Have you seen them together?'

'I . . . look, Tina, you can read lots of wrong things into any situation.'

'Ali, you are my best friend, I trust you. Please tell me what you have seen, please. Christ, I only said that as a throwaway remark, I never believed it. I said it to hurt him and maybe shock him out of his hypnotic state, but . . .' I think back to how he was when I accused him. 'But maybe I was right . . . oh God, am I? Am I?'

'Look, Tina, what I think I saw could make things worse by telling you. I am confident Glyn is not sleeping with her. You are imagining the worst already.'

'Ali, you can tell me anything. I need to know. Now you've let it slip, you can't not disclose.' I slump back into the chair, I feel even worse now. Must be the shock of what I'm about to hear.

'Gossip was what started the troubles in my marriage and it never went away after that. And that is what it was. Malicious gossip. But it was believed and everything went downhill afterwards. I don't want that to happen to your marriage.'

I know all about her marriage, but her husband was nothing like Glyn. He had always been a bully and control freak. I don't want to drag that up, but to compare the two of them is unfair.

'Do you think he is sleeping with her?'

'God, no. I don't. That's not what I saw. It was nothing like that.'

'Then what was it like?'

'Tina, I wish I hadn't opened my big mouth. I saw them in town; he was helping pack her bags in the boot. She climbed inside the car and wound the window down and he . . . well, he bent down and she kissed him on the lips. It was just a peck, I think. I saw Glyn pull away.'

'A kiss?'

'Yes, and like I said, it can be misread by anyone wanting to cause malice. Who knows if she saw me at the pelican crossing and thought it a brilliant idea? She might have arranged the whole thing for precisely this situation.'

'So, he is having an affair.'

'I never said that, and this is why I didn't want to mention it to you. She might want to. But I don't believe Glyn would. Never. And you must believe that too otherwise she is having the desired effect, casting doubt and wrecking your marriage.'

'She's doing a brilliant job of that all right.' I shoot out of my chair to leave and the room spins.

'Tina,' Ali shouts chasing after me down the front path. 'What are you doing? I don't think you should drive, you look and sound terrible. Have you been drinking?'

'Have I been drinking? At this hour? Don't be ridiculous, all this stress is driving me to drink, but no I haven't been drinking.' I grab the fence to steady myself. 'I am doing what I should have done a long time ago. Finding out who the bitch is and why she is trying to destroy me.'

'I'm sorry, Tina, I really didn't want to tell you.'

I wipe my eyes with a tissue I find in my pocket and roll the window down. 'I'm sorry for forcing you to reveal it, but I am glad you have.'

Ali's voice is soft. 'Call me if you need me for anything.' She hangs on to the car door as I pull away. 'Tina, can you forgive me?'

I grab her hand through the open window. 'I'm not angry with you. I will phone you later.'

CHAPTER TWENTY-FIVE

I wake up to find myself slumped in my car, my head resting on the steering wheel. My mouth dry like a desert and my head groggy. Gradually I straighten up, disorientated. Where am I? I'm parked down a side street that I don't recognise. I take a long drink from the water bottle in the cup holder. Through the fog in my brain, I know I need to do something important. What was it? I get out and stumble, my legs struggling to bear my weight. I look round but still I'm incapable of locating my position. I don't recall how I got here. I was on my way to the office. I rummage in my handbag for my phone. Google maps will pinpoint where I am.

I have a list of missed calls and voicemails from Glyn and one text saying. *Where are you?????* I dial into my voicemail and listen to my messages, cringing from one to the next as Glyn's voice fills the car. My hands shake as I hit delete and wait for the next one, much the same as the previous one. Glyn is irate to say the least. In a way, I'm grateful I am not there in front of him. I can feel his anger pouring from the phone. There is one from Ali, imploring me to phone her and stressing to do it before calling Glyn. I listen to the fifth message from Glyn and this time I take in the time it was sent. 6.30 p.m. — I forgot to pick up the kids. How did I forget my kids? I dial Ali, quickly.

'It's me, God, Ali, I totally forgot my kids. Is everything alright? Are they OK? Did Glyn pick them up?'

'Tina, I can't believe you forgot them? How could you?' she yells at me.

'Please, Ali, don't, I feel so bad.'

'Christ, Tina, nothing should ever override your kids. You of all people with your paranoia should know that.'

I drop my head into my hands and rock back and forth crying with guilt. 'I know. I know. Glyn collected them, didn't he? Please tell me he did. I've had furious voicemails from him, but he doesn't say. All he says is, "How could you, Tina. How could you be so self-indulgent that you forgot the kids?"'

'And he's bloody right. Christ, you have really made a mess for yourself now. I am furious. Why didn't you call me?'

'I couldn't! I passed out, I've just woken up, I don't even know where I am.'

'What do you mean passed out? Have you been drinking? You looked like you had, I asked you. Are you lying to me? You've just handed it to her on a plate, how stupid are you?'

'What do you mean?'

'I don't know how, but she took them. I didn't even see her. I wasn't there. Katie came home sick and I knew you said you were picking yours up. She told nobody. You called the school, don't you remember? She's telling Glyn you called and told them she would collect them. By the time Glyn became concerned there was nobody at school. He called me and I couldn't help him. We've been frantic, Tina. Can you imagine what's been going through our minds?'

'You know I wouldn't do that. She's the last person I'd ask.'

'She took them. And she didn't tell anyone. Not even Glyn. He was out of his mind when he got home and his parents asked where they were. He's been trying to get in contact with you. Nobody could find Megan for hours either.'

'WHAT!' I yell so loudly my voice breaks.

I slam the car into reverse and screech out of the side street, oblivious of the traffic, fastening my seat belt as I tear down the main road.

I cut her off and dial Glyn. 'Tina! What the hell is going on? Where are you? Why didn't you bother telling me you'd asked Megan to collect the kids?'

He is extremely hostile with me. What I don't understand is why Megan failed to notify him? What was her plan? 'I didn't ask Megan to collect them. Are they OK?'

'Are they OK? Now you ask that! Hell, Tina, I've been in a right state. And Matt's been to hospital.'

I nearly crash into the car in front, hitting the brakes just in time to avoid a pile up.

'What do you mean! Why? What's happened? Oh, my God, what's she done to them? Glyn, what has she done to Matt? Is he OK?'

'Shut up, Tina, just shut up about her. Matt is fine, he fell down the stairs in her basement chasing the cat or something, he's bruised but not hurt. No thanks to you.'

'No thanks to me? Why did she not take them straight home? Why did she not contact you?'

'You asked Megan to collect them. You even contacted the school and informed them. And then you forgot to inform me and because I was unable to get hold of either of you, well you can imagine what I was thinking.'

'Didn't the school tell you she had them?'

'Of course they didn't, it was closed by the time I called them. And we couldn't find Megan, that was the problem.'

'So you thought she had done something to them? Now do you believe that she's dangerous?'

'Stop it, no, of course I didn't think she'd harmed them. I JUST DIDN'T KNOW WHERE THE HELL THEY WERE!' I cringe at his words, my ears hurt from his shouting. 'Can you imagine getting home and finding them gone with no way of contacting you? How was I to know Megan had them? I thought you'd had an accident with them. When I phoned round, I was told a woman who wasn't you had picked them up. She is the last person I thought you'd ask to collect them from school. Then I tried her mobile, thinking you might be with her for some crazy reason, but she didn't answer, I thought you'd done something to her.'

'Stop shouting at me. I don't understand. I never asked Megan to pick them up. She's lying. She's lying, again, Glyn. Why would she not bring them straight home? Don't you think that's odd? And why didn't you just go over the road and ask her where the kids were?'

'I told you. Aren't you listening? Tina, her phone died. There's no malice on her part just misunderstanding.'

'What a load of bull. For God's sake. Don't you see how she's manipulating everything?'

'Shut up, Tina, just thank your lucky stars that she did collect them. Otherwise, we might be having a different conversation seeing as you went AWOL.'

I have no defence.

There's a beat before either of us speaks.

'Are they at home now? Is Matt back from the hospital?' I say.

He sighs. 'Yes, and my parents don't know what the hell is going in this house.'

'Are the kids OK, Glyn? Tell me they are OK?'

'They are fine, Tina, they know nothing of the horrors we've gone through. Megan is helping Mum prepare dinner. They are all OK . . . this time.'

I can't speak. Megan is in my house preparing dinner with my mother-in-law? I cut the call because right now I want to scream. And I do until my throat burns. Thumping the steering wheel over and over until my fists hurt. He conveyed it so easily, like it was an everyday occurrence, Megan popping over to make dinner for my family.

CHAPTER TWENTY-SIX

I enter my house, and from the silence that descends and the look on everyone's face, I am persona non grata.

I smile apologetically and move straight over to my in-laws to welcome them but they glance at me and then quickly to Glyn. I'm surprised his mother doesn't say anything. She's never taken to me, not really, there's always been a bit of *you're not good enough for my son* type of attitude. I don't know why they think they are any better than me. They had a small win on the lottery ten years ago and moved to Australia and bought a place on the outskirts of Melbourne.

My mother-in-law turns to Megan, who I see is sat in my usual seat next to Glyn. Her hair pulled back in a ponytail and wearing a lot less make-up. She looks radically different. Less Barbie, more homely. More together. I don't feel envy but something like it, it's something stronger. Hate? Definitely. Megan has slid neatly into my place easily. I imagine she doesn't especially care what Glyn's parents think. That's all peripheral, she cares what I think and that's kind of sickening.

'Well, it's nice to see you, Tina. How are you feeling? Megan tells us you've been having some mental health issues,' my mother-in-law says. I bet she's loving all this drama.

Glyn's anger is reflected in his eyes, they burn a trail of utter fury in my direction. I look away and glance to the floor, full of shame and remorse, unable to provide an explanation for what has happened to me.

I wonder if the signs have always been there but I haven't bothered to look closely enough. We have, or at least I thought we had, a terrific relationship. Our sex life was always healthy and steamy, even after the children. We made each other laugh. We rarely argued. But maybe it isn't as I thought. Maybe it isn't strong enough to withstand trouble. Trouble in the shape of Megan or possible illness like mental health issues. It is a marriage of smoke and mirrors. A chocolate teapot sort of marriage.

My heart thumps as I prepare to speak and I sense disaster looming. 'I'm sorry about what happened. I have no excuse.' I look at Matt and Laura who both ignore me. Laura sits next to Megan and rests her head against her shoulder. It cuts me like a knife, but I don't flinch. Whatever I say, apart from an apology will sound feeble. 'I don't have a mental problem. Despite what you might have heard to the contrary.' I tag that on for the benefit of Glyn's parents, though I doubt my own sanity right now. I don't want to tackle this with the children around.

Their silence continues. Evidently, they are waiting for a revelation from me that will clear all this up. But what the hell can I say to clear my name? As a lawyer, I know whatever I say now will incriminate me. Therefore, I choose my words carefully. I have no evidence I was drugged, which I'm pretty sure I was.

'However crazy all this sounds,' I begin, 'I did not ask you, Megan, to pick up the children. That is certain. And please allow me to continue,' I say as she makes a move to interrupt me, 'I am wondering why you didn't tell Glyn that you had the children? Why didn't you bring them straight home from school? Why did you go off the radar like that? And why did Matt fall down the stairs in the basement?' I hiss this last sentence like a snake about to strike.

Nobody says anything to me.

I want to grab my kids to reassure them that Mummy has not abandoned them, but I'm fearful they will shrug me off. I couldn't bear that, not in front of them all. Christ, have I failed miserably at parenting?

Megan says, 'I can see you're distressed and confused, Tina, especially with all the difficulties you are having remembering things. Certainly, your behaviour lately has been a little erratic. But I can assure you that you did ask me to collect the children. I have the text on my phone.'

Glyn clears his throat. Is that the best he can do? Really?

Her words set my teeth on edge. I don't even have her fecking number on my phone, so that is a lie. I raise my hands in a gesture of surrender and shake my head. Tit for tat, I won't do it, even if I look guilty by not fighting. I won't do it. I won't provide her with the satisfaction. An inner instinct tells me not to press this point right now.

I glance over at Glyn. He has a right to feel annoyed with me, but shouldn't he be trying to be more supportive than he is? What about asking if I'm OK? That would be a start. Sitting there with the enemy is not helping my state of mind and now he has his parents as back up. I should stand on the table and shout that he ought to support me not hurl me to the dogs because something has gone off track in our marriage. I should seize him by the scruff of the neck and yell, 'This is serious, Glyn, this is really serious, you need to focus on what is happening. Why can't you see what is happening?' But I won't do that, either.

Matt removes himself from the table and wraps himself round my legs. I gather him up and grip him close but Laura doesn't look at me. We walk into the lounge together where I flop on the sofa and cry into Matt's snuggled body. What happened to me today? One thing is for certain. I was neither drunk nor did I take any pills. So what the hell happened to me?

'Mummy, I didn't fall down the steps.'

'What do you mean? Daddy told me you did.'

He shakes his head and stares at his hands all bunched up on his lap.

'What did happen, Matt?'

'She pushed me.'

'Who pushed you?'

'Megan.'

'What? Are you sure, Matt? You need to be sure. Maybe you slipped and she was near you and you thought she had pushed you when in fact she was trying to catch you. Do you think that's what maybe happened?'

He shakes his head.

'Did Laura see it?'

He shrugs his shoulders.

'What does that mean, Matt? Was Laura there when you fell?'

He shrugs again.

I stroke his head. 'I won't say anything to Laura and if you're frightened she will get into trouble for not telling, she won't. But I need you to tell me what really happened. Can you do that, Matt?'

He twines his fingers together. 'We went down to the basement, she said her cat was stuck and we had to help it. Laura went first. I was coming down the stairs after her. Then she pushed me. I banged my knees, Mummy. I hurt them. Look.'

He pulls up his trouser leg, I lend a hand. When I see the state of his knees and his legs, I want to roar out of the living room and kick that bitch across the street into her own fucking home. An invisible belt wraps itself round my waist, squeezing, firmly, until I want to retch. My wrath is contained only by the concerned look on my son's face. It pulls me with the force of a train but his angelic face puts a leash round me.

What would she gain from hurting the children? It's me she wants to hurt. I remember seeing some laxative tablets in the bin in the secretaries' office the day Sally went home ill. What lengths will this woman go to harm me? I bet she gave them to Sally. I open my phone and check my call list.

I check my text. *That* text to Megan stares right back at me. I search my contacts with nervous terror mingled with terrifying horror when I see her name together with her mobile and landline number. How? How is she in my phone contacts?

Did she know where I was today? Did she do this while I was out cold? Birthdays are not difficult and not original passwords either. Christ what an idiot I am. She must have my Apple ID from when she hacked my emails and used iPhone finder to track me.

A tiny voice in my head tells me Laura could also be in danger. And Glyn. And maybe Ali, too.

I look at my watch. I hate the thought of leaving them tonight. But I have no choice I must find out about Megan.

* * *

By the time I wander back to the kitchen the little get together has broken up. Megan has gone home, and Glyn's parents are doing the washing-up, with Laura helping. The atmosphere is still frosty. I must swallow my frustration for another day. Nothing will be accomplished tonight. I hear Glyn in the basement. I don't go down, for now, I want to maintain my distance.

'I'm sorry,' I say, holding out the olive branch to Glyn's parents.

I get a sort of limp squid kind of smile and a nod of heads from them both. Clearly, they are not letting me off that easily, so I don't say any more. I'm not in the mood.

I spend the next hour organising bedtime and working my way back into Laura's affections. I try not criticising Megan, the last thing I want is a fight. I've scared my children and everyone around. I've messed up. I snuggle up next to Laura in her bed admiring her nails, slowly she lets me back in and cuddles up to me. I hold her tight and say I'm sorry and the tears run down my face. My guilt swamps me. I tentatively have a go and see if Laura will reveal to me what happened at Megan's house.

'Sweetie, did you see Matt fall down the stairs today?' I stroke her hair and keep my voice soft, hoping not to project my anger but it keeps catching in my throat. An unrelenting invisible force squeezes my chest as I try to keep my voice even.

'He fell on his own, why is everyone asking me?'

Surprised, I say, 'Everyone? Who . . . else has questioned you, sweetie?' My voice breaks. Why would she say that? Does someone else suspect Megan of foul play? Sensing I might gain an ally, I press on. I manage to keep my voice steady but my whole body is twitching. I don't know what to do with it. My hands want to grab Laura and shake her until she tells me who it is that has been asking. 'Who, Laura, who asked you if you saw Matt fall?' I feel frozen in time, scared my movements might scare her to clam up.

She fidgets and turns her back a little towards me. I'm grateful because I can't keep my features suspended any longer. As soon as she turns her back they crumble like a pie crust.

'Laura, you can tell me, I won't be cross with you.' My mouth is dry and my tongue sticks to the roof of my mouth.

'I told you, he fell,' she shouts.

'OK, OK, did you see it?' I persist. Feeling as if I'm choking on the words I want to spit out. It takes all my concentration to assure myself I'm doing the right thing by being patient with her.

'Mum! I told Megan the same thing, I didn't see it. I turned round and he was on the floor. Crying. As usual,' she says, rudely, as if she's embarrassed her baby brother cries when he injures himself. As if she wouldn't. But I say nothing in response to this. A voice in the back of my mind tells me to keep calm.

'OK, sweetie, don't get upset. Mummy is just sad he was hurt, that's all. I would be the same if it had been you.' I almost laugh. It's evident it was Megan who pushed him. Just as I thought.

'You should have been there to pick us up.' She shuffles her body and curls up into a ball.

Her words are like a slap. I recoil physically from their impact. I am pathetic to allow this stupid bitch under my skin. I don't want to upset Laura further, but I can't help feel there is more she wants to say. I should wait until tomorrow. I can't. The need to know is too powerful. I play around in my head with a couple of versions of what I want to ask until comfortable with the gentlest approach, I say, 'If there is something bothering you about today and what happened to Matt, you need to tell me.' I bite my lip mentally cursing myself. Have I messed up? Have I pushed too hard?

'I didn't see much, I was looking for the cat. She said it was trapped but I couldn't hear it. I thought that was odd. I think I turned round just as Matt fell. I think she tried to catch him not push him, but now you're making me see different things. Megan likes us; she wouldn't hurt us. She says you hate her and that you're trying to stop her having friends. She's nice, Mum, really she is.'

I let out a long, quivering breath feeling as though my guts have been ripped out by a ghostly hand.

CHAPTER TWENTY-SEVEN

I plonk myself down in the sitting room in front of the TV and flick the channels to keep busy but am unable to focus. I look at my watch. Glyn is going to find it weird when I say I'm going out tonight. I can hear the three of them talking in the kitchen, their voices hushed, so I don't hear them. I keep out of their way especially after the frosty atmosphere I detected when getting myself a drink just moments ago. I don't want to discuss this any further. I'm home. The kids are safe. I can understand Glyn being pissed off, but his parents really need to back off. I'm not apologising again to them or even talking about it. She is playing with me. No. She is playing with everyone.

Glyn enters the room silently and sits down in the armchair opposite. I jump when I see him there, still in his office wear, open neck shirt and rolled up sleeves. He must be roasting; his shirt has become transparent under his arms. A slight breeze floats through the sash window. I hear his parents talking in the hallway making their way upstairs. I call out, 'Goodnight,' but they don't respond.

I turn pointedly in my seat to look at him. 'So, I take it you've sorted the spare room out for your parents?' I say, to initiate the conversation, my voice trembling. I can't help thinking how handsome and serious he looks as he drums his fingers on the arm of the chair. I can see a myriad of thoughts flashing across his mind and an unreadable countenance and beneath it all I know he is judging me.

'You scared the shit out of me today,' he says dramatically.

We've been through all this so why is he still being so damned nasty? He could say, 'Tina, I was so concerned for you today.'

I pluck at the strands of thread from the cushion feeling strangely self-conscious. I would never have felt like this in his company before all this started. Normally, after a spat, I go over and sit on his lap, kiss him and sink deep into his chest with a profound sense of pleasure. Presently, I feel I'm not welcome. It's weird that I am scared to approach him in case of rejection. I feel ugly and lonely and desperate.

'I know, sorry.' My face is full of anxiety with a trace of hostile justification. 'I don't know what happened to me today.'

'Well, maybe now is the time to tell me, don't you think?' says Glyn in a snappy tone, I don't much like. He might as well have slapped me; his words sting and the colour rises in my face.

'Sorry. The thing is, I don't know what happened to me today and that's the truth.'

'You have to tell me, whatever it is. I need to know.' He folds his arms across his chest. 'I'm waiting.'

'I passed out. In the car. Somewhere near Hale after I left Ali's house this morning. I have no idea how I got there or what happened to me. I think I was drugged.'

He scoffs and rolls his eyes. 'I couldn't reach you. We had no idea where the kids were.'

'Well, that was Megan's fault, wasn't it? She didn't reveal her whereabouts to you because she wanted to stir it up.'

His face remains impassive. 'Well, she already explained that, didn't she? When I spoke to Ali, she said you appeared drunk, out of sorts. Did you take something?'

I feel panic closing in around me. My shoulders drop. 'I just told you I think I was drugged. You won't believe me, but

I took nothing. I had a coffee at home and my energy drink and started to feel unwell at Ali's. I thought it would wear off. The next thing I knew I woke up feeling like shit in the car with most of my day missing.' I hate that I sound as if I'm making excuses. 'Why haven't you cross-examined Megan, I think her lame excuse of not bringing the kids straight home is bullshit. Oh, but you're happy to accept that, aren't you? But not that I was drugged. Why? Why is that?' I hate the way I sound.

He raises an eyebrow. 'I don't believe you because it's so unbelievable. Megan thinks you're taking diazepam. Admit the truth because you looked awful when you got home. Your eyes gave it away. Stop lying to me.'

I close my eyes for a second to try to fend off the panic growing inside me. 'I told you I'm not and you're being ridiculous now. Stop listening to everything she says. I hate that you don't believe me.' My reply is full of tetchiness. I'm rattled. The text I received about social services has scared me. Should I be worried whoever sent that might really call them? It wouldn't look good for me and there are so many bloody witnesses to my irrational behaviour of late.

'Are you?'

'No, you won't even try to believe me, will you?' I look away. I force myself to swallow my fear because what I see in his face hurts too much. I leave the sitting room and head for the kitchen to grab my car keys.

'Oh, are you leaving again?' he says following me. 'Seems that whenever things get too hot to handle you bugger off.'

I can't look him in the eye. I don't know who he is any more. He's changed. I hear him calling after me but I am rushing out of the house.

'Tina! Where the hell are you going? Stop! Come back. We need to talk about this.' He dashes to the car, his feet crunching the gravel. He's yelling for me to stop. I reverse out of the drive. 'Tina, if you go now then . . . then it's over between us. I can't cope with any more of this madness.' I look at him as I shoot past, I heard him. I zoom up the road and park up outside Ali's house.

Ali's mouth opens wide and snaps shut. I start to lay into her the moment she opens the door, feeling betrayed and hung out to dry. Her eyes narrow. 'Tina Valentine, don't come around here having a go at me. I was concerned for you. You did look drunk. I'm on your side and worried about you. I should have called him the minute you left, but I didn't. When the kids weren't home, of course I told him. I was bloody worried something had happened to you and the kids.'

'Oh, Ali, my marriage is on the line because Glyn thinks I've truly lost it and now I'm pill popping. My daughter thinks Megan is *nice* and, according to her, she only wants to make friends. I, the wicked witch am preventing this because I'm cruel. I'm not having a go, really, I'm not. I wish you hadn't told him, that's all. She's telling him I'm taking pills and showing signs that I am. I don't know what to do. She seems to have every angle covered.'

'Tina, you're all over the place.'

I drop onto the stool behind me as if I've been shot. Ali looks at me like you would a wounded animal, tears glisten and her hand trembles as she wipes them away. 'I'm worried about you.'

I hug her tight; it's all I can manage, I don't know what else to say. 'She is winning, and I don't know how to stop her. I am shrivelling up inside like a water starved plant and she is the one holding back the water. I can't allow this to happen. I must find out what is in Braitling. I'm a brilliant divorce lawyer because I never back down. To the contrary. I fight. I forge on with tenacity and doggedness. And yet I can't seem to fight this because every time I come up against a brick wall. The truth is I am consumed by it. I can't think about anything else. My work is affected. I've messed up with Glyn's parents, too. They never liked me much before and now they regard me as the devil personified.'

Ali hugs me tighter and pulls away. Her arms hold onto mine and she scrutinises me.

'I'm losing everything, Ali, my family, and probably my job when Howard hears about this latest stunt, I can't lose

194

you. Sorry for having a go, I'm so messed up, I'm lashing out but I don't mean it.' A deep hurt inside cuts through my heart and twists my belly into unforgiving knots. I haven't felt so alone and depressed since my mother died. I can't accuse Ali of betraying me. I just can't. I can't quite believe that I, Tina Valentine, am in such a bloody mess. I made one bad move a long time ago. One bad decision, which was forced upon me and here I am. On the verge of losing everything I have strived to build. Apart from this, I have never broken the law. I've paid my taxes on time. Believed in the justice system wholeheartedly. But now it seems that I am being framed for something which wasn't really my fault. Not really. Dammit. If only I could remember everything. But none of this changes the fact that I am in a big hole and need to get myself out of it before I'm buried.

I want this all to be over and go home. To go back to my life as it was. To start rebuilding the tatters of my life that has collapsed.

'You're not losing me, Tina, and you are not going to lose your family. So, who cares about Glyn's parents?' She shrugs, and I manage a pathetic smile. 'They live in Australia and they will never like you, no matter how fabulous you are. Glyn is their God-like son, nobody would ever be good enough for him. So, forget trying to change what you can't.'

I am so grateful for her friendship. 'Thanks.' I mean it more than it sounds right now.

'Don't apologise any more. Get to the bottom of this. You need to see that private detective. And you need to find out what this is all about. You don't have time to lose.'

* * *

I ring Glyn telling him that I know my sudden departure makes no sense but that I must meet someone who will help me explain all this mess.

'I know you'll think this is another of my crazy stunts, but please, you must believe me, Glyn. Please don't give up on us. Don't give up on me. I know right now our lives are a mess and you think I'm to blame for all that is happening. But I love you. I love our family. I know you didn't mean what you said. I'm not giving up on us.' The silence on the other end makes the hairs on the back of my neck stand up. I slip on to the M6 heading north. The address where I'm meeting the private investigator, Liam, programmed in the satnav.

'No, I didn't mean it, Tina. You know that. I'm trying to get you to realise what you're doing is not normal. I said it in a moment of anger with you.' I think back to the conversation I had with Matt the other night when he told me someone was in his room. That was the same night the French windows were unlocked. She left them unlocked on purpose. So I would know she'd been in. How many times has she been inside my house without my knowledge? Glyn's voice breaks into my thoughts. The weight of our conversation heavy between us. My hands tighten around the steering wheel. I know this is all getting out of hand. I know how crazy I appear. I take a deep breath ready for what he will say next. 'Tina.' I hear him sigh. 'Please don't tell me this is you going rogue and doing some detective work on Megan.'

I'm about to say no, but I want to solve this and I want him to know I'm doing all I can to get us back on track. Lying to him will only make it worse for me. Especially if Megan has read my emails. I must be upfront with him. 'Glyn, just listen to me, she's trying to blame me for all that has happened and it wasn't me. I need to prove that. I also need to find out why she is attacking me.'

'Fuck, Tina. Have you hired a private detective?'

So much for keeping it under wraps. The only way Glyn would even think of me hiring a private detective would be because she's read my emails and told him.

'She told you, didn't she? Christ. I can't believe she's hacked my emails, again.'

'I thought you wanted to resolve this. Now you're accusing her of hacking your emails, again, but you changed the password. I saw you. She's not a computer hack, Tina. Listen to how you sound.'

I resist the urge to cut off the call.

'What the fuck, Tina?' Glyn rarely swears, oh, occasionally he'll use the f-word if he's broken something or hurt himself, but the anger with which he uses it now is filled with so much rage it makes my heart stumble. 'Have you completely lost your fucking mind? Oh-my-God, you have completely lost the plot.'

'It's not like it sounds. It's only to find out background information. I need to find out about Megan, who she is and where she comes from.' Even to me that sounds pathetic. I resist the urge to explain my actions, but the tears spring to my eyes. I swallow and blink them away. I want to cry not because we are arguing, but because I'm scared.

* * *

I wait for Liam in the pub where we've arranged to meet. In the end I didn't want to go to Braitling, I couldn't face it and Liam told me there was no need. He had all he needed and was travelling back up North. He lives in Wigan. We chose to meet in the Swan with Two Necks.

As I wait, I write down every bit of suspicious behaviour towards me:

- *Rachel and Megan's friendship.*
- *Megan renting the house across the road.*
- *The laxatives and Sally going off sick with sickness and diarrhoea.*
- *The electronic files and paperwork vanishing then reappearing.*
- *Megan wearing clothes like mine.*
- *Megan taking the kids and not telling anyone.*
- *Flirting with Glyn.*
- *Having a relationship with Howard.*
- *Somehow drugging me, probably in my protein drink.*
- *Entering my house without our knowledge.*

- *Hacked emails.*
- *Why? Why? Why?*

A short man with a ginger beard, jeans and hoody appears at my table. 'Are you Tina Valentine?' he asks in a heavy southern Irish accent.

'Yes.' I suggest he sits down in front of me with a gesture of my hand. He's not what I expected. I think the Irish accent had me imagining somebody like Liam Neeson or Colin Farrell. He's a long way from either of them.

'I thought it was you. You look nervous like you're expecting the police to come storming in here.'

'Do I? Well, I've never hired a private detective before.' I think of the mental debate I had with myself about whether I should or shouldn't call him a private dick. I shudder. Definitely not.

'It's not illegal to hire a private detective, Mrs Valentine. Don't look so worried about being seen with me. Although what I've found might worry you a lot more than our meeting.' He pulls out an A3 brown manila envelope and places it on the table in-between us. I want to laugh at the incongruous action and can see why Glyn thought this all one step too close to the men in white coats knocking on our door. 'I've found out a lot on the subject. There's plenty in there that is not applicable to your situation. I've highlighted the points which I feel are what you need to read first. If you need me for anything else. You have my number.'

I hand over my own envelope, filled with three thousand pounds. Money well spent, I hope.

I sit in my car and pull out the papers. A knock on the window makes me jump. It's Liam. I wind down my window a long way down. He really is short. 'Is there something wrong?' I ask worried he might want more money.

'I don't want to make you fret, lass, but I feel I should make sure that you read carefully what's in there. I suspect this woman could be very dangerous. I just wanted to warn you.' He points two fingers at me and blows his lips as if firing a gun. 'You know where to find me, Mrs Valentine.'

What the fuck was that all about? Was he serious? I pull out everything and read.

The woman in the photograph that I saw in her house I recognised. I know this woman but I don't know how. There's a photograph of Megan, her mum and dad with that woman taken in a smart lounge with flowery sofas and wallpaper. I imagine this was the older woman's house. There's a familiarity about it. Why does that photo give me the chills? Most of what's in here, she told us herself. There's also a photograph of Rachel with Megan's mother at a picnic on the beach taken a long time ago. The last paper makes me cringe the most. Megan was institutionalised for a period of time after her father died. Paranoia, it says in black and white. She was convinced her grandmother was murdered by someone she knew. There is nothing in the police report to suggest any such thing. I look at the grandmother's information once again. This time I read it more carefully and suddenly waves of nausea engulf me. Just who is Megan Pearson?

CHAPTER TWENTY-EIGHT

When I get back home, the house is in darkness. Everyone's asleep. My first thoughts are to crash in the spare room, but Glyn's parents are in there. Besides, I want to tell Glyn, only I'm not sure how to begin.

'Glyn?' I slip quietly into our bed. 'You didn't mean what you said earlier, did you?'

He mumbles something. I can't make out what he says. He seems exhausted. 'No, I didn't mean it.'

I snuggle up to him hoping he won't pull away. I need to talk to him. 'Glyn, I need to talk to you, please.' I hold my breath. If he pulls away from me, I don't know what I'll do.

We're spooning. 'What, Tina?' He doesn't make an effort to turn round but that's OK, at least he hasn't shrugged me off. 'Did you find what you were looking for?' His voice is quiet and weary sounding.

'Are you OK?'

He turns round quickly but stays close. We look at each other in the semi-darkness, the light from his iPhone on charge casting a glow over us. 'Fucking hell, Tina how can you ask that? Sometimes I wonder if you remember anything we talk about.'

'Sorry, I didn't mean . . . look, I think you should read what I've found out about Megan. She's been institutionalised, I told you she's crazy.' I see his eyes roll and he's about to pull away but I grab him. 'Glyn, please don't. I don't understand why you don't believe me, but right now I'm not bothered, I just want you to read what I've discovered. Please.'

He exhales a long breath. 'Sometimes, Tina, I just want to shake you so hard to see if you will wake up from this dammed miasma of lunacy you're going through. How can you be sure this guy isn't making stuff up? He could say anything to you.'

'He hasn't made it up.' Why would someone make this stuff up? I just can't win here.

'How do you know that? You found him on the internet. You gave him a name and a town and what? Have you checked him out? Have you? He's probably a con man. Taken your money, and I don't want to know how much that's cost, and made up some story for you. I bet he said she's dangerous.'

I keep calm. I realise that Megan had fed him all this in readiness for my meeting. 'Then, I guess there's no reason for you to read what I have. I can't defend myself, can I? She's got in there first. Look, our problems started when she turned up. Haven't you realised that?' I go rigid waiting for his response.

'No, Tina, our problems started when you banged your head. They just happened to coincide with Megan's arrival. I can't believe you can't see that. If you cared about me and the kids, you'd see that and go back to the doctor for a scan.'

That was below the belt. 'Of course, I care about my family. That's what I'm fighting for. I love you.' I pull him close and snuggle into his chest. I want him to hold me tight and make me feel safe, for him to give me something that shows me he still cares even though he thinks I'm crazy. 'I don't want to lose you. But I'm on my own here. You're not helping me. Why don't you believe me?'

'Tina, all I see is you running round like a headless chicken accusing Megan of everything that's going wrong for you, and to top it all you accuse me of sleeping with her.' He wraps his arms around me and I melt into his embrace. Whatever we're fighting, I know deep down he's there for me.

'I don't believe you slept with her. I only said it because she's driving me fucking crazy flirting with you and you seem oblivious to the fact. Oblivious to how it makes me feel. I don't want to argue any more.'

'I don't want to argue any more either. It's affecting the kids. I'm sorry if you feel I don't believe you. I'm sorry if you feel I've hurt your feelings, that was never my intention. I just don't want to encourage you on this foolish quest of yours. I miss you, Tina. I miss us and I miss what we had and I won't lie. I've said it before but I'm fucking terrified what's happening to you. Please ring the doctor tomorrow. Please.'

'OK, I'll call in the morning.' I genuinely mean it when I say I will call. If it will help put his mind at rest, I will make an appointment tomorrow.

'OK, let's do this together. I'll go with you. Will you let this all drop?'

In a whisper of a voice I say, 'OK, I will.' I hate the lie. I close my eyes and say a little prayer because I'm not dropping it.

* * *

The following day is not how I expect it to be. Right from the moment I wake up I suspect something is horribly awry. I receive a text from Howard advising me to get my arse into the office NOW! Then another one asking me *Is this the right number for social services?*

Shaking with biliousness, I throw myself from the bed and grab a thirty-second shower. Crazy, I barely need to dry myself I'm in and out so fast. I don't think the water had a chance to wet my skin. I throw on my most formal black business suit with a crisp white shirt and jacket. I twist my

hair into a chignon, apply a little make-up and natural lipstick. No matter how much blusher I put on, I still look pale.
No, I look grey, my skin looks grey and the natural lipstick
disappears amongst the greyness of my skin. Petrified and
fossilised. Looking at my reflection, I work on de-stressing
my hardened facial muscles with my fingertips, but it's no
use, the visage reflected back is ossified. My facial muscles
have become inflexible, and my jaw hurts from all the teeth
clenching. Those two texts have terrified me. I haven't told
Glyn about the last social services text. I can't bear to imagine
what he would make of it.

I have a bad, bad, feeling about this meeting. I don't
know what to do about the other text. I leave the house early
leaving a note for Glyn explaining where I've had to go.

It's seven o'clock when I walk into the office. It's quiet.
A light emanating from Howard's office is the only illumi-
nation in the corridor. With trepidation I make my way
towards it. My feet feel heavy and leaden, a rush of heat
swoops up my back, across my shoulders and up the back of
my neck and I begin to sweat.

That sixth sense I have is working overtime. If this was
a horror film, I would be petrified and expect a hideous creature to be waiting for me in the illuminated room. I enter.
Christ, I was right, there is a hideous creature in here waiting
for me. Megan.

I smile but my frozen features don't move and all I manage is a grimace. Suddenly a whoosh of blood rushes through
my ears and I can't hear clearly, my beating heart thrashes
out a rhythm all its own like one of those crazy jazz bands
where all the musicians appear to be playing to their own
tune. Time grinds to a halt. My brain tries to make sense of
the tableau in front of me. Then it picks up time once more
and I feel I'm on a roller coaster.

Howard gesticulates for me to sit down. His mouth is
moving, but I don't hear his words. I sit. Actually, I perch
with hands on my lap.

'Tina . . .'

Now I can hear, I see that on his desk is the Miller file. It's open and all the papers are scattered across his desk, but he holds one single sheet and waves it at me. His face is scarlet and his eyes bulge as he yells. 'Do you recognise what this is, Tina?' Megan sits motionless by his side, I don't hazard a glance.

I shake my head; how can I know, I don't possess bionic vision.

'It's a debenture. Remember what they are?'

Of course, I remember what they are, I'm not stupid. It's a security issued against a company's assets. 'I do, but I don't see what that has to do with the Miller case or me.' I nod in the direction of the file.

'Don't you? Really? Permit me to clarify. This debenture was for Mrs Miller as a director of her husband's company to issue against the company and was supposed to be registered at Companies House. But you missed the deadline. And guess what? He has filed his own.'

The world spins. As a director of the company she could have achieved protection against the insolvency of the company; she was probably aware he would try to sell it off. In which case he wouldn't be able to do so without first paying her the amount she placed on the debenture. I don't want to know how much money she has potentially lost. I can't bear thinking of it. But hang on. I never had this paperwork. I never saw it. This is the first time I have heard about it.

'Howard, this is the first I know of this. Mrs Miller hasn't told me of any money she lent to the company.'

'She emailed you the information. Prior to her wanting a divorce, Mr and Mrs Miller put in a huge amount of money into the business because they knew they were about to secure the Coca-Cola contract and would need to reinvest. They disposed of properties and lent money to the company. It was Mr Miller who informed his wife of the plan to secure the money. But then she found out about his affairs and the marriage fell apart, she was smart and wanted to protect her investments.'

Christ, that would make sense, the debenture must be registered at the same time as you lend money to your company. This means that the directors loan account, when secured by a debenture, must be repaid in full out of the company assets in the event of insolvency before VAT, PAYE and trade creditors receive one penny. And it must be registered within a set time scale.

'She was a director of the company. He wouldn't be able to sell the company without paying off the debt to her or obtaining her permission. And here is the email spelling it all out. You've fucked up, Tina. You have screwed up monumentally.'

'How . . . ?'

'How did I find it? Well, isn't it commendable we have Megan? Mrs Miller phoned me. Screaming at me. She went on to Companies House and saw Mr Miller had got there first and she wasn't registered at all. It was you, Tina, after talking with her who suggested she get in there quick. Here is your email to her and here is her reply authorising you to register. But you didn't. You were too hard-pressed trying to find out who Megan is and her bloody background. I think you're having a breakdown, Tina.'

I pause a moment to steady my breathing then stand up to protest but what good will it do? There is the evidence. But I never saw any of it. And Mrs Miller didn't once mention it to me. I didn't have that conversation. 'Why did she not ask me when we had our meetings? I don't understand how this can be the first time I have heard of this. I don't overlook critical pieces of information, Howard. You know that.'

'Go home. Don't come back, Tina.'

'But I need to ascertain the underlying cause of this . . . you know my emails were hacked. We had that conversation. I don't make mistakes like this, Howard. I won't be blamed for this. I want to find out how this happened. I need to find out.'

He cuts me up, 'No you don't, you've already done enough damage. Get out,' he yells, throwing the piece of paper onto his desk and sighing heavily. 'Go and don't come back.'

I suppose my partnership is not going to happen. Of, course it's not. I've fucked up. I've ruined my career. As I vacate the office, embarrassed and confused, I stare at Megan. If looks could kill she would be pinned to the wall with a hatchet through her head.

CHAPTER TWENTY-NINE

I get home in a daze and pull onto the gravel drive. Glyn is still home. I check my watch, is it only that time? I storm upstairs without saying anything to anyone. So much has happened since I left, how can it only just be that time? I don't know how I got home. I can't remember the journey or leaving the office or even driving the car. I've blown it. My partnership. My dreams and hopes, everything. What will I do? I have no job. And I probably won't have a career after this. Who wants a divorce lawyer who just made a basic balls up? I was doing so well. I had big clients. Celebrity clients. Rich clients. Exceedingly rich clients. And now I must tell Glyn. Oh, Glyn. I groan. I think I'm in shock because I can't feel anything. I should be trembling, crying, screaming. There's nothing. I am as still as a corpse.

Just then my phone pings with an email and I leap to the side with shock. Perhaps it's Howard with a change of heart. Joke. He's been too harsh? It wasn't all my fault? Mrs Miller should have kept on top of it herself, after all it is her security, why rely wholly on your lawyer? I sigh, as if. People do, they leave it all for us to sort out. 'Well we are bloody human too, we do make mistakes,' I shout, finally. I don't make mistakes,

which is the galling thing about this bloody mess. And it is.
A BLOODY MESS.

* * *

When I slipped into the house and up to our room, I tex-
ted Glyn that I needed to speak with him after the kids
got picked up by Ali. That it was really, really, important.
Because I looked like a zombie passing through the house,
he believed me.

I crawl into bed and open the emails on my phone because
I am unable to switch off. My brain works at speed. There are
hundreds of thoughts firing at me about possible ways out of
this situation. All stupid ones, of course. The only problem
is that my body is exhausted. Lethargic and the only thing it
wants to do right now is sleep. Oh, God, there's an email from
Alexander Bamfield. I notice quite a few have come through
over the last few days that I haven't opened. I scowl. Why is
he bothering me so much? Leave me alone! I don't want to
deal with Alexander. I have more pressing issues to deal with.

Ten minutes later, Glyn finds me in bed with the duvet
wrapped round me, smothering me like a cocoon. I can't do
this, I can't tell him I've been sacked! On top of everything
else going on he will leave me. I know he will! I have unrav-
elled like a yarn of wool tossed down the stairs. How has this
happened to me? Glyn's hand pulls the duvet down, and I
roll into a ball too ashamed to confront him.

'Tina, Howard phoned me in a state of apoplexy. He
said you forgot to register a debenture?' His tone is disbelief;
he's waiting for me to clarify and tell him Howard has it all
wrong and that I don't make those mistakes. But I have. So
I have nothing to say.

I take a sharp intake of breath and hold on to it until my
chest burns and I can't any more. 'Apparently.' A whoosh of
air escapes me and now I feel dizzy.

'Tina, he says you're sacked. He has yelled non-stop that
Mrs Miller wants to sue, and this will damage the firm and

you are to blame. Is he right? I can't believe it; I'm hoping this is one of his crass, mental jokes.'

Howard has in the past been the meanest of men by engaging in what he calls 'jokes' on all of us. In his mind he wants to test everyone's strength of character by making up some crazy situation about a client to note how we would contain the problem. He's so good at it, we fall for it every time. Sadly, this is not one of those times.

My face is pressed into the pillow and with a muffled voice I say, 'I don't think this is a joke.' I turn to look at him. I can read in his expression how low I have fallen in his estimation. It seems so long ago that I was this dynamic lawyer climbing the ladder of success. Like a game of snakes and ladders I have slid to the bottom on the throw of the dice.

Glyn drags the chair from the corner of the room where I usually dump my clothes. He sits with his elbows on his knees and his head in his hands as if to make sense of it all. I am ashamed and scared. I turn my face free from the pillow and watch him. Looking for some sign of support. I have a huge urge to touch him; I need to feel he cares, I reach out and try to pull his arm free, but he won't let me. The ground we made up last night has gone, disappeared into a huge sinkhole.

I miss my husband. I love him and this time I really fear he has lost his love for me. My hand drops over the side of the bed and I feel so very alone.

'Megan was in the office this morning; did you know that?'

Glyn shakes his head. 'No. Why are you still talking about her when there are bigger issues at hand?' He lowers his hands from his face and looks at me. 'Tina, you know your career is over if this gets out and it will.'

'I bet it will. She will make sure it gets out.'

He stands up abruptly. 'Tina,' he yells, 'will you fucking give it up! There is no conspiracy against you. You said you'd let this drop. You have done all this. You're unwell, Tina, you are delusional. I'm going to call the doctor.'

I freeze. He believes I'm delusional? He believes *her* and Howard and that stupid precocious Mrs Miller, well I won't blame Mrs Miller, to be fair she did send the emails. I fling my legs over the edge of the bed, renewed energy coursing through my veins. I can't let it go. I can't!

'Delusional? Did you say delusional? Where is your support? Where is your blind faith in me as your wife and work colleague and mother of your children?' I push him out of the way. 'I know I said I'd go to the doctor. But I know there is nothing wrong with me.'

'Tina, it's because I do care that I am having to persist. This has gone on too long, and you can't see it because you are in the middle of it all. I should have stepped in long ago. I blame myself, I allowed it to go on for too long and now look where we are? You do need to go back to the doctor and ask for a brain scan or something.'

I snort and walk past him, the very idea. The very thought of it! The very bloody notion that there can be no other explanation to all this but my mental capacity! Not one single doubt that Megan could be behind all of this.

'A brain scan? Are you mad? You all need bloody brain scans. I am the only one that sees what is going on here. She's taken you all in. Every one of you. And you think I'm mad? Terrific. Bloody terrific.' I pull off my suit and throw it on to the floor in a heap. I dress in jeans, T-shirt and hoody and as I walk past Glyn, I stamp all over my clothes in pure frustration. 'That's what I think of you lot.' I have a headache, but I don't have time to worry about that. I need to galvanise myself into action and get to Braitling. I've decided whether I want to or not I have to go. I storm out of the bedroom.

In the kitchen I pull open my handbag and tip out the contents on the counter. I won't need any of this crap. I repack it with my purse, my umbrella, my headache tablets and a bag of sweeties I grab from the top shelf in the kitchen cupboard. I switch on the coffee machine and pull out my flask cup; as I finish making my coffee and securing the lid,

Glyn walks in. I pull the charger from the socket, ram it in my bag and face my husband.

'I am going to pack an overnight bag. Then I am going to Braitling and I will come home with proof of what I have found seeing as you think the detective made it all up. I may be away for a few days, please don't worry, I'm sure you won't, you have Megan to keep you company. So, I will leave the children in your capable hands.' My tone says not to interfere with me; I am on a mission and nothing you say is going to stop me.

The doorbell rings and I run back upstairs, I stop half-way up.

'OK, OK, I'm coming,' he shouts in an irritated voice. I stand at the top of the stairs.

I don't recognise the voices and this worries me. I dart to Laura's bedroom at the front of the house and peer out of the window. The police. Shit. What has Howard done? He wouldn't have me arrested? Would he? I must get to Braitling. I can't be arrested! I can't!

Glyn tells them I'm not home and that he doesn't know where I am. Gone for a walk he says. Well at least he hasn't escorted them upstairs and handed me over. That's a little bit promising.

They're gone.

I run and grab my overnight bag, fling a few essentials in and rush downstairs. I don't have time to waste. They'll be back. I need to go.

'What did they want?'

'You.'

I'm not surprised, but I still am all the same. 'What for? Is it Howard? Has he phoned them?'

Glyn looks at me bewildered. 'No, it's not Howard, Tina. Megan has reported you for breaking into her house.'

Bitch! I shrink backwards. 'She has no proof. She can do nothing. I told you she was out to get me. Why would she do that? She can't prove I broke in.'

'She has, though. She videoed you on her phone. It's date stamped, it's proof. She says you stole from her. You stole her keys to break in and you stole from her house.'

'I stole from her! What did I steal? Surely, you can't believe this, Glyn.'

He snorts. 'Don't make me answer that, Tina.'

'Why on earth would I steal from her?'

'She is claiming you have a vendetta against her and has reported your behaviour at work. She's going for you, Tina. You have brought this on yourself. I told you.' He raises his voice. 'I told you this might happen. Not only have you botched your own career, but she is now going to bury you. With a criminal record you will never find a position in any law firm even if you were lucky enough to worm your way in somewhere.'

'But I didn't steal from her. Glyn, you know I wouldn't do that. I would have told you if I had discovered anything there to take because it would have been evidence against her.'

'Just like you wouldn't forget registering the debenture?'

I pull a face at his remark. I don't know what to say. I'm dumbfounded. How can this be happening? I feel as if I am falling into Alice's rabbit hole.

CHAPTER THIRTY

The journey to Braitling is tedious, and I drive on autopilot following the directions of the male Australian voice of my satnav. Sometimes I like to diversify my route by taking short cuts, which cause us to argue like a married couple, he insistent I do a U-turn and me ignoring him. It irritates the hell out of me but at the same time I weirdly enjoy it. Not today, though. Today, I do as I am told because today my mind is whirring with probabilities. Why would a woman come into my life, unexpectedly, and try to sabotage my family and my career? Why? Why? Why? What connection to Braitling does she and I have? I know there's a connection there but my memory won't reach it.

* * *

I arrive in Braitling some three hours later. The welcome sign notifies me to slow down and that it is twinned with some town in France, which I can't pronounce. It all looks so familiar suddenly. I nip down a side road and park up out of the way. I habitually used to park here. The only problem with Braitling is the parking, it always has been. It's a little cooler today but still warm with cloudy skies; I leave my jacket in my car and stroll to the centre of the village two hundred or so metres away. There's a small river running through the middle of the village with a tidy, neatly clipped green verge on either side and benches to sit and pass the time away. I sit down and watch a family of ducks gracefully glide past. It's such a charming village with sandstone houses and picture postcard shops — the sort of village that has tourists flocking in to take in a piece of quaint Englishness.

I push my hands into the pockets of my lightweight hoody and gaze down the road. Memories flood back all at once and instantly I recall another time.

The time when I met Deborah Duarte and how she reconstructed my life.

I walk to a small, picturesque B&B and book myself in. I shudder at the thought of not being at home with my kids and Glyn; I abhor the fact that I've abandoned them at the mercy of Megan.

It was the pills that implicated me, I know that now. If she hadn't planted them, then I might never have seen the truth. I nearly missed it, I was too quick to toss them in the bin and get rid of them. It wasn't until they lay there staring back at me, the last remnants of a pharmacy label torn off and Meg . . . the partial name glared back at me. And there it was, with startling clarity I knew I hadn't been going off my head these last few weeks.

Driving down here I ran through everything that has happened since she arrived. It's amazing how quickly someone can manipulate people's minds into thinking differently about a person. Before I had the lightbulb moment, I genuinely thought I may have started to suffer from dementia or Alzheimer's or that my anxiety had retrogressed. I realise she had fed them to me in my protein drink. Thanks to Glyn informing her that I was taking them to boost my energy.

I also remember the day the cursor on my computer moved on its own. I did a little digging and found that someone with a little techy knowledge and IP address could easily infiltrate my PC. After that it was only a matter of pulling all my suspicions together, including finding the packet of laxatives in the small, silver bin tucked away in the store cupboard that I found not long after Sally was ill. I suspect she thought nobody would ever look in there. Why would they? It's never used. Except I used it when I went in the store cupboard and dropped a box of staples which burst open covering the carpet, unable to put them back in the box, I simply binned them. And there was the box. As big and bright as a neon sign. Not that I could prove anything with it. But it was a start and from then on, I slowly started to allow myself to remember what happened ten years ago. The information from the detective started the process when I saw the photograph of the woman in the photograph.

In my B&B I flop on the bed and try not to remember what happened to Deborah Duarte. I don't want to think about it just yet. But the images begin to get clearer and clearer inside my head. They've been falling into place since I read Liam's dossier on her. I've opened Pandora's box, and Braitling seems to be the key. To stop my memory running riot, I pick up my phone and dial home. *Please don't let Megan be there.* The home phone rings and rings and rings. Nobody answers. Why not? Where are they? I try Ali, again, her phone rings and rings and rings. An image of my family and friends altogether with Megan presiding over them floods my brain. Where the hell are they? I'm losing it. Of course they are at school and work. I press two fingers from both hands against my temple to ease the beginning of a headache. Dammit.

To keep on track I list what I know to be evidence or suspicion. I pull out my old list that I made while I waited for Liam and add to it.

- *The diazepam with her partial name on the label. This is evidence which I've kept.*
- *My computer cursor moving by itself.*
- *Passing out and waking at the wheel of my car and a text sent from my phone while unconscious.*

215

None of the above can be used as evidence, maybe the diazepam, but it's weak and I'm sure she'll have a satisfactory explanation. I can't afford to trip up. I must get more proof. Concrete proof. Proof that cannot be refuted in court.

The memories of Deborah push to be released.

I suddenly develop a craving for alcohol. This used to be my default to forgetting before I discovered therapy. No mini bars in a B&B. I'll have to go out for a bottle, which might not be a bad thing.

Half an hour later, I sit on my bed once again and open a cold bottle of white wine pouring it into a plastic cup. So classy. Oh, God. I don't care.

I ring home, again, it's 4.00 p.m., someone ought to be home by now. Laura answers the house phone and takes me by surprise. 'Mummy! Where are you? We're having a barbecue.' Her voice brings a smile to my face.

Who is, we? 'Hello, darling that sounds like fun. Who is we, Laura?'

'What?'

'Who is having the barbecue?'

'We are, silly.'

'I know that, but with who? Is Ali there with you?'

'No. Megan is here. She's helping Grandma. Do you know where the long tongs are? Daddy can't find them,' she asks, her sweet voice clutching at my heart.

'No. No, I don't.' I do know, but I'm not telling them. 'Why do you need them? We cook our food inside. The long-handled tongs are for the charcoal barbecue outside.'

'But Megan is doing a *real* barbecue and she needs them and *I'm* helping.'

I want to scream. *Why is Megan doing a barbecue at my house?* What is Glyn thinking of? And why are they home at this time? 'That's nice. Laura, can you put Daddy on the phone?' I'm holding the phone so tightly against my ear I nearly push it into my head.

'Oh, he's gone out with Grandad. There's only us girls in the house.' She giggles.

216

Us girls? 'Laura, who told you to say that expression, *us girls?*'

Laura giggles again. 'That's what Megan calls us.'

What a stupid fucking expression. 'Is Matt with Daddy?'

'Yes, there's only us girls here, Mummy. Do you want to talk to Megan? Or Grandma?'

'Err, no, no. Laura, tell Daddy to call me when he gets home.'

'OK. Love you, bye.'

The phone goes dead.

CHAPTER THIRTY-ONE

It is 4.30 p.m. Alexander Bamfield Solicitors are across the road from the B&B. I finish my wine and venture back outside. I don't know what to expect and I dare not think too hard about what this might all mean. I walk to a coffee shop, order a latte and sit by the window. I like to watch the world go by from coffee shop windows. They have a cosy feel to them. That half bottle of wine has gone to my head; I need to clear it before I go in. Wouldn't do to go in slurring my words. I take out my phone from my bag and check for messages. Nothing.

I look at the solicitor's office and remember the last time I was in this place. It's difficult to understand how the events of that day happened, how the universe conspired to help me back then. Yet now it is trying to destroy me. I often wondered if I hadn't opened the letter that came to our house that day how my life would be right now. It was a rare day that I reached the post before Mum. She always binned the post, convinced it was a form of spying.

I'm feeling terrible now I'm remembering. I don't want to feel terrible. I don't have time to feel terrible or the strength to deal with the feelings that are beginning to churn inside me all over again. I straighten the coaster under my coffee cup, stand up and adjust the chairs nearby so they are all equidistant to the tables. I wipe round the coffee cup and remove the smudged lipstick. My hand shakes so I ball it into a fist. I breathe in through my nose and out through my mouth. In through my nose and out through my mouth. I do this until my heart rate slows and the terrible feelings begin to subside. In through my nose and out through my mouth. Does the universe work on a tit for tat basis, I wonder?

* * *

At 10.00 a.m. ten years ago, I entered Bamfield Solicitors; the receptionist ushered me into a stuffy office. I walked in and found Deborah Duarte sitting across the desk from a very old, serious-looking man with a goatee beard and bushy eyebrows. He welcomed me in. I took the seat next to Deborah and was told all would be explained.

When he started talking, I saw that he was one hundred per cent on the ball, his appearance not reflecting the sharpness of his mind. He never smiled, not even at Deborah, he nodded. He nodded a lot when Deborah instructed him with her wishes to make changes to her Will. I simply sat there listening and looking round the room and wondering why I was there. At this moment in time, I had no idea who she was and how I was connected to her. The office was ancient. Unchanged for years, it was probably furnished like this when Mr Banfield first set up his practice some forty years before. The carpet was threadbare in places. Not that you would notice, only if you stared long and hard. I doubt many would waste their time looking at the floor.

I remember Deborah saying her son lived in Cheltenham. I sat back in my chair and waited to be spoken to. Mr Bamfield flipped some papers back and forth making notes.

The thing is, before reading the letter from the solicitors asking me to come to their office to discuss my deceased father's estate, I'd never heard of Deborah Duarte. What estate? My father had nothing. He abandoned us and left us nothing and died with nothing. As far as I was aware, anyway. I had enough on my plate looking after my mother. What horrors was my father going to drop on me from his grave?

After the meeting with Deborah Duarte, my anxiety went off the scale. Whoosh, just like that. 'Unbelievable,' my therapist said.

'Always has to be a first time for everything,' I said. That's when I began taking diazepam, against my doctor's advice. 'Drink green tea,' he said. 'Meditate,' he said. 'Do more exercise,' he said. I wasn't in a mental state to do any of those things so I begged for the pills threatening to do something silly unless I had them. Normally, I don't think doctors fall for that. But this one was getting sick of me and as I had already been in the surgery for an hour, he wrote out the prescription.

Mr Bamfield handed me a file.

I opened it and read about Deborah's son. I wasn't sure what it all meant. The man was in crippling debt. What did that have to do with me? I broke out in a cold sweat thinking they were trying somehow to place the debt on my deceased father and coming after me now he was gone. I managed to keep a level head and said very little. Grateful that my brain was quick and knew this couldn't actually happen. So why was I there?

It turned out Deborah Duarte was my father's second wife. She was nominating me sole beneficiary of her estate, which Mr Bamfield explained was over a million pounds. She had disowned her son whom she hadn't seen for years after she stopped lending him money for the last time. We did the necessary paperwork. I signed. She signed.

I took one of the pills that morning. Maybe it was the pills fault, because later when I left the office it was lunchtime, so I went to a pub to celebrate and had a glass of wine. Then another. And maybe another after that, I don't remember that's the problem. I have a gap in my memory. Missing time.

For days after the missing parts irritated me. I knew something had happened in that void. Something bad.

I went back to the doctor, concerned my memory loss might be linked to what Mum had.

'I wouldn't worry excessively,' the doctor said. 'They're probably not real blackouts more like foggy blackouts. Alcohol and the pills can temporarily affect the ability to transfer memories from the short-term to your long-term memories.'

'But I need to remember, I know it's significant that I do.'

The doctor nodded and gave me a look like I was just another idiot patient that didn't read the leaflet that comes with the medication. Always read the leaflet. It's there, in bold, NOT TO BE TAKEN

WITH ALCOHOL. *'Sometimes a trigger can free a memory. A taste. A smell. A place. That sort of thing. Go back to where it happened, it might help.' The doctor smiled limply at me. I didn't smile back.*

All I've ever remembered is me, standing at the top of some stairs looking down at a body.

CHAPTER THIRTY-TWO

Now, ten years on, Alexander Bamfield sits across from me. 'Thank you for coming, Tina.' He looks at me from beneath his bushy eyebrows. His goatee beard has gone. 'It's been extremely difficult getting hold of you, I thought you might have left the country?'

I can't sit still, I play with my bracelet. 'No, but you did surprise me when you got in touch. Your email was so . . . err . . . serious.'

'Indeed, it was. You see a family member of Mrs Duarte's has been in to see me.'

There's a silence. I don't know what to say.

He gazes at me for several seconds and I want to fidget in my seat.

'Have you seen or spoken to anybody of the Duarte family, Tina?'

I get the impression he thinks I have. 'No, nobody. Why do you ask?' I look expectantly at him, willing him to tell me something instead of looking at me as though I was guilty of something. Am I? I think I might be. Alexander Bamfield leans forward, his hands clasped in front of him.

'Deborah Duarte was a dear friend as well as a client of mine for many years. I knew all about the problems she had with her son and how hurt she was when all he appeared to want was her money.'

I nod. 'I see.' I know all this. I remember all this. What does it have to do with me?

'Deborah didn't want to leave her home to an animal charity or any other charity. She felt guilty about your mother and what happened to her after your father left. I suppose it was her way of saying sorry.'

'Sorry?' I say harshly. I can't help it, I hit staccato. 'Sorry for what? For driving my mother mad? My father abandoned us for her and left us with nothing. We lost the house, and my mother had to work two jobs to pay the rent and keep us while I finished school. Sorry? Please don't give me that rubbish about feelings and guilt. She wanted to soothe her conscience before she died and that was why she left the house to Mum and me.' My body moves in the chair all twitchy and jerky like a junkie in need of a fix.

'If you felt so strongly why did you take the money?'

'Why? Why do you take the money, Mr Bamfield? Why do you charge such crazy fees when you know most people can't afford to use you? Because it's all about the money, isn't it?' I am so agitated I do my breathing exercises to calm myself down. 'I needed that money. Oh God, I thought it was a sign that someone was looking out for us. My mother, thanks to my father, was crazy, mad as a hatter, but I looked after her. Regrettably, she developed cancer just to compound her problems. And through some mad, crazy woman's notion, she remembered my father through rose-tinted glasses. She wanted to come to live in Braitling where she'd had summer holidays with him when they were young and in love hoping he'd come to find her. So, when it was offered, I bloody took the money. I didn't know Braitling was where my dad and his new wife lived when Mum and I came here, thankfully, neither did my mum. I couldn't tell her that. All I wanted was to buy Mum a house in Braitling but we couldn't afford it. So we rented and that's where she died. Where she thought she'd been the happiest. So when I inherited, I took the money. She owed me. She took my father from my mum. She was selfish breaking up a marriage. She owed me and I didn't and don't feel guilty about that money.'

An expression of shock crosses his face, and I don't care. 'I see. I didn't realise you felt quite so strongly about Mrs Duarte.'

'You don't remember, do you? I never showed any grand appreciation that day. I wanted that money, of course I did and she bloody knew it. She tried being nice to me that day. Remember? Nice! The cheek of the woman. I just accepted it. Why? Because we had the last laugh, didn't we? My father was dead and she was dying. I know Mum was sick, but she was going to outlive terminally ill Deborah.' My rage feels as powerful as a contraction.

Alexander Bamfield holds up his hand like a stop sign. 'I don't wish to hear any more, Tina. We can leave it there, thank you. But I've had a visit from Megan Pearson. Deborah's granddaughter.'

My stomach cramps viciously.

CHAPTER THIRTY-THREE

I collapse back into the chair; this was getting so twisted and tangled. Megan Pearson. Deborah Duarte's granddaughter?

'Megan tells me quite a story. That Deborah phoned you to tell you that she had changed her mind, and you went over there and there was an argument and then . . . an accident.'

We sit in silence.

I feel my self-control slipping like feet on a pebbled beach. 'Mr Bamfield,' I say. 'I was unaware that Megan Pearson was Deborah Duarte's granddaughter. Until recently, I had never met Megan. What do you know about her?'

'Megan is charming; I've met her a few times. After her father died, she came to see me about what she had seen one day at her grandmother's house. Of course, she didn't know your identity. If you remember, it was confidential. Mrs Duarte didn't want anyone to know to whom she had bequeathed her estate. She was trying to protect you.'

I snort. Protect me, my foot. 'You mean protect her reputation.'

He sighs.

'OK, if that is the case, then how has Megan found me?'

Mr Bamfield looks shocked, his heavy brows furrow. 'That information has not come from this office, I can assure you.' He clears his throat. 'So what you are saying is that you have met with Miss Pearson?'

'I have, but I'm puzzled, why is she using the name Pearson?'

'It's her mother's name. Too many people knew her father's story and his family; she wanted to disassociate herself from them. Her mother committed suicide you know.'

'Did she fall out with her parents? What happened?'

'No. Her mother died soon after Adrian Duarte had been called in by the receivers and lost the house. She couldn't handle the shame. He started another business as a book restorer, had a shop and workshop in Cheltenham that eventually also had to close. Duarte's Book Restorers. The shop was small and hidden away just off the main street in Cheltenham. Not much visibility but probably close enough to command a large rent, I imagine. He wasn't a businessman at all. I guess it was a specialist place, so not important enough to warrant being on the main street. I don't think he had much experience. His mother despaired.

'Some of the restoration he had been working on were put up for auction, but they didn't raise much. His mother bailed him out many times. But, in the end, she felt she'd become a moneylender. He never visited her or rang her after they fell out, only when he wanted money. When she became ill, he made no effort to come and see her.'

'What happened to him?'

'He died some years later; they ended up in social housing and on benefits. Megan looked after him, I believe. He dragged her from place to place. Poor child had no fixed abode.'

'So she's resentful of what happened? Is that what you're saying?'

'She never said that to me. Megan tried getting her father to look for work, but he fell into a deep depression. After he died, there was nothing to detain her in Cheltenham so she moved from the area. She moved back here to Braitling and met up with Rachel, who had been her mother's friend. I think she stayed with Rachel. They had a huge fight about something and that's when Rachel moved up to Manchester, I think.'

'Has Megan been ill?' I don't want to stress what sort of illness I'm referring to.

Alexander Bamfield shrugs his shoulders. He sets the pen that he's been twirling in his fingers on to the desk. It's the same fountain pen I remember. 'She had a stay in one of those rest homes. She signed herself in, she wasn't admitted by her GP, you understand. Megan, you have to understand, went through a lot when she was very young. She lost her mother then she lost her home. Her father declined into more debt and depression and became dependent on her from an early age. She was messed up. Her grandmother wanted to bring her to live with her but he wouldn't allow it. He wouldn't let her visit her grandmother. She used to make excuses and come to stay with Rachel so she could visit her without her father knowing. She suffered from anxiety and depression after her father died. I believe while she lived with Rachel things got a little difficult. After Rachel left, I don't know what happened to her. I did hear . . .'

'Go on, please.' I understand her pain. It's hard to understand why a mother you love and loves you, leaves you all alone in the world. I too cried for my mother knowing she wasn't ever coming back to me. Dominoes, that's what comes to mind. My dad and Deborah's affair destroyed so many lives. But why does Megan hate me so much?

'I believe, and don't quote me on this, that Megan was quite controlling of Rachel. Or so that's what I've heard.' He shrugs. 'I'm not one for gossip. Maybe you can ask in the village. My concern is what Megan told me about her grandmother.'

I knead my stomach with my fist. 'What?' I laugh. 'That as a child she saw Deborah and I argue and the next thing Deborah suffers a fatal accident and I'm to blame? Surely Mr Bamfield as a solicitor you know that you need more than that to accuse anyone.' I look expectantly at Alexander Bamfield hoping that's all he has.

'I have to ask you the question you understand. Of course, if there was any foul play, I must report it to the police now that I've been made aware of it. And, as it happens, I never mentioned the accident Deborah had was fatal.'

'I don't know anything about a phone call or going to Deborah's house after the meeting we had here at your office. That was the one and only time we met.'

He nods and scowls. 'I did say that to Megan and that the coroner didn't find any unusual causes of death apart from a fall. The stair carpet was severely damaged by her cat, as you will recall it was suggested she tripped and fell.'

'I remember you telling me. I don't know any more than that.'

'I'm curious how you know she was talking about *that* accident.'

All the air has gone from my lungs as I think quickly. I know I've put my foot in it and I am beginning to know how I do know *that* was a fatal fall. I must assume I was told, so I go with that. 'I was told she had a fatal fall and I am assuming you are referring to that. Why else would Megan discuss it with you in such a way?'

CHAPTER THIRTY-FOUR

I walk through the village checking in several shops and asking discreet questions about Megan. I'm out of luck. Nobody knows of her.

Finally, when I'm about to give up, I walk past a tiny side street, there's a sign above a door, Beauty by Bella. I've tried coffee shops, restaurants, clothes shops, but not beauty salons. I remember her nails and wonder, what if?

Bingo.

No sooner have I sat down having my nails done and mention Megan that Bella — adorned with false eyelashes, extensions, nails, tan and brilliant white teeth — off loads. I wonder what it must be like to wear so many false attachments.

She settles herself in front of me, begins my nails and the words just pour out at an alarming rate. She talks with no pauses for responses or breath. 'Oh, yeah, Megan, she's a lark. I've known her for ages. Used to come in here *all the time*, when she moved back, you know? She's had everything done. God, she's so unhappy with her body. Crazy, isn't it? I mean, the girl is pretty, nothing wrong with her. But, you know, between you and me, I think she has body issues. She's messed up. In the head, you know? Was in one of *those* places

229

for a while.' She sets her fingers to her temple and twirls them. 'Cuckoo, you know what I mean?'

I want to ask questions, but I can't get a word in.

'Anyway, she was doing a beauty course, like me, you know, but she never finished it, dropped out. I was cross with her, what a waste, I told her. But Megan was unable to settle at anything. She did a few jobs. Worked for an IT company and dated the owner, I thought that was weird. He was an oddball sort of guy. You know what I mean?' I nod. 'He was dull and always on the bloody computer; the guy had no conversation. I don't know what the hell she saw in him.'

She breaks for air, finally.

The pieces start to fall into place. 'So, Bella, did she mention her grandmother at all?' I ask.

Bella rolls her eyes. 'Did she? Oh yeah. What colour do you want? I like purple, purple is really in at the moment. I like this shade of purple, it's intense, don't you think? It's the most popular colour right now.' She laughs. 'Only because I love it,' she says dragging out the word love. 'I push my clients to wear it. Shall we go with it? OK, let's go purple.'

Before I can say anything, she's shaken the bottle and is about to paint my nails purple. It's not that I don't like purple. As a colour I do, but it reminds me of when I was twelve. 'Err, red, let's go for blood red, shall we?'

'Great choice, my favourite. After that it's Barbie pink, love Barbie pink nails, don't you?'

'I thought you liked purple best?'

'Huh? Oh yeah, but I like red and pink too.'

I try to stay focused but she's exhausting me. 'OK. So, what did Megan say about her grandmother?' I can't believe this font of knowledge is not curious to my questions.

'Well.' She lowers her voice. There's nobody else in the salon. 'She found papers after her dad died when she was clearing the house. She discovered a letter from her grandmother that told her dad he wasn't going to inherit anything because he'd already taken shedloads of money from her.' She looks at me to see if I'm following.

'Right, I see, go on.'

'You know her family was loaded, right?' She puts my right hand under an ultraviolet light.

'Yes, yes I do.'

'Right, well, anyway.' She starts on my left hand. 'This letter, Megan thinks tipped him over the edge. He was depressed and couldn't work. In my opinion he didn't want to work. Felt sorry for himself is what it sounded like to me. Anyway, I think from what she said, it pissed her off because she had to look after him and he had been counting on the inheritance. You know, she quit school at sixteen that sort of malarkey.' She lowers her voice to a whisper. I lean forward to hear her. 'I think she hated him for doing that to her, you know, ruining her life. 'Cause Megan is really bright, I mean smart, smart. When she came here and started dating Mr Miserable, she completed an online course for a paralegal. Said she had a plan. Said she was going to get everything back that was hers.'

CHAPTER THIRTY-FIVE

I find myself outside Deborah's old house. The wheelie bins stand outside ready to be taken back in. I look at the house from the opposite side of the road. The front garden is still well looked after. I forget who bought the house after I sold it. Mum and I never lived here. The thought of living in the same house as her and Dad didn't appeal.

I wander round, up and down the pavement trying to remember that day. Deborah did phone me to tell me she'd changed her mind and that she wanted to explain something. I remember that much. Of course, I wasn't going to admit that to Bamfield or anyone.

I want to look inside to see if anything will trigger a memory. No cars stand on the drive and there is no sign of life inside. Gingerly, I walk up to the front door and knock. I wait, telling myself this is a bad idea but that I have no choice but to go through with it. I have no idea what I'm going to say if somebody opens the front door. *Hi, I think I might have done something bad in your house, once. Mind if I take a look round to remind myself of the details?* Nobody answers. I walk round to the back and look through the windows. It's so different, modern, white walls, grey furniture, a lot less clutter. It looks so much bigger this time round. There's nobody home it seems.

I wonder if there might be a spare key hidden somewhere in the garden. I always leave a spare key hidden just in case. Or I have my handbag stolen. It's worth a look.

I check the door frame and move some rocks by the back door that form a small rockery covered in purple verbena making the whole area look cushioned. I find nothing. I know where I keep my key, and it's nowhere near the house. There isn't much traffic down this part of the village, a few cars have gone by. There's no sign of children, either. I check the time. They will be back from work soon, I imagine. I purse my lips, where would you hide a key that's not obvious. There's a sundial on the lawn. No. Too obvious. A shed, maybe? I wouldn't. I pluck at my lip, thinking. The solar water feature! Obviously! I look round the edge and see a slim piece of string anchored down into the lawn by a tent peg. I pull it out of the water and remove the key.

Quickly I put the key in the lock and wonder what I'm going to do if they arrive home whilst inside. I try not to think of that right now. I'm getting quite professional at breaking and entering. The key turns and the lock clicks. I turn the doorknob. The door opens easily with a slight squeak. I hesitate before entering. When I'm inside, I push the key into my pocket and close the door quietly. I don't know why I do that, there's no one here. The answers I'm looking for must lie in this house, I just have to find them. It's so different, though. It shocks me a little. I've no idea why I thought it would not have been decorated. Very elegant and stylish. I wonder what type of couple lives here. Young and professional with lots of disposable income I think while walking through the kitchen into the hallway. A flutter of thoughts drift through my mind, gently like bird's wings. I continue towards the stairs and without thinking I walk into the lounge and I'm back. The impact of the memory jolts me to a standstill. I grab the back of the sofa as I am flooded with memories as clear as the view through the window.

'You can't change your mind; you just can't,' I say.

'I can, Tina, I'm sorry. I was rash in thinking I could cut out Adrian and my granddaughter. I wanted to hurt him like he'd hurt me. But the more I've thought about it, I just can't do it. I'm sorry,' Deborah says.

'Sorry! You destroyed my mother and our lives and then you dangle a carrot pretending you want atonement and then you take it back? You are a cruel bitch, Deborah Duarte. I don't know what my father saw in you.'

Deborah leaves the room and goes upstairs. 'Please leave, Tina,' she says, walking slowly up the stairs, using the banister to pull herself along. She has arthritis in both knees. 'I'm sorry to have caused you so much distress, I never meant to hurt either of you.' From the landing she says, 'Your father left your mother; I didn't force him. But we were in love. Very much in love.'

I stand at the bottom looking up and her words grate on me. How cruel. How mean and nasty to give something and then take it back. And to say that to me. To me! The woman is vicious. Cruel and cold-hearted.

The sheer climatic force of emotions I felt that day strike me again now and cause my legs to give way beneath me. I move, slowly and sit on the bottom step looking up the stairs. And just like that the fog clears: And I remember. Everything.

CHAPTER THIRTY-SIX

I stand at the bottom of the stairs, raging. Thoughts of my mum running riot in my head.

I storm out of the house, slamming the back door. Striding down the back lane towards the village, I seethe. She didn't care, she probably only did it to anger her son. Her stupid, leechy son. I'm filled with an overwhelming desire to smash something. Break something. I pass a wheelie bin left out on the grass verge of a house three doors down. Grabbing it, I swing it round and let it go crashing into a car parked on the other side of the road. Immediately the alarm screams out. For a moment I'm terrified at the depth of violence I feel. How could she? How could she?

I stand still for a moment looking at what I've done. When I was young I used to like twirling round and round until I was so dizzy I couldn't stand up. That's how I feel now. The feeling makes me sick. I sit on the grass verge outside the house whose wheelie bin I've just lobbed across the road. I hate the feeling growing inside me, it's awful. I pull out my tablets and swallow a couple with saliva, and wait for them to kick in. The alarm still rages. Strange nobody has come outside. If tackled about it, I shall say some teenager in a hoody did it.

I look round. There is no one about. I pull my hair off my face and grab a bobble from my handbag and tie it back. I've never had any luck in life. Never. Some people are handed life's niceties on a plate as though their fairy godmother is constantly watching and pinging her wand to grant their desires. *Chime! You will have a great family life! Chime! You will enjoy an amazing career! Chime! You will have wealth! Health! And all you desire! Chime! Chime! Chime!*

What did the universe want for me? A family pulled apart by a greedy, wealthy woman! *Chime!* A mad mother! *Chime!* A mad and sick mother! *Chime!* A promise to help the mad, sick mother before she dies! *Chime! Lies! Chime! Chime! Chime!*

The tablets are kicking in. My thoughts are random and not making any sense. I should only have taken one. But two cushions everything so much more effectively.

I hear a car horn in the distance cutting through the fog inside my head. A voice. Strident and insistent in the distance breaking through my cotton wool jumbled thoughts. *'No. No. No,'* it says, over and over. *'It's not right. None of it. Lies. All lies. It's wrong. It's all so bloody wrong.'*

Is someone here? Nearby? Of course there isn't. It's all in my head. The voice is getting louder and more insistent. I put my hands over my ears. It's useless because it's already inside my head. I hear my mother's voice. *'Don't listen to them. Don't answer the phone. They're spying, trying to get inside our heads, don't you hear them? Don't you hear them shouting inside your head?'*

I hear them today. Today they are screaming at me. I can't bear it. I can't! I take another tablet. Stop. Stop. Please stop! I stand up looking round. I must go back to the house. I have to sort this out. I need to tell her how wrong she is to do this. It's mean. Nasty. She's nasty. She needs to know she's nasty. I race back turning the bend in the road too quickly and bump into a little girl carrying a skipping rope.

I let myself in through the back door. I can't hear anything but floorboards creaking. She must still be upstairs. I race up the stairs taking them two at a time. I'm breathless when I get to the top.

'Deborah! Deborah, where are you? We need to talk. This is all wrong. You can't do this. You can't!'

Deborah comes out of her bedroom. She looks irritated. I can't hear what she's saying. All I can hear are the voices shouting, louder and louder. *'No. No. No. You're mean. You gave it to us and now you want to take it away. Like my dad. You took him away.'*

236

'Tina, I think you'd better leave. I'll be going to see Alexander Bamfield tomorrow to sort this mess out. I'm sorry.'

I see her face. Hard. Uncaring. I spike up as if I've had a shot of adrenaline to the heart. Sorry. She's sorry. Bloody cow. Deborah comes over to me and speaks. I don't hear anything. I want to shake her so hard my hands hurt with the need to grab her scrawny shoulders and dig my nails into her old, crinkly skin and shake, and shake and shake.

As she walks over to me, I grab her shoulders, firmly. She stops and looks at me in disgust as if I'm not good enough to touch her.

It happens so quickly.

Nasty. Mean. Selfish. All these words pile up in my head until . . .

I push her so hard she bounces off the wall ending up in a heap at the bottom.

I come down the stairs and stand above her. I feel no remorse. No pain. No regret. She had it coming. She did. She ruined our lives. Twice. I bend down and find no pulse. I put my face to her mouth. No breath. My automatic reaction is to call the police. An ambulance.

I don't.

Instead, I walk out of the house.

CHAPTER THIRTY-SEVEN

The moment I remember what happened, I want to get out of this house and as far away as I can from Braitling. I don't want to see Alexander Bamfield again.

No one ever suspected.

It's gone peaceful inside my head now that I know. But I won't do anything about it.

My mouth feels momentarily parched and no matter how much water I drink I can't seem to get rid of that feeling. I fill another glass from the kitchen sink then rinse it out and leave it on the drainer before I leave.

I get to my car, unlock it and turn on the ignition. I'm numb. I fasten my seat belt. I need to get home. I set my satnav and put the car into reverse. My phone rings through the Bluetooth and startles me. I set the brake. Glyn's name comes up on the dashboard.

'Hello?'

'Tina, are you OK?'

'Yes?' I say, oddly surprised by his question then realise he can't know what I've just discovered. His voice sounds off. Something is wrong. The hairs on my arms stand up. 'Glyn, what's wrong, what's happened?'

'You need to come home. Right now. Do you hear me?'

I scowl, why won't he tell me? 'I am. What's wrong? Tell me.'

'You're in Braitling, aren't you? You actually went.'

'Of course I'm here.'

'It doesn't matter. But you need to come home right now. Do you hear me? No excuses. No stopping off anywhere else. Just come home.'

'WHAT THE FUCK HAS HAPPENED, GLYN? WHAT?'

His voice is calm, but I detect the slight wobble. I know him too well. My foot is on the foot brake and my hand is ready on the release. But I can't move. It's as if I'm suddenly paralysed. Paralysed with fear. The only thing still functioning is my mind and my voice. In my head I have terrible thoughts.

'Tina, I want you to relax and stay calm. You have a long journey and you need to stay focused. I just want you to come home. Now.' His voice has the sound of someone battling to keep their emotions under control.

He's killing me.

'Glyn, I can't, I can't drive home not knowing what's wrong. I know something has happened. What's wrong?'

'Bloody hell, Tina, you ask what's wrong? Have you forgotten what you left behind when you shot off in your car like a bat out of hell? Have you? Have you forgotten us? Look, just get home, please. Christ, I can't believe how we're arguing. I don't know you any more. I thought I could count on you. I thought I knew what was going on in your head. Who are you? I've had Howard on the phone looking for Megan. Saying you've done something to her. Have you?'

'What? No! I haven't seen Megan. Where is she?'

'We don't know and—'

I brace myself; I have a horrible feeling I already know what he's going to say. 'And what?'

'When you left, it's as if everything imploded. Everything has gone crazy here. I'm not saying any more. Get home.'

'Don't you trust me to be able to deal with whatever it is you're not telling me?'

'It's not a matter of trust, is it? It's can *you* handle it. I shouldn't have said that.' There's a small pause. 'We've had the police here. Again. They were looking for you, and they've been back. Megan called them. She told them you had attacked and threatened her. They're concerned for her safety.'

'I haven't done anything to Megan. You must believe me. You know me, Glyn. I couldn't hurt anyone.' I stop abruptly. That's a lie. I hurt Deborah. I pushed her down the stairs. I killed her. I murdered her. I did that. Me. Tina Valentine. But I haven't hurt Megan. I know that. Can I be sure though? Can I? I think I can but then again, how can I definitely say I am sure. What if I've had another blackout?

'Megan told them you broke into her house. It's been trashed like there was a fight. She said it was you. She has a photo of you breaking in the other week.' There's silence before he speaks again. 'Look, I don't want to argue any more. I'm confused. Just get home.'

I let out a small sigh. 'Glyn . . .'

'No, I'm not saying any more. Just come home. We need to sort this out. I want my Tina back. I miss you. I miss what we had. And right now, I need you here, we need to sort this out.'

'This is your fault, Glyn.'

'My fault!'

'Yes,' I say, 'you shouldn't have employed her in the first place.'

'It's not your fault or mine. You're ill, Tina, you need help,' he says.

I knew he wouldn't absolve me; I wanted him to, the old Glyn would have.

I release the handbrake and put the car in drive.

This is torture. I know something is horribly wrong at home. But now I don't want to know. Glyn is right. If he tells me something horrible, I'll likely have a crash. I'll have to curb my thoughts. God, what the hell has happened to us?

'I want to come back,' I say. 'I want us to be the same, again. I love you. I'm sorry if you think I've been horrible to you.'

'That's irrelevant now.'

'Is it? It's not to me, to me it's very relevant.'

'What is it you want me to say,' he says clearly irritated.

'An acknowledgment that you love me would be nice,' I say just as irritated. Does he think I have a handbook on 'How to handle a psycho woman who threatens your family?' I'm as much in the dark about how to deal with this as he is. Just because I'm a woman he seems to think I should know all the answers.

'Come home, please.' The line goes dead and the radio kicks in. I turn it down as I drive out of Braitling and head home.

I'm not religious, not at all, but right now I want forgiveness for what I did. How could I have done it? I know I won't ever own up to this. I have a family, a husband and children. I'll go to prison. They'll lose their mother. No. I'll keep this inside me. After all, what good would it do now?

CHAPTER THIRTY-EIGHT

I drive on autopilot, stopping once on the motorway for the toilet and grabbing a coffee. I haven't eaten all day, but I'm not hungry. Everything is a mess, and I don't know what to make of what I've discovered. As I eat up the miles on the motorway, and to stop myself from thinking about what's going on at home, I run through what I've discovered.

I killed Deborah Duarte.

Megan Pearson is Deborah's granddaughter.

Megan overheard Deborah telling me she was going to change her Will back in favour of her dad. Megan has a letter from Deborah telling her father what she was going to do.

Megan has told Alexander Bamfield what she heard and shown him the letter.

Megan is out for revenge.

How far will she go?

Has she told Glyn?

I clench my stomach as a wave of nausea hits me. I focus and do my breathing exercises. Taking small sips of water from my bottle until I begin feeling it ebbing away.

I need to think.

It's starting to rain. Big, heavy, drops smash into the windscreen. My wipers frustratingly whack them away so I can see the road. A summer thunderstorm. I see brake lights ahead; everyone is slowing down. The heavy clouds soak up what little light there is left.

Slick roads are treacherous, I need to drive safely. I need to get home.

I'm starting to calm down a little as my breathing exercises kick in.

I pull off the motorway, only a few miles left. I force my foot down and lean forward to see better through the fat raindrops, the velocity with which they are coming down matches my speed.

Suddenly the thought of Megan in my home with my children squeezes me with dread. I've managed not to allow those thoughts any freedom while I drove on the motorway, but now I can no longer hold them back. They come crashing through like a herd of charging bulls and just as destructive. My skin prickles with terror and I'm engulfed with terrible thoughts. I squeeze the steering wheel.

I hit the brakes at a red traffic light.

It stays red. Red. Red. 'Come on, come on, change you bastard, CHANGE!' I scream as if I can make it change. I'm irrational with fear and dread.

Just as I lose patience and push my foot down on the accelerator it changes. I race through, the revs on my car scream as I push it to the max.

Pulling into my road, I slow down. My heart is pumping furiously. My palms are hot and sweaty. My knuckles hurt from gripping the steering wheel tightly.

My phone rings, I glance and see no name. Curiosity makes me answer; I don't usually answer unknown calls.

'Tina, hi.' It's Megan.

I slam the brakes on. The car stops and I'm jolted forward. A cold finger of fear runs down my spine.

'Megan. Where are you? What do you want?'

She laughs. 'They're looking for you. The police that is. Social services, too. Glyn isn't looking for you; he's looking for someone else. You hurt me, Tina. They want to ask you about that, do you know where I am? Do you think you can find me?'

What the fuck is she playing at? I can't think clearly. My thoughts spin out of control, images flash in front of my eyes. Deborah. Alexander. The stairs. Deborah falling. Oh my God! Matt! He fell down the stairs. Did she push him on purpose? Was that a message I was supposed to pick up on? Oh my God. Oh Matt.

'Where's Matt?'

'Well done, that legal brain of yours is working well. Not clouded by the pills today, is it?'

'So, you do have Matt?'

'Yes, I have him. And I'm sure you want him back. In one piece. Social services want to know what you've done with him.'

This conversation can go one of two ways; I make the decision to keep it stable. What I want to say, I need to keep to myself, for now anyway. I rest my forehead on the steering wheel cursing under my breath what I want to do to her.

'Is Matt OK?'

She laughs. 'Oh, so concerned about your family, Tina.' There's a facetiousness to her tone I don't like. She reminds me of my mother when she was at her worst. Full on crazy. 'It's really shitty, isn't it, when your family is being destroyed by someone you don't know, purely for their own gains?'

I try to protest that I don't know what she's talking about and stop myself, realising it will probably make her angrier and what's the point? We both know the truth. I killed her grandmother and took her inheritance. Therefore, by default, killed her father, too.

I breathe in through my nose and out through my mouth.

'I don't know what you think you know, but you're mistaken.' I press my forehead hard against the steering wheel until it hurts. The pain keeps me centred.

Megan gives a snort. 'Wrong? I don't think so. Besides, what is it you think you know?'

'I spoke to Alexander Bamfield.'

'Is that so? Then you know what I know.' There's too much drama in her voice. Too much malevolence under the surface.

'All I know is what he told me. That you went to see him, claiming to be Deborah Duarte's granddaughter and claiming you overheard a conversation that allegedly she and I had.'

A police car and ambulance race past, I consider whether to catch their attention.

'Allegedly? Are you using legal jargon on me? It won't work, you know. Besides, everyone thinks you're mad. Even Glyn. We've spoken at length, and I've convinced him you have the start of dementia like your mother. He's already concerned about the children. Your mother-in-law agrees with me.'

She'd agree with anyone against me that's not news.

'How can you know what you heard that day? You were a child; you misunderstood. You've got it wrong.'

'I haven't got it wrong. You forget I have the letter Grandma sent Dad.'

Shit. I slam my forehead against the steering wheel a few times.

'Knowledge is power, Tina, and I hold all the power. Everyone believes me. You see I know so much about you that I've seized all your power. A bit like Superman with kryptonite. You were so brilliant, running a home, two lovely kids, husband that adored you and a career about to take off big time . . . and now you possess nothing . . . and I have everything.'

I return her facetious laugh. I hadn't planned on losing my temper. But suddenly, I'm voicing it, all the words bottled up in my subconscious burst forth. 'Oh, right, you believe that? You genuinely think Glyn is going to dump me and take up with you? You're the crazy bitch, here, Megan, not me. You're barking, loopy, off your head and bloody delusional if you think you can take over my life for yourself.'

I can feel the tension sizzling between us. I look up and see my face reflected in the windscreen. My hands shake violently as I try to keep control of myself. If I could, I would climb through the phone and rip out her throat. Bitch.

I shift in my seat, my eyes on my reflection. 'Look, Megan, we need to talk face to face, we need to clear this up. What your grandma said in that letter wasn't altogether true.' There's silence on the other end of the phone. For a moment I think she's rung off, then I hear her breathing. 'She told me she'd written to your father and told him of her change of heart, but that day, where you think you heard what you heard, you are missing out a chunk of conversation.' I see a cyclist coming towards me, soaking wet, he rides through a puddle and suddenly, spectacularly, flies over the handlebars. He must have hit a pothole filled by rainwater. They're rife round here. I want to go and help but I can't cut my call. He gets up, looks at his front wheel and marvellously, loses his temper throwing his bike on the floor and giving it a good kick before storming off in the rain.

'Obviously you think I'm stupid and will believe whatever you say.'

Obviously, I thought that too. But that would be too easy.

Suddenly her voice gets louder, and I turn the phone volume down on my steering wheel. Her voice is hectic and high pitched now. 'No, Tina, I heard it all. Because of you . . .' Her voice falters. 'You destroyed my life, you took away everything. And I am going to do the same to you. It's called karma.' She laughs. 'You believe in karma, right? You love saying it when you win a case, don't you?'

'Where are you, Megan? Tell me.' I can't bear the fact that she has Matt. He'll be scared and frightened. 'Tell me where you are.'

'Think. Think. Think, Tina, where would I go where nobody would think of looking for me at this time of night. Tick-tock, tick-tock, time's running out.'

I speak rapidly, 'For what? Why is time running out? What do you mean? What are you planning? Tell me where the fuck you are!' I grapple with my phone and text Glyn. *Is Matt with you?*

I get an answer straight back. *No. Where are you????*

'You know where I am, Tina, come and rescue your boy.'

'What are you talking about? Rescue him? Surely you wouldn't harm a little boy. He has nothing to do with this.'

'Little boy, old lady, they're all the same, aren't they? I mean, if it delivers you what you want then surely it doesn't matter, right?'

'Are you threatening my family?'

'Maybe. Why don't you come and see?'

I turn the car round and head back to the motorway, breaking all the speed limits along the way. My foot flat to the floor. I don't stop at traffic lights. Speed cameras or junctions. I just drive. I need to get to Matt. Oh God if she hurts Matt, I'll kill her. I squeeze the steering wheel.

I get an incoming call from Glyn. I need to speak to him, dare I cut Megan off? I must. I press Accept, she'll probably think I've lost signal, anyway.

'TINA! Where are you? I saw you stop in our road. Where the hell have you gone? You must get home, quick.'

'Glyn, I know. I know Matt has disappeared. I know Megan has him. I'm going to get him back.'

'What the fuck are you talking about?'

'She's got him at the office. It's the only place I can think of. I'm heading there now. Call the police. Tell them that crazy bitch is trying to hurt our little boy. Do it now. Do it now, Glyn, before it's too late. I told you she was mad. I told you and you didn't fucking believe me.'

'Megan isn't at the office. The police have already checked.'

'What!' I lose control of the car. Suddenly I'm veering all over the motorway, car horns are blasting all over the show. I see red tail lights glowing as brakes are stamped on and frantic drivers dart across lanes to avoid me. I catch it before it goes into a spin, at eighty miles an hour in the pouring rain I'm driving a lethal weapon. I can feel my back end losing traction. I withhold the temptation to hit the brakes again.

Instead, I take my foot off the accelerator to drop the speed and guide the car back into a straight line. I see the next junction come up, fast. Swerving across the lanes I come off, turning sharply round the roundabout and back on to the motorway heading for home.

Megan calls back. I answer. 'Oops, wrong way? Have you worked it out now?'

CHAPTER THIRTY-NINE

A torrent of ice-cold fear descends over me as I navigate down our road, not speeding but not exactly going slowly either. I skid to a stop in the drive, sending golden gravel flying.

I race through the front door and see that the children aren't there. 'Where are they?' I scream. 'Where are they?' Glyn's parents jump at my tone. His mother is crying at the kitchen table. I rush towards Glyn. He grabs my arm and drags me out of the kitchen.

In front of the basement he yells at me, 'You tell me? What have you done with them?'

I shrug free. 'What the fuck are you talking about? You think I have them? How? I've been in Braitling. That lunatic has them and she's threatening to hurt them.'

'Fuck's sake, Tina. Megan doesn't have them. She's here, she's been here all the time. She's been upset and worried to death. She's having a lie down.'

'I'm OK, Glyn. I heard her come in. Tina, you must tell us what you've done with the children. They'll be frightened and scared. You don't want to really hurt them.'

I'm too stunned to do anything; the weight of everyone's eyes on me brings me to my knees. I lash out at her ready to tear her limbs from her body. Glyn grabs me and pulls me to one side. 'Tina, this isn't helping. Where are the children?'

I study his profile. I'm conscious of my heart beating rapidly and the need to stop it racing out of control. I dip my hand in my coat pocket and pull out the papers from the private detective. I pivot away from him and slip on Dog. 'Dog! Oh my God. Matt will be desperate without Dog. What have you done with my children, you bitch?' I rush towards her again, but Glyn intercepts me a second time dragging me downstairs into the basement.

I scan the room, my vision is clear as is my mind, the only thoughts I have are to rescue my children at all costs. When I move towards her, Glyn stops me.

The three of us stand in a circle. I need to focus. I need to stay in control. The slight twist of her lips is nearly enough to send me over the edge. I'm aware my fists are clenched. I can feel the blood filling my veins in readiness. I'm at tipping point.

The basement is silent. I can hear my breathing. Her eyes are wide. We watch each other. She's waiting for my next move. I don't know what that's going to be. Glyn's pale, standing legs apart, ready for whatever I throw at him.

I move backwards. My fingers grip the neck of a bottle. 'Read those papers I gave you. Read them,' I insist. He looks at them in his hands and pulls them out of the envelope.

Megan looks at me. My chest heaves, my heart out of control. I need to get out of here. I can't believe my husband thinks I've done something to my children. Glyn shakes his head as he reads.

'Did she tell you that the diazepam found in my drawer was hers? It has a partial of her name on it. Sally was off sick and I found a packet of laxatives in the bin. She had a relationship with an IT guy and that was how she knew how to hack my computer. She's been in a mad house. She had a breakdown. She blackmailed Rachel to get a job at the office when she found me. Rachel's been spying on me for her since she started at the firm. Rachel was her mother's friend and it's through Rachel that she knows so much about me and Ali and the kids.'

'Oh, come on! How would she blackmail Rachel?'

'Rachel's husband is here illegally. She told Megan, who threatened to tell the authorities if she didn't help her. He's not ill, Rachel just couldn't do it any more and that's when Megan came for the job. That's what the private detective found out. That's why I wanted you to read it.'

'Is this true, Megan?'

She laughs, 'Of course it isn't.'

'Someone broke into our house. You.' I point a finger at her. 'You watched our children sleeping. Matt saw you. You messed with Laura's ribbons so Matt would get in trouble.' I stab my finger at her, again. 'You waltzed around our garden and in our house when we were out, wearing my sun hat. You were seen,' I bark. She says nothing, but her eyes are locked on mine. 'You used Find My iPhone to track me tonight, didn't you?'

All these things that have happened she did them. Look at the proof you have in your hands, Glyn. I have the packaging. The police will find fingerprints on the box. Your fingerprints not mine.'

Glyn shifts his weight from one leg to the other. He looks confused. 'Megan is this true?' He waves the papers in front of her.

A laugh escapes her. 'What?'

I swivel towards her, my fingers fastened on the neck of the bottle behind me. 'Where are the children, Megan? What have you done with them? Look, if you tell us we'll let this all go. We won't call the police. Just please tell us where they are. They're only little. They'll be so frightened. Please. You've hurt me. You've destroyed my career. Is that not enough?'

She faces me head on. 'I think you know where they are, Tina.'

Glyn points at the papers. 'Are you not denying what's in here?'

'What do you think?' Megan replies. 'Why don't you ask your wife about my grandmother?' She raises an eyebrow.

'Never mind your fucking grandmother, where are my children?' I demand before Glyn can speak.

'I'm not the only one lying, am I, Tina?'

'Are you standing here telling me that everything Tina has said is true? That you planned all this?'

Finally. Glyn has matched up the dots.

'Glyn, the kids will be at hers. In her basement. That's where they are, isn't it?' I march towards the door shoving her out of the way.

She spins round and blocks my path. 'Let's just be honest here, Tina. Why don't you tell Glyn what you did to my grandmother?'

'Megan, are the kids at yours?' Glyn interrupts, but I'm still marching up the stairs, the bottle of wine still in my hand.

She thrusts a hand in front of me baring my way and stepping up the stairs in front to block the exit.

Glyn's face changes. Anger sweeps over his features. I can see he's realised how duped he's been by this woman. He studies Megan as I prepare how I'm going to tell Glyn what I did. Not that I care. I need to get out of here and save my kids, but Glyn is already ahead of me grabbing hold of Megan's arm and yanking her down the stairs. 'You lied to us all. You made my wife out to be crazy when all the time it was you and now you kidnap my children? I ought to throw you under a bus.' Glyn's voice is raw with rage. She topples over and into his arms.

As soon as she's out of the way I race up the stairs. 'I'm going to get the kids. Keep her here until the police get here,' I shout, pulling my mobile from my back pocket and dialling.

'She's delusional if she thinks she's going to find them at mine,' Megan adds with a laugh.

Glyn and I freeze.

I run back down and raise my hand to strike her. Glyn stops me, pushing me to one side. He grabs Megan by the

252

shoulders and shakes her. 'That's enough. Tell us where they are. I won't let Tina hit you, but I will smash your fucking face in unless you speak now.' He thrusts her against the wine racks. A few bottles wobble and fall, smashing on the floor. Red wine creeps around our feet.

Her face goes blank. 'What are you going to do now? Beat me up and go to prison for GBH? You'll lose your licence too. No, I don't think you'll do that to me, Glyn. It's not your style. Why don't you tell Tina how you kissed me and how you liked it and how you wanted to fuck me?'

The world stops spinning. I reel back as though she punched me in the stomach. I look at Glyn.

'Liar,' he hisses.

Megan collects herself. She's back in control. 'She's as crazy as I am. I want you to tell him Tina what you did to my grandmother.' She snorts, 'Tell you what, Glyn. You tell her about our kissing and she can tell you about her killing.'

I look at Glyn for an answer. The bottle slips from my hand smashing on the floor tiles. I sway. The room sways with me. I hear Glyn make an animal sound deep in his throat.

He explodes, 'I didn't kiss you, Megan. You kissed me. You sat on me. You put your hands down my trousers. I didn't do anything but prevent you.' He looks at me but I can't read him. But I believe him. I believe my husband.

'I believe you,' I say in a whisper. A tear falls down my cheek.

I look at Megan, her eyes have gone dark.

I raise my voice, 'God, you are just as vile as your bloody grandmother. It was her dying wish that I inherit. That woman took everything from me, my dad, my mother's sanity, our home and our life. She wanted atonement by giving us the money, and I bestowed it on her by accepting.'

'You killed my grandmother for her money,' Megan shouts. 'Tell him what you did. I saw you. I was the little girl with the skipping rope on my way to see her, but I saw you instead. I saw what you did.'

'This is so messed up. You were a child, you can't possibly have seen what happened.' My eyes flick from her to Glyn. 'I'd gone to see her grandmother when I heard she wanted to talk to me, she never told me she wanted to change the Will. She asked me to help her down the stairs when she caught her foot on the carpet and fell. I didn't lay a hand on her except to grab her as she fell.'

'You're fucked up. You can't even tell the truth.'

Glyn looks at me. 'Tina?'

I don't look at him. I keep my eyes on her. 'That is the truth. I left because I was frightened, I might get blamed being the beneficiary in her Will.'

Glyn's brow creases, but I don't waver. She has no proof and I will never admit to what really happened.

Megan sneers. 'You lying bitch.'

Glyn grabs her by the throat. 'Enough!' he thunders. 'Tell us where the children are.'

'No.' She sounds almost bored. 'Not until she admits to what she did.'

Glyn keeps his hand wrapped around her throat and turns his head to me. Megan squirms to escape.

'She isn't going to tell us, Glyn. Do something.' I can't stand another moment of this.

'Call the police,' Glyn says and shoves Megan into the alcove. I dial 999. He turns to grab some rope and the next moment he's on the floor with red wine sloshed all over his face. She's smashed him over the head with a bottle.

We stand staring at one another for the briefest of moments. I put my phone back into my pocket. I want to run and check he's all right, but I know I need to find the kids.

The words leave my mouth and I know it's the wrong thing to say but I can't help myself.

'They locked you up for a reason, you crazy bitch.' I feel disembodied and charge at her. She slams against the wine racks. She glares at me as her head slams backwards. Bottles fall and smash around us. 'I pushed your grandmother. Is that what you want me to say? Well I've said it now. Tell me where my children are, you psycho bitch.' I step back, away from her.

She moves forward, just one step. My jaw tightens. She's glowering at me. I'm staring at her. I catch a movement from Glyn. I stand where I am, not intimidated by her.

'I'm not *crazy*.' She jabs her finger in my chest. 'You're crazy if you think you can get away with murdering my grandmother. I'm not imagining things. I know what I saw.' She moves another step forward. We're nose to nose like two animals about to fight. My nostrils flare. I see hers do the same. She's taller than me. Silence falls between us. Both of us frozen. Waiting for the other to make the first move.

I come to life.

'The thing is, Megan,' I keep my voice low. 'I already have.'

She takes me by surprise and lunges for me. I step to the left and push her away racing up the stairs. She grabs my foot but I kick myself free and climb. I slam the door and pull the bolt across.

The rain is hammering down as I race out of the house. I remember I haven't a key to get in and I'm not going to be able to break down the door.

Back in my kitchen I grab her handbag from the work-top where I saw it when I arrived. 'Call the police,' I yell at Glyn's parents as I run out. 'Don't open the basement. Call them and tell them Glyn is being held hostage.' His dad stands up immediately, no questions asked. I see him rush over to the house phone.

I pull my phone back out but I can't make a call it's raining too hard.

At her house I push the front door key into the lock and slam open the door. I mop water from my face, race towards the basement door. 'Laura? Matt? Where are you?' I scream into the empty house. The same cat from before screeches past me and out the front door. My clothes are sodden, cling-ing to me. I brush my hair off my face with my hands. 'Laura? Matt? It's Mummy. Where are you?'

I wait a moment and catch my breath. My heart pumping. My chest heaving. Listening for any sounds. My stomach turns, what if she's killed them? I slide the bolt back from the basement door and yank open the door.

It's dark. A musky smell hits me instantly. I run my hand over the inside wall to find the light switch. I flick it on and go down the stairs. There's open space either side. 'Laura? Matt? Are you in here?'

The light bulb pops and I'm thrown into darkness. Slowly I creep down, measuring my foot against each step so as not to fall down the stairs or over the side. I sit down and carry on down on my bottom. It's so dark it's impossible to see anything. Slowly, I pull my phone from my back pocket and flick on the flashlight. I scream as a hand grabs my foot. My phone flies from my hand, I hear it tumbling down the few remaining stairs. 'Shit.'

'Mummy?' A tiny voice fills the dark empty space. My heart rate accelerates.

'Matt? Matt? Oh my God.' I grab his hand and slide down the rest of the stairs wrapping him up in a bear hug. 'Where's Laura?' I reach down fanning my hand across the floor in search of my phone. I find it. The screen is black but the flashlight is still on. The screen has smashed and bits of glass shards cut into my finger.

'She's over there, Mummy, she's hurt her leg.'

I hear a movement and rush over holding Matt's hand, tightly. 'Oh my God, Laura, are you OK, you look awful.' Her face is pale and her leg lies in a strange position. I touch it and she screams. Suddenly she starts crying and crying unable to stop. I sit next to her, holding her, cradling her in my arms. This was all my fault. This happened because of me. I hear the sirens outside and thank God it's all over.

'Mum, I feel sick. I've thrown up. Megan pushed us down the stairs.' The acrid smell of vomit is all over her.

I turn to Matt. 'Are you hurt?' I ask him, frisking him as though he was going through security in an airport.

'No. I lost Dog,' he says and I hear his voice break. He starts to cry. 'She said she'd thrown Dog in the bin. I want to rescue him, Mummy. Please?' I pull him down on top of me and cry.

'Dog's OK, he's at home. Mummy found him. He's safe. Like you are, sweetie.'

I hate what I'm going to have to do next. Taking a deep breath, I pull Laura close to me and say quietly, 'I have to go for help, Laura. Mummy needs to go and get the ambulance people to come and help you. I can't carry you. You'll have to wait here.'

'No!' she yells.

I stroke her hair. 'I won't be long. It's OK, the police have Megan. Daddy's with her too. He won't let her come here. They're at our house. It will only take me five minutes to run over and back. Can you be brave and wait for me?'

'Use your phone to call them.'

'Look.' I show her my phone. 'All the apps are gone, the screen is broken, the only thing working is the flashlight.' I don't want to move her in case I do her more harm.

'I won't be long.' I kiss the top of her head.

I pick up Matt, shine the light in front of me and climb back up the stairs, through the house and out. Outside I take a deep lungful of air. Put my phone in my pocket and hug Matt close to me. Kissing him as I run through the rain back to our house.

The paramedics take him from me and Glyn's mum rushes inside the ambulance with him. 'Where's Glyn?' I ask.

'With the police. Tina—' She stops me and puts a hand on my arm. 'I'm so sorry for not believing you.'

I don't have time for this and frankly, I couldn't care less if she feels shit about what she did.

I tell a paramedic where Laura is and what's happened to her. I see Glyn a few feet in front of me. He gives me a small smile and watches Matt going into the ambulance followed by his mum. I see him searching for Laura and the smile dies.

I shake my head to stop him thinking the worse. When I'm by his side, I wrap my arms around his waist. 'Laura is OK, she's broken her leg. I've told the paramedics, they're going for her now. I'm going to catch them up. I just wanted to see if you were Ok. How's your head?' He has a bandage wrapped around his head. A small stain of blood visible on his temple.

'Tina. My dad opened the basement door. She told him I needed medical help that I was bleeding badly. She's gone, Tina.'

I feel the blood drain from my head. I steady my breathing. 'No. I don't believe it.' I jerk away. 'Laura!' With all my strength, I run.

I pass the paramedics on their way to Megan's house. 'Call the police. Tell them Megan is here. HURRY!'

In an instant, I'm back at the front door. I remember the way to the basement. Without light I move forward careful not to crash into anything. I don't know where she is. She'll be dangerous. I realise I don't have a weapon of any kind to protect myself.

I open the basement door. I daren't call out to Laura. I don't want to frighten her. I look down the stairs. I'll have to go down in darkness. I blink as my eyes adjust. The basement is still in darkness. The familiar damp smell assails me a second time.

I listen to any sounds as I make my way down. Down. Down. I reach the bottom and I'm thrown to the floor as her body impacts with mine. I hear her fall near me. I haul myself up. Back on my feet I run in the direction of Laura.

Megan yells, 'You bitch.' Her shoes squeak.

I need to get to Laura. Frantically I get my bearings, and move in that direction. I see her at the last minute before I fall over her. I bend down, it's so dark down here I don't notice she's gagged until I kiss her. I tear it off and hush her to be quiet. She's crying, her tears wet my cheeks.

I hear sounds upstairs and pray for the police to get to us in time.

We won't make it if they don't hurry.

She can't see us in the darkness, but I can hear her shoes. I know where she is.

Then it all happens so quickly:

She's upon us instantly. I stand up, in front of Laura. She comes for me and something stabs me in the arm. I push her away. It's a reflex action. She has something sharp in her hand. My arm bleeds, I can feel it soaking my top.

There's no other way out of here.

I won't be able to get Laura out. I must lure her away from my daughter.

A flash of light hits my eyes, she's put on the flashlight from her phone.

My hip bangs into a box. I try to move it with my foot. To use it somehow to get her away from Laura. It's too heavy. I lunge against it and push, and push, and push towards her until I've driven her to the side, close to the staircase, away from Laura. She jumps out of the way. We're near the stairs now. Upstairs it's gone quiet. Have they gone? Didn't they think to look down here? What sort of police are they?

'I can see what you're up to. Playing mother bear protecting her cub.' She charges towards me.

I round the heavy box and she grabs my ankle and twists. I let out a cry of pain. The woman is insane. My hands flay around the steps looking for something. Anything to use as a weapon. Her hand on my ankle twists more. I shake it viciously to free myself, pumping back and forth, the third time I make contact with her and she falls against the box.

'Do you know what's in here?' she says recovering herself and flipping the lid off the box. She pulls out a letter. 'Grandmother's letter, telling us that she was going to change the Will back making Dad her sole heir. That she was going to speak to the existing beneficiary — that's you — informing them of her change of heart. And I saw you at her house the day when you killed her, before she had time to post it. I found it amongst her papers when she died. We both know the police are upstairs making their way to the basement.'

I see the glint of the knife she has, but it's not a knife, it's my silver letter opener. I stand up, my ankle gives way when I put weight on it.

'No one will believe you now—'

As she speaks, I hear Glyn calling my name at the top of the basement. Megan looks up, distracted. I make my move, stooping down to hurl my body weight at her. The letter opener drops from her hand. I hear a scream as Laura appears from behind the box. She grabs the letter opener. Glyn rushes down the stairs. He's turned the lights on upstairs and their glow reaches down a little. 'Tina, Tina are you OK?' Lying on top of Megan I grapple with her. She punches me in the face. I roll over. I hear Laura scream then all is quiet. All is still.

Glyn reaches us. Grabs Megan's phone from underneath her with the flashlight still on and shines it at us.

'She was going to hurt you, Mummy. I had to help you.'

Megan lies in a pool of blood. The letter opener sticking out of her neck. I quickly feel for a pulse. There's a faint one.

The police appear at the top of the stairs. Glyn informs them what's happened then wraps us both in his arms. I pull the letter from Megan's hand and scrunch it up into my pocket.

The paramedics check us all, my arm is bandaged, it's not a deep cut but I'll need stitches. Laura lies on a bed in the ambulance, her leg in a splint and Matt sits on Glyn's knee clinging on to Dog as we make our way to the hospital.

CHAPTER FORTY

Maybe one day I will tell him the truth of what really happened in Braitling. It's a month ago now that we fought for our children's lives. We're OK. For now, anyway. There are still some trust issues between us, but I think in time we'll get past them. Neither of us want to be without each other. I've got my job back at the firm and I've been made partner.

When someone gets inside your head it's impossible for them not to leave something behind, like a virus on a computer. Glyn believes I was set up and that's just as I want him to think.

That reckless action of mine with Deborah almost lost us our children. At that time, I had wanted nothing more than to take back what I thought was mine by rights. After all, my father was Deborah's husband and by rights I was entitled to an inheritance. But it was more than that. It was not allowing Deborah to screw Mum and me again. It was not allowing her that power over us a second time. Back then I had not thought of the consequences, then or in the future. I had purely thought that I would do whatever I needed to do to keep myself in the Will.

Megan will be spending time back in the psychiatric hospital she was in before, except this time she's been sectioned.

The day she arrived at the office and started talking of secrets and Braitling, I was instantly on alert. I did a search on her from Manchester library. I'm not stupid enough to do it from home or the office, there's always a footprint. It's not hard to find out about people in this day and age. Social media is a mine of information. By the time I collated all the details on Megan Pearson all I had to do was wait for her to make a move.

I knew what I could and couldn't do, I'm a good lawyer, I'm not an idiot. I let her pursue me. I let her meddle with my paperwork and interfere with my marriage. I was in control all of the time. I let her think she was driving me crazy and everyone around me were taken in. I do feel rotten about Ali, but that was a necessary evil.

As if I would have really allowed a meddlesome, bubble brain get one over on me. Please. This was the only way I could either kill her or get her locked up as insane. Nobody would believe her story then.

Glyn would never have believed my fall from grace unless I had fallen apart quite so spectacularly. That's why I knew finding the diazepam in my drawer would seal my fate on that score. I pretended I hadn't told him I'd been on the drugs after Mum died. I knew full well I had. But I had to act out that I was so ashamed of getting hooked on them at that time that I would never have confessed that to him. As I said before, he has a brilliant memory.

The partial name on the packet was my mother's middle name. Elizabeth Megan Fisher. I simply tore the label leaving enough to incriminate her. It was unbelievably coincidental she was called Megan. This presented an opportunity too good for me not to utilise. The pills were Mum's. When Mum died, I packed her room up without taking much notice what went in the boxes, they're stored in my basement. The sell by dates on the packet would have given the game away if they'd been checked, I guess, but I gambled nobody would look that closely. And I was right. So leaving them in my drawer and telling Sally in a hushed voice, which I knew Megan could hear, that I was so stressed I could do with some diazepam was perfect. She simply *assumed* I would have some. It was genius. As I've always said, any good lawyer would never presume to assume — ever.

Maybe if I'm ever brave enough, I will tell Glyn that I planned to kill Megan with diazepam.

I wasn't sure if she knew how Find my iPhone worked, so I made sure she was around when I mentioned to Glyn, he could monitor me that way if he thought I was having problems remembering. That's how she knew I'd been to Braitling and whereabouts I was on the motorway on my way home that night. I made it easy for her. I had to give her enough rope to hang herself. I knew there would be history on her phone showing she'd tracked me. Everything I needed to convince the police she was the crazy one.

I also happened to mention how lost I would be without Sally. She fell for it and as predicted, Sally became sick. I loved the way Sally rallied to my defence with the phone call fiasco and saying the diazepam in my drawer was hers. That had been me calling her but I blamed Megan. I remember Megan's face when confronted, she didn't have a clue what game I was playing. I think she genuinely thought those things actually happened by chance. Me, really on diazepam? Someone actually making the phone call to Sally? What an arse.

That night when I got home I was ready for her. I played the disorientated, terrified mother, but I knew she'd never really harm the children — she was just full of hot air. I already had enough on her to have her sectioned. I must admit, her escape from our basement surprised me. I think she worked it out at that point. Certainly, from the look on her face in her basement, I was prepared to believe that was the case. What I wasn't ready for was Laura jumping in and stabbing her in the neck. Sadly, she missed the main artery and the stupid bitch survived. Oh well, she'll be locked up for a long time if ever she gets released at all.

Sometimes when the things you love the most in this world are in danger. You do what you must — to save them.

THE END

ACKNOWLEDGEMENTS

This book has come a long way and had many manifestations. It came about while on a London trip, sat at a pavement café around the corner from Kensington Palace. I marvelled at the colourful houses across the street and their prices. An old lady came out of one of the houses, I got talking to her and she told me all about her family and her life story. It generated a nugget of an idea and after playing around with different scenarios inside my head I came up with *Behind Closed Doors*.

This is a work of fiction and there may be some inaccuracies to do with the legal world, but I have to the best of my ability researched as much as I could so, I hope you will forgive me if I have slipped up in any way.

I am beyond grateful to my publisher Ruby Fiction/ Choc Lit who believed in me and made my dreams come true. Their friendly approach and kindness have made the publishing process very enjoyable.

I actually love editing! Which brings me to my editor, a marvel and a genius and so very kind, thank you so much it was a real pleasure working with you.

A massive hug and tremendous thanks to The Tasting Panel readers who read and loved my book: Dimi E, Elena B, Jenny M, Stacy R, Gillian C, Wendy S, Carol D, Rosie F,

Selina D, Carol F, Jenny K, Sharon W and Shona N. A huge thank you for all the wonderful words you wrote about *Behind Closed Doors*.

It's a funny feeling when the real world reads your book. You live with it for so long inside your head to let it go into the world is like your child going to school on that first day — very daunting.

Thank you, Stephen for being so patient with me, for the many times I have written and re-written my manuscript and you tell me, 'I can't read it again!' But you do anyway. You've picked up when I waffle telling me, 'You're waffling.' Or the heroine is, 'too hard, make her softer,' then 'now she's too soft make her tougher.' He's always right. And I always listen.

THE CHOC LIT STORY

Established in 2009, Choc Lit is an independent, award-winning publisher dedicated to creating a delicious selection of quality women's fiction.

We have won 18 awards, including Publisher of the Year and the Romantic Novel of the Year, and have been shortlisted for countless others. In 2023, we were shortlisted for Publisher of the Year by the Romantic Novelists' Association.

All our novels are selected by genuine readers. We are proud to publish talented first-time authors, as well as established writers whose books we love introducing to a new generation of readers.

In 2023, we became a Joffe Books company. Best known for publishing a wide range of commercial fiction, Joffe Books has its roots in women's fiction. Today it is one of the largest independent publishers in the UK.

We love to hear from you, so please email us about absolutely anything bookish at choc-lit@joffebooks.com

If you want to hear about all our bargain new releases, join our mailing list: www.choc-lit.com/contact

ALSO BY SADIE RYAN

STANDALONES
THE SECRETARY
THE PROPOSAL

Milton Keynes UK
Ingram Content Group UK Ltd.
UKHW010635030624
443491UK00004B/105

9 781781 896792